Flight of the U-463

Published by Pinger Publishing, Omaha, Nebraska
www.PingerPublishing.com

Hardcover ISBN: 978-1-7341816-1-6
Paperback ISBN: 978-1-7341816-2-3
Mobi ISBN: 978-1-7341816-3-0
EPUB ISBN: 978-1-7341816-4-7

LCCN: 2019916784
Library of Congress data on file with the publisher.

Printed in the United States of America
10 9 8 7 6 5 4 3 2 1

Flight of the U-463

Timothy Donald Pilmaier

Pinger Publishing
Omaha, Nebraska

Contents

Chapter One: Epiphany... 1

Chapter Two: Canaris 10

Chapter Three: Rendezvous................................ 31

Chapter Four: Holiday 39

Chapter Five: Oenophile 47

Chapter Six: Harvest... 57

Chapter Seven: Construction 65

Chapter Eight: Launch 73

Chapter Nine: Sailor 80

Chapter Ten: Metallurgy.................................... 90

Chapter Eleven: Sicherheitsdienst.................... 104

Chapter Twelve: Condor 123

Chapter Thirteen: Photograph 133

Chapter Fourteen: Reconnaissance 143

Chapter Fifteen: I-30....................................... 154

Chapter Sixteen: Crestfallen............................ 169

Chapter Seventeen: Doubt 178

Chapter Eighteen: U-463 190

Chapter Nineteen: Covet................................. 205

Chapter Twenty: Treachery 212

Chapter Twenty-One: Opportunity.................. 221

Chapter Twenty-Two: Discovered 237

Chapter Twenty-Three: Foxhunt...................... 248

Chapter Twenty-Four: Runaway 258

Chapter Twenty-Five: Plunge........................... 270

Chapter Twenty-Six: Border 282

For Dad

Chapter One: Epiphany

January 21, 1942 23:15
Western Approaches to Great Britain
U-216

The cards had been dealt. They lay facedown on the table in the Petty Officer's Mess. Peter Teufel reached for his hand. He had been holding his own in this poker game, up at times and down at times, but, overall, he had maintained his stake. After all, he was only a *Matrosengefreiter*—an ordinary seaman apprentice—newly arrived onboard. His reward for qualifying his first watch station as engine room aft was a seat at the nightly poker game.

Peter picked up his five cards and eyed them with a straight face. He spread the cards slowly without changing his expression. Two kings, a nine, a seven, and a deuce. *This is a fine starting hand.* Slowly, he laid the cards facedown on the table and picked up his cup of coffee. He was scheduled to stand watch in twenty minutes, so this would likely be his last hand of the night.

As the other three players mulled over their options, Peter observed their actions, their mannerisms. He was looking for any telltale signs that might indicate the strength of their hands. Unconsciously, he noticed the boat, the rumbling of the diesel engines throughout the sub. Peter mused that the submarine felt very much alive with the rushing sound of the ventilation system as it passed air through the compartments.

The cool fresh sea air flushed away the dank air from that day's submergence.

Running on the surface, the two *Germaniawerft* four-stroke, six-cylinder diesel engines propelled the vessel and turned the generators to provide electricity. The electricity provided a charge to the batteries and powered all of the electric loads on the boat. Fans, motors, control circuits, and lights were all powered by the diesels, either directly or indirectly from the batteries when submerged. Peter knew these relationships. His training had taught him well. He marveled at his environment as the lights in the Petty Officer's Mess shone down upon the four sailors.

Peter was one of the new men onboard. He kept to himself and focused on qualifying his various watch stations. He had not really made any friends with the crew and, while he was a sailor in the *Kriegsmarine*, he was different. Unlike the others, he had a secret. A dangerous secret that he could not share. One, that if revealed, would result in his death. Protecting this surreptitious information was the one thing that kept him alive. Kept him in the game—one even more important than poker.

The betting began with the man to Peter's left. Giese emphatically tossed down two *Reichsmarks*. A large opening bet for this game. The man to Giese's left folded his cards with a look of exasperation. After a few moments of consideration, the man to Peter's right, Hauptman, called the bet. Peter picked up his cards, looked at them, and laid them down slowly. He placed his two *Reichsmarks* in the center of the table.

"I call," said Peter.

The remaining players tossed their unwanted cards, except for Giese.

"I will play these," Giese said smugly.

Muttering a profanity, Hauptman drew two cards. Peter evaluated the situation carefully. Giese must a have a straight or a flush. Either that, or he was bluffing. Not likely, after having observed Giese's play for the last few hours. He must have the hand. As for Hauptman, he must have three of a kind, since he called the big bet. That would not beat Giese's probable hand, but it certainly beat the two kings in Peter's own hand.

Peter tossed three cards into the muck and drew three replacements. He viewed his hand and laid all five cards face-down on the table.

Giese gruffly grabbed five *Reichsmarks* and firmly placed them in the pot. A broad smile spread across his face.

Hauptman looked at his cards and then at Giese. He, too, wondered if Giese was bluffing. The draw did not improve Hauptman's position, but three nines was still a good hand. A hand that he would usually pay to see if it could be bested; however, the price to see Giese's cards was too steep. He folded.

"I raise," Peter said immediately. "Your five and ten more, *Herr* Giese".

Now it was Giese's turn to think. He believed that he was in complete control of this hand. Dealt a spade flush out of the chute and with the kid Teufel drawing three, his flush must be the best hand. But the kid was so quick to raise? To call the pot, with the antes included, would be a pot of almost forty *Reichsmarks*. That's more than most sailors make in a month! After a moment, Giese concluded that the quiet youth was bold and brave. He must be bluffing … *Or he thinks that I am bluffing?*

Giese called, threw in his ten *Reichsmarks*, and rolled over his spade flush.

Peter chuckled, shaking his head from side to side. "That is very unfortunate!"

Giese reached for the pot as he exclaimed, "Ah hah! It is going to be sweet liberty in Lorient!"

"Hold on, *Herr* Giese," Peter said. "The pot is not yours. I have two pair."

Giese was shocked. Then confused before a grin spread across his face.

"Ah, *Herr* Teufel, two pair do not beat a flush," Giese stated firmly, as if speaking to a little boy who had made a childish mistake.

Peter slowly rolled over his hand on the table. "I believe that two pair does beat a flush—when the pairs are two red kings and two black kings."

For a moment, no one moved. Then Hauptman burst into laughter. He had been watching the hand with interest and was surprised that Teufel had actually drawn two additional kings; however, it was Teufel's final play that made him laugh.

"Giese!" Hauptman said. "The kid played you like a fool!"

Giese quickly stood up, his face reddening in anger, staring at Peter with great venom. He slammed both hands on the table and shouted, "You son of a bitch, Teufel! You slow played me, you little shit! I am going to beat your ass for that."

Tension was high in the Petty Officer's Mess. Peter stood to address Giese. He knew that perhaps he had gone a bit too far with his "two pair" ploy but it was a moot point. He knew that this was going to get ugly quick.

Throughout the boat a klaxon blared, followed by a shout from the officer of the deck, "ALARM! Enemy ship sited! Man all battle stations!"

January 21, 1942 23:37
Western Approaches to Great Britain
HMS Churchill

Seaman Blakley was the first crewman of the *HMS Churchill* to see the U-boat. The *Churchill*, an old four-stack, American-built destroyer, was returning to England after suffering battle damage from a German air attack two days prior. With one of her four-inch guns out of commission, the radar wrecked, and her sonar damaged, she was limping back to Portsmouth for repairs. The old destroyer was traveling at very slow speed, listening with her limited sonar as best as she could for enemy submarine activity.

Assigned as the aloft port lookout, Blakley was bundled up for the night air. The night was cool but not cold with relatively calm seas; however, visibility was hampered by banks of thick fog. Peering through his binoculars, he glassed the port quarter of the *Churchill*'s heading.

Blakley panned his binoculars from side to side, scanning the surface of the ocean. As he glassed the sea, something caught his eye. A shadowy shape, somewhat darker than the background, was emerging from the mist. He stared intently until he detected the stream of white foam that was the wake of a craft on the surface. A U-boat!

"Bridge. Aloft port lookout. U-boat on the surface aport!" Blakley shouted.

The officer of the deck, Sub-Lieutenant Hamill, acknowledged the report and snapped himself around to look out upon the port quarter. He, too, could see the enemy submarine. It appeared to be traveling at twelve knots, quartering onto the *Churchill*'s heading.

"Helm, come left to heading 190 degrees, ring up ahead full," Hamill commanded. He picked up the handset for the ship's loudspeaker: "Action stations! Action stations! German U-boat sighted. Prepare for surface attack and ready all depth charges. Set depth to fifty meters."

January 21, 1942 23:41
Western Approaches to Great Britain
U-216

As the HMS *Churchill* picked up speed and turned to port, the bridge lookout on the *U-216* spotted the destroyer: "Destroyer off of the starboard bow, sir!"

The officer of the deck, *Leutnant zur See* Hans Kahler shouted down to the control room: "Alarm! Destroyer off of the starboard bow. Range two kilometers. Dive, dive, dive!" He grasped the diving alarm and activated it as he slipped down the hatch.

In the Petty Officer's Mess, the confrontation between Teufel and Giese immediately dissolved as both men sprinted to their diving stations. Upon the table lay a pile of unclaimed *Reichsmarks*. They would remain there, untouched, until the winner claimed them … if the winner was *alive* to claim them.

Peter ran aft toward the engine room where his diving station was located. As he jumped feet first through the hatch, he could hear the two diesel generators sputtering to a stop. The engine room watch, a senior petty officer, was shutting the main air induction valve. Another petty officer was aligning the electric motors for submerged propulsion. Peter reached into a storage locker and retrieved a set of headphones. His diving station was as the engine room phone talker.

Peter looked at the senior petty officer who had finished shutting the main air induction valve. The man nodded at Peter and he keyed the mic on his headphones.

"Control, Engine Room. The engine room is rigged for dive."

"Engine Room, Control. Rigged for dive, aye," replied the control room phone talker.

Several men raced past Peter headed to their dive stations in the aft torpedo room. Peter could feel the U-boat begin to tilt forward. The dive had begun. It was a race to get under the waves before the threat above could pounce on the submarine. The electric motors hummed as they propelled the submarine into the depths. A blast of air announced the venting from the ballast tanks. From the time the alarm sounded until the submarine was under water took thirty-two seconds.

Peter listened intently on his headphones. The phone talker in the control room was, in Peter's mind, "on the ball." Peter chuckled to himself at the phrase "on the ball," pleased at the common American idiom.

The control room phone talker was indeed on the ball. He was connected to every compartment on the U-boat from the heart of the submarine. He would key his mic when orders were given and when conversations were taking place to keep the rest of the crew informed.

From the control room talker, Peter learned that the threat was a destroyer charging down on them. Range, bearing, and speed were passed along. He quickly performed the calculations in his head. Sighted at about two kilometers, the destroyer probably had a speed in excess of thirty knots or approximately fifteen meters per second. That would give the *U-216* just over two minutes to dive to safety, of which over thirty seconds had already elapsed. How deep could the *U-216* dive in a minute-and-a-half? Not as deep as Peter would like.

Peter continued to man the phones. He looked around the engine room and noticed a change from only a few minutes before. During the poker game, fresh air flowed through the boat as she cruised on the surface. Now fresh airflow had stopped and the sealed vessel started to smell of diesel oil, sausage, and old socks. The temperature had begun to fall slowly as well. Being submerged in a U-boat for an extended period of time could be very uncomfortable.

The first depth charge exploded thunderously close. The submerged tube of German steel shuddered and rolled fifteen degrees to starboard. A second explosion followed shortly after the first with similar effects on the submarine. Over the phones Peter could hear the captain, known by all as the CO, *Oberleutnant zur See* Karl-Otto Schultz, calmly issuing orders.

"Take her down to two hundred meters, helm hard to starboard to heading 350 degrees," the captain commanded. "Rig for silent running."

Four more depth charges exploded: *Klick-WHAM, Klick-WHAM, Klick-WHAM, Klick-WHAM.*

Peter could hear damage reports being relayed to the control room. A minor leak in the forward torpedo room, broken lights in the control room, and a leak on the air line to the forward ballast tank near the entrance to the battery compartment were all reported. Repairs were underway.

Peter was scared, really scared. Perhaps the most scared he had ever been in his life. This was only his second patrol on the U-boat and his first depth charging incident. He had imagined what it would be like, but his imagination fell short of reality. He looked at the senior petty officer who smiled and nodded back to Peter with a *This is nothing* look on his face. That look didn't comfort Peter one bit.

Four hours and sixteen depth charges later, Peter heard on the headphones, "Secure from diving stations. Set the normal submerged watch." The boat was now at periscope depth and there was no sign of the destroyer.

Peter let out a sigh. It had been a tough four hours. Perspiration ran down his back and his nerves had been stressed considerably. He stowed the headphones and headed forward. As he entered the Petty Officers' Mess, he saw the pile of *Reichsmarks* still sitting undisturbed on the table. As he did, Giese stepped into the compartment from the control room.

"You look like shit, *Herr* Teufel. First depth charging for you?"

Peter just nodded and leaned back in his seat to stretch.

Giese continued, "Get used to it, Peter. You will come to know when the depth charges are *really* close. We got off easy this time."

"Those were close enough for me."

"Teufel, take your money. You won it fair and square. But, Teufel, your nickname is *Two Pair* now." Giese headed aft, turning with a smirk. "Time for me to go on watch … Two Pair. I will remember that trick, might even use it myself one day."

Peter sat at the table in silence. Other sailors came into the compartment and crawled into their bunks, sipped coffee or began reading. Peter, however, was lost in thought. The depth charging had shaken him. More so than he would like to admit. There were enemy sailors on the surface who were hunting the *U-216* and, more importantly, trying to kill Peter Teufel. In his mind, that was not good.

An announcement over the ship's loudspeaker broke his train of thought: "Surface the boat!"

Peter reached in his pocket and pulled out a Turkish cigarette. He lit a match and took a long drag. His mind drifted back to his predicament as smoothly as the smoke drifted out of his nostrils. Here he was college-educated, raised in a wealthy family, destined to do great things, and now he found himself at war, a simple seaman on a German U-boat. This was no place for anyone to be, but especially not Peter Teufel. How had his life gone so wrong? What was he doing here in the middle of the war on a German submarine?

After all, he thought, *I am an American for Christ's sake!*

Chapter Two: Canaris

October 1, 1938 17:30
Plzeň, Czechoslovakia
Kobalvitz Beer Hall

Twenty-year-old Peter Teufel sat comfortably in his seat in the outdoor garden of the beer hall with his friend Leopold Goetz. The two of them had taken a weekend trip to Leopold's hometown of Plzeň. Technically, as the son of a United States diplomat, he was not supposed to leave Germany, but a little college side trip couldn't be resisted. Leaving the day before, they had taken the train from Stuttgart through Nuremberg on to Plzeň. After spending last night with the Goetz family, the two college students were out and about in Leopold's hometown.

The weather was superb for this time of year, warm with just a few clouds drifting across the sky. Peter finished his last bite of Czech goulash and washed it down with a Pilsner Urquell He held up his hand and with his thumb and index finger signaled for two more drafts. The waitress winked and nodded at him and headed for the bar. She was pretty and quite shapely. He liked that.

"So, Peter, what do think of my city?"

Still watching the waitress, Peter replied, "I like it. I like it a lot."

They both laughed and continued to drink the fine Czech beer. Around them, the beer garden was abuzz with loud conversation. The crowd was excited, but, to Peter, they did not seem happy. He asked his friend what was going on.

"I think that Plzeň must have lost their football match to-day. They were playing a team from Prague for the champion-ship. The big match must not have gone our way."

They must take their football very seriously. Still, something was bothering Peter. He sensed more agitation rather than disappointment from the patrons in the garden.

The waitress appeared at their table and bent over to set two more beers in front of them. Peter got an eye full of her ample cleavage as it stressed her blouse to its limit. He stared at this for longer than he should and then realized that she had seen him. He saw her smile as his cheeks began to burn with the beginnings of a blush.

Peter met her eyes and then looked quickly down at his beer. Attempting to hide his embarrassment, he asked the young woman, "What's all the excitement about?"

"The Germans. Haven't you heard?"

"What about the Germans?"

"They have moved into western Czechoslovakia; the *Sudetenland* is being occupied by them. They are on the outskirts of Plzeň as we speak."

"Really? An occupation? Then again, the Germans have always laid claim to western Czechoslovakia. They believe it is part of Germany."

"It most certainly is not!" she huffed and turned quickly away from the table.

"Nice going, Peter. I doubt that you will be dancing with that one tonight."

Peter took a long pull from his beer and wondered about the news of the German occupation of the *Sudetenland*. It was true, he believed, that the Germans had laid claim to the land for years, thinking it a part of Germany. It was really no surprise to him that they had made such a move. The newspapers in Stuttgart had been reporting on this debate for months. Now they have what they have been asking for and that should be that.

The next morning, Peter awoke feeling the effects of perhaps a few too many Pilsner Urquells. In the kitchen he found

Leopold sitting with his father, who was reading a newspaper at the table while Leopold's mother moved about the kitchen making breakfast.

"Coffee?" she asked.

"Yes, please."

"This man, *Herr* Hitler, is a menace." Leopold's father shook the paper. "This is only the beginning."

"The Germans love him. Father, he is rebuilding their economy."

"By occupying Czech lands! I should say so!" said the elder Goetz. "This will get worse. Mark my words. He will want all of Czechoslovakia, then Hungary, Romania. No one will be safe."

Peter noticed that Mrs. Goetz appeared to bristle at the conversation. She unsuccessfully tried to change the subject. "Heading back to school this morning Leopold?"

"He wants access to the Mediterranean. He is hungry for power," the old man continued.

"Yes Mother, we need to get to the train station by noon."

The elder Goetz continued, "He will continue this expansion. He is a threat to stability in Europe, I tell you."

"Father, he just wants to restore Germany for the Germans."

"They teach you that in college? You should open your eyes a little wider in class and pay attention to what is going on around you or you will find yourself defending a trench as I did in 1916."

Breakfast was served and they ate in silence.

Peter and Leopold boarded the train at the crowded Plzeň train station. There were people milling about the station, most with stoic faces. Literally overnight, this part of the world had changed and, apparently, the change had the people of Plzeň worried.

Peter sat back as the train departed the station. The engine chugged methodically as the train picked up speed along the tracks. Twenty minutes west of Plzeň, near the town of Nýřany, the train whistle blew three times and the train began to slow. Peter looked out the window but could see no train station. An unscheduled stop. Why?

Into Peter's car passed the conductor, followed by a German military officer. The conductor looked upset and a bit nervous in Peter's estimation. The conductor announced that all passengers were to exit the train for a security check.

"Have your papers ready for inspection. This will only take a few minutes," the conductor said with a weak smile on his lips.

Peter and Leopold disembarked. As he stepped off of the train, Peter could see that the train was halted at a crossroads. On the road were several army vehicles, staff cars mostly, but there were also tanks. Dozens of German soldiers milled around the vehicles, setting up barricades on the road.

He stood in line with the other passengers awaiting his turn. Each passenger met with a German officer who inspected their papers. A few questions, a quick check of their travel documents and identification, and most passengers returned to the train … most.

A man and a woman from Peter's car were subjected to the same inspection, but there was a problem. The officer was not happy about something. They were escorted out of line and walked to the road to speak to another officer.

It was Leopold's turn next. He handed his documents to the officer.

"Is Stuttgart your final destination?" the officer asked.

"Yes, sir. I attend college there."

"Very well, all is in order. You may board the train."

Peter stepped forward next and handed his papers to the officer. The German was a tall slender man, sharply dressed in his uniform and all business. This was not the time to be the chatty American tourist.

"American?"

Peter replied in perfect German, "Yes, sir. Traveling with my friend to Stuttgart."

"Why are you going to Stuttgart ... uh, *Herr* Teufel?"

"I am a student at the Stuttgart Institute of Technology. We were on holiday in Plzeň, sir."

The German officer eyed Peter for what seemed like a very long time. Peter wondered if going to Plzeň had been a mistake. He wasn't supposed to leave Germany. He had been briefed on that at the embassy and his father had reminded him of it several times.

"Teufel, a good German name. Board the train."

"Yes, sir." Peter followed Leopold to their railcar.

Together they boarded the train. They quickly discussed their experience with the checkpoint. Peter learned that the checkpoint was new to Leopold, who had made this trip several times. Twenty minutes later the train proceeded on its way. Peter noticed that several previously occupied seats were now empty.

December 16, 1938 10:07
Stuttgart, Germany
Stuttgart Institute of Technology

Peter was a bit startled when the professor announced that class was over. He had been studying the properties of alkaline earth metals for his organic chemistry class and was fully engrossed in his reading. As other students stood to exit, Peter marked the page he was reading and slowly closed the book. Winter break was just starting. It was time to catch a train to Berlin to see his parents.

He walked out of the classroom, waved goodbye to his professor, and headed towards the stairwell. Down three flights of stairs, he headed out of the sciences building into a cool damp day. A quick stop at his dorm room and he was back on the street heading for the station a short walk away. He carried a garment bag over his shoulder as he paced down the wet sidewalk. Arriving at the Stuttgart *Hauptbahnhof*, he purchased a ticket to Berlin and headed towards the train.

As he sat in his seat, Peter recalled his last train ride from Plzeň. He wondered if there would be another stop along this route to check papers. Getting on the train he had been delayed, but he had finally been allowed to make the passage. His mind wandered on towards Berlin. Christmas was coming. There would be family dinners and, of course, holiday parties to attend. It was always that way around Christmastime.

Peter enjoyed living here, maybe more so than any place that he had lived. He had liked Japan, but it was well, just different. Virginia was better. There was so much to do in Virginia: baseball, movies, museums. All things that he enjoyed. But Berlin had everything Virginia had and more. Berlin was a diverse city, where history and culture abounded with great food and pretty girls. No baseball, but that was a small concession for the life he had.

Peter thought about his future. He liked his life here. He had only one more year at the Institute and he would have his mechanical engineering degree. What should he do then? Go back to America, get a job here in Germany, or maybe travel Europe for a year? So many options, but he had time to make up his mind. A year was a very long time, he thought.

The train came to a stop in the Berlin Central Train Station. As he stepped off of the train, he walked towards the exit to the terminal. Outside, he saw his father waving at him, standing next to an embassy car.

"Father!" Peter approached the older, smiling Teufel—his father Erik. The two Teufels talked casually as the car pulled out of the station and toward *Invalidenstrasse*, south to cross the river Spree, and into central Berlin. As they crossed the river, Peter could see the United States embassy to the east. The car continued on to the Teufel's apartment. He was home for a few weeks and it felt good.

Two nights later the two Teufel men were alone together in the study of the family's apartment. Dinner was finished and Peter's mother Anne was in the kitchen addressing the larger-than-normal pile of dishes. Erik poured himself a drink, two fingers of Old Charter Kentucky Straight Bourbon, neat. It had been a long week for him. He offered Peter a glass, but Peter chose a beer instead.

"So … school is going very well for you I see."

"Yes, Pop, I'm in the top 10% of my class."

"Parents never tire of hearing that. You know, Peter, things are changing."

"How so?"

"The world is changing and I don't think it is for the better. Europe is headed towards war and Germany will be involved, I have no doubt." The elder Teufel took a sip of bourbon. "Since Bill Dodd left, the new man, Ambassador Wilson, has been doing his best to keep the United States on top of things, but now he has been recalled. They haven't named a replacement yet, but I've been informed that it will not be me."

"That doesn't seem right, Pop. You've been here five years."

"I've told you before, there are diplomats and there are politicians. I am a diplomat. They will want someone younger." He paused for a moment and then continued. "I am fifty-eight, son, and I am tired. I have served my country well, but now is the time to get out of this business and get back home."

"Back home where? Virginia, Nebraska?"

"Since your Grandfather Tanzer passed, leaving your grandmother alone, your mom has been aching to get back to Nebraska. She's followed me around the world for so many years, it's about time that I acquiesce to her wishes for a change. Besides, I am ready to retire, to relax a bit."

"When are you two leaving?"

"Soon, son, soon. We haven't set a date yet, but it will be only a month or two. Of course, we'll find you a fine engineering school to attend in the States. That shouldn't be a problem with your grades."

"I am not leaving now. I only have one more year of school in Stuttgart."

"Don't be silly, Peter. You are coming with us. Germany is no place to be now."

Peter slammed his hand firmly on the table. His eyes rolled and his expression showed petulance.

"I am not a kid anymore, Pop. I'm twenty years old. I like it here, I have friends here, and I am finishing school at Stuttgart."

"Peter, didn't you hear me? War is coming and Germany will be involved."

"I don't think that is the case, Father. The Germans only wanted the *Sudetenland*, which is mostly Germanic anyway. If they do go to war, they will just dig trenches in Czechoslovakia like the last war, not in Germany."

"Hasn't college taught you anything? Haven't I taught you anything? After all I *do* work in European political affairs, Peter."

"I am learning plenty in college, but I think that I have learned everything that I can learn from you, Pop."

Erik bit down hard on his lip. Normally, such an insolent statement would draw an immediate and harsh rebuke. This time, he took a slow sip of his drink and pondered how to proceed. This conversation was not going exactly the way that he wanted it to. The boy was partially right. He was twenty and he was learning plenty in college, but it sure hurt him to think that Peter believed that he could learn no more from his father. *That is youth speaking.*

He took a deep breath. "Son, I know what is coming. It is my job to know. Europe will be at war, next year or the year after. This man, Hitler, has designs on a greater Germany. Czechoslovakia, France, the Netherlands, maybe Poland. But ultimately, all of Europe will be at war."

"Pop, I only have a year left in school. If what you are worried about happens, it will probably happen after that, and somewhere other than Germany. I'll be fine. You have no need to worry. I am not worried."

"Peter, be reasonable. We can make you go."

"You cannot! I am an adult."

"We will not pay for your final year of school, unless it is in the States."

"I don't need your money! I have Grandpa's trust. He left money for me, *FOR ME*, to go to college and I am going to Stuttgart!"

God damn it. How had this conversation gone so wrong? His "boy" was technically an adult, but he sure didn't act like it. He had always been independent, but this was different. Maybe he had learned *too much* at college. Erik decided to back off and approach this another time. *Let the boy think. He is a smart boy; he will come to his senses. He just needs to stew on it for a while.*

December 23, 1938 18:30
Pariser Platz Berlin, Germany
Hotel Aldon

Peter Teufel stood in the receiving line dressed in his tuxedo and feeling like he would rather be just about anywhere else than at the US embassy's annual Christmas party. He had tried to talk to his mother about skipping the event, but she had been adamant. *This is your Father's last official state function and you will be there,* she had said. And so he was, but he wasn't happy about it.

Next to him stood his father who, with no sitting Ambassador, was charged with carrying the banner of the United States. *State functions, what a bore.* Peter had been to many over the years. Picnics, Easter egg hunts, Christmas parties—they were all pretty much the same. Lots of introductions and handshakes along with food, drinks, and socializing. He used to enjoy it as a kid, but now he would rather be in one of Berlin's better beer halls. At least now he was old enough to have a beer here, or a glass of wine. It might make the time pass a little easier.

All around them in the Grand Ballroom of the Aldon Hotel, people sipped their cocktails and engaged in social niceties. The press was there, too, reporters and photographers from several countries. It was always interesting to Peter what some people thought of as newsworthy.

Peter listened as the orchestra played softly in the background. It was Beethoven. He would rather hear some jazz, Benny Goodman or the Dorsey Brothers, something with a little hop to it, but this band was playing the dusty old perfunctory selections probably picked by his father. As soon as the receiving line was complete, Peter would grab a bite to eat, get a glass of wine, and find a way out of this place.

Peter mindlessly accepted handshakes from the attendees as they passed by, each giving their *Thank You*s and *Merry Christmas*es to his father and mother. The ambassador from England, Sir Nevile Meyrick Henderson; the French Ambassador, Robert Coulondre, and various German dignitaries all made their way through the line. Even an emissary from Mexico was in attendance. Peter thought that it was strange that no Japanese diplomats were in attendance. He'd thought that he might get a chance to freshen up on his Japanese tonight. His Japanese club at college was not a big hit. Only three other people showed up; two were professors who did speak the language, but the other student showed up to learn Japanese. He had tried his best to teach Leopold Goetz Japanese, but Leopold was no linguist. At least he had turned out to be a good friend.

Peter turned to his Father. "No Japanese diplomats tonight?"

Erik spoke quietly into Peter's ear. "Not invited. Our countries are not seeing eye to eye these days. But I suppose that you already knew that."

Peter missed the dig. Wanting to pass the time and perhaps open up a dialogue with his Father, Peter continued. "Sure are a lot of dignitaries here tonight, Pop."

"Many suitors, but only one maiden."

The reply confused Peter, but he laughed. What did he mean?

"Yes, the upper crust of the political, diplomatic, and military of Europe are here tonight. I trust that you will be on your best behavior, right son?"

"Yes, Sir."

The line was moving again, more hands to shake, more introductions to people that Peter did not and probably would not need to know. His Father elbowed him as a man in the dress naval uniform of the *Kriegsmarine* approached. "That is *Konteradmiral* Canaris, head of the *Abwehr*, German intelligence. A powerful man here," the older Teufel whispered.

Peter looked down at the diminutive man moving towards him. Only about five-foot-three-inches tall, the man looked up at Peter's father and spoke in perfect English: "Good evening Mr. Teufel, a pleasure to see you again. Please meet my wife Erika and my daughters, Eva and Brigitte. Thank you for the invitation to your festivities."

"It is a pleasure to meet you," Erik said as he grasped Mrs. Canaris' hand with both of his.

Peter looked on as his Father in turn performed the ritual as he had done so many times before, introducing Anne and then Peter in turn. Years of etiquette training and practical application. At the appropriate time, Peter reached for the Admiral's hand and extended his courtesies. He then shook young Brigitte's and, in turn, Eva's.

Their eyes met for an instant and Peter could see, if not almost feel, that Eva was pleased to meet him. The handshake took a half second too long before she let go. *How old was she, seventeen? Perhaps eighteen?*

And then they moved on. Up next was a duke from Liechtenstein or Luxembourg or some such place. It didn't quite register with Peter. He only noticed that, as the Canarises proceeded down the line, Eva gave a slow over-the-shoulder glance back in his direction. *I might stay a little longer than I expected.*

Two hours later, Peter found himself sitting alone at the bar of the Grand Ballroom of the Hotel Aldon. The party was still going strong, but he believed that it was time for him to make his escape. He looked about the ballroom and watched the socializing. His father, bourbon in hand, talked with several foreign diplomats. With all of the formalities completed, it was apparently time to discuss international relations. Peter was glad that he did not have to participate in that.

He had thought that the evening might be interesting, as Eva Canaris had been interested in him; however, it was not to be. They had danced a waltz and sat together to talk for a while, and he had learned that she was only fifteen years old. She did look older, but the fact was that she was a kid. He had been a gentleman the entire time, even though Eva had hinted to him in no uncertain terms that she would let him be less gentlemanly if they could slip away alone. Fortunately, her little sister Brigitte soon arrived to tell Eva that their parents said that they were leaving. Now, alone and a bit relieved, he ordered one more glass of wine.

"Scotch, a double," Peter heard a woman say.

He turned to his right and looked down the bar. A few feet away stood a beautiful woman. Dressed in gray slacks and a simple light blue blouse, she was clearly in her twenties. Long dark hair flowed over her shoulders and onto her back. Around her neck hung a camera, a fancy one at that. One of those new 35mm jobs. He was eyeing her with great interest as she waited for the bartender to pour her scotch.

She turned, looked at Peter and smiled. Her eyes were blue, so beautifully blue.

"Are you a reporter?"

"Photographer." She laid her hand on the camera, which rested between her breasts.

"Covering this grand event must be exciting."

She chuckled at that and picked up the scotch.

"Yes, very exciting." She rolled her blue eyes. "Just paying my dues. I am Marilyn, Marilyn Miller." She extended her hand.

Peter stood up and clasped her hand and introduced himself. "Peter Teufel. Care to join me, Marilyn?"

"Thank you." She slipped easily onto the bar stool next to him.

"Why aren't you out there taking pictures?"

"I already got the pictures I needed. I took some of the receiving line, of the short speech that the American ambassador gave, all the formal stuff. No one wants pictures of men drinking and smoking cigars. No, my work is done for the night."

"He is not the ambassador. There is no current ambassador. That guy is just standing in."

"How do you know that?"

"He's my father."

They spent almost an hour talking and laughing together. Marilyn was easy to talk to and she was very intelligent. Peter learned that she was from Dubuque, Iowa, and that she had graduated from Skidmore College in upstate New York with a Bachelor of Arts in Journalism. Two years older than he, she was working for the Associated Press, traveling the world covering the news through her photographs. All very exciting, he thought.

As they talked, Peter kept looking into her deep blue eyes. She was the most beautiful woman that he had ever met. He was now very glad that he had stayed at the party longer than he had originally planned.

"Marilyn, would you care to dance?"

"I would love to, but it is strictly *verboten*. We are not allowed to mingle with the newsmakers. We get free food and free drinks but that is where it ends. Unless ..."

"Unless what?"

"Unless you know of another place where we could go to dance," she said, with a smile that told Peter that she liked him. They agreed to meet in front of the hotel in five minutes.

Peter looked around the grand ballroom and located the table where his mother was sitting. He swung by her table to let her know that he was leaving to go meet up with friends. She reminded Peter not to stay out too late. He kissed her on the cheek and headed to the coat room to get his overcoat. His mother was not awake when Peter made it home at dawn the next morning.

December 27, 1938 21:30
Bank of the River Spree Berlin, Germany
Der Dunkle Ort

Peter sat alone with his beer at the bar. Quiet and out-of-the-way, *Der Dunkle Ort* was one of his favorite places in Berlin. He looked out the window next to his table and watched the river flow by as soft jazz music played by a three-piece combo drifted through the bar. It was crowded for a Tuesday night, but not too crowded. Peter didn't want to be with anyone except for Marilyn, but she had left for Paris that morning to cover the French ringing in the new year.

It had been a wonderful three days with her. They had seen the sights of Berlin, danced nearly till dawn, enjoyed the food at one restaurant after another and, for the first time in his life and hers, they had made love. It was clumsy and a bit awkward the first time, but they got better at it. And now his heart missed her so much.

They promised to stay in touch, but her job required her to travel around the world. Her home office was in New York City and she gave him the address. If he wanted to write to her, he should write to the office and it would be forwarded on. He asked her to come to Stuttgart soon to see him if her work brought her anywhere close to where he lived and she agreed. But they both knew that this was unlikely.

He reached down and lifted his beer to his lips. It was then that he noticed her. Across the room, sitting at the bar was Eva Canaris. *What was she doing here? She is underage.* He knew that Germany had liberal drinking laws, but not this liberal. She was sitting between two men nearly twice her age and they were arguing. She did not look happy, but the two men did. One kept putting his arm around her, which she promptly removed. She did not look like she was enjoying the attention.

Peter wondered if he should intervene on her behalf; after all, she was only a kid. Part of him knew that it was none of his business. Girls like Eva, apparently, got into predicaments like this.

At that moment, one of the men reached down and placed his hand on Eva's thigh. That was enough for her. She slapped him forcefully, swung out of her stool, and made her way to the door. The man sat, stunned. The other man burst out laughing. That was it. The first man shoved his laughing friend, and both men leapt off their stools and followed Eva out of the bar.

"Ah, shit," Peter muttered as he stood and made his way to the same exit. *This isn't going to end well.*

A long path from the doorway ran along the steep riverbank about forty yards to the street. There was snow on the ground, but the path was clear of it. Peter could see that the two men had Eva, each holding one of her arms, and she was struggling. She was screaming for them to let her go.

Peter ran headlong towards the attacker closest to the riverbank. Lowering his shoulder, he plowed into the man at full speed. The man released Eva and stumbled over the steep bank next to the river. Losing his footing on the snow, the man fell on his ass and slid down the slope.

Peter turned to see the other man still struggling with Eva. She was screaming at the top of her lungs for him to let her go. The man swung her around and threw her into the snow next to the path. She gave a loud "ugh" as she hit the ground hard. The man then looked at Peter and snarled.

"This is none of your business. Now fuck off."

"Leave her alone. She is only—" Peter was saying but the right cross caught him on the side of the head before he could finish.

It was Peter's turn to stagger. The man rushed him as Peter was regaining his balance. The man was bigger than Peter and knew how to fight. He gave Peter a royal beating like he had never had before. Peter held his own for a moment. He even cut the man's earlobe with his watch band after throwing a punch that missed the man's face. This only seemed to anger the man more. He dropped Peter to the ground with a punch to the stomach. Punches and kicks rained down upon him like thunder as he did his best to fight back. All the while Peter could hear Eva screaming and crying. And then the beating stopped.

Neither of the combatants saw the *Ordnungspolizei* as they rushed down the path to intervene. Two of the police officers wrestled the big man to the ground, another went to Eva, and the fourth grabbed the man who was crawling on his hands and knees back up the riverbank.

Peter, battered and bruised, rolled onto his back and groaned. He touched his hand to his lip. It was bleeding and swelling quickly. He hurt in several different places, but he didn't think that anything was broken. He looked up from the ground and made his first eye contact with Eva. She was still crying but she was beginning to settle down. He could see that she recognized him.

"Peter?" She sounded grateful.

The whole lot of them were transported a short distance to the Berlin police station. Each side was allowed to give their story. All of the storytelling stopped when the police identified the victim as Eva Canaris. Released shortly thereafter, Peter slowly made his way home.

December 30, 1938 11:15
Berlin, Germany
Teufel Apartment US Embassy Housing

Peter looked up from his textbook as his mother answered the knock at the door. His father had left for the embassy over an hour ago. Perhaps he had forgotten something. She opened the door and Peter could just see two men in suits and overcoats.

"Mrs. Teufel?"

"Yes."

"I am Kirk Jurgens. I am here on behalf of Admiral Wilhelm Canaris. Is your son Peter home?"

"What ... what is this about?"

Jurgens smiled politely but his demeanor was all business. "I am not able to give you any details, Mrs. Teufel. Just that the Admiral wishes to speak with your son."

Anne turned and looked at her son. He could see a look of concern on her face.

Twenty-five minutes later, Peter was escorted into a gray stone building in central Berlin. The building was austere, simplistic in its form, fit, and function. There were no signs on the front of the building. The double doorway that served as the entrance was guarded by armed men, soldiers of the *Wehrmacht*. He ascended the steps with Mr. Jurgens and was escorted through the entrance into the foyer. The inside of the building was as gray as the outside. Nazi flags hung on the walls along with a picture of Adolph Hitler. Peter was escorted to a stairway that led to the second floor and there he walked down a long corridor that terminated with another set of wooden double doors. A sign on the door read, "*Konteradmiral Wilhelm F. Canaris – Abwehr Chief.*"

Abwehr was German military intelligence. This was surely related to the event involving Eva Canaris from a few nights ago. Was he in trouble? Had Eva spun a different tale to explain what she was doing at a bar with two strange men? Had she told her father that Peter was responsible? One of the doors opened. Peter was told to enter.

Inside, the admiral sat at a large ornate desk. Peter looked around the room. He noticed that there were no windows, giving him a closed-in feeling. The door closed behind him. They were alone. The admiral was writing. Peter stood a few feet in front of the desk and waited. Finally, the admiral put down his pen and slowly looked up at the young man in front of him.

"You were a participant in an event the other night that has caused my family some measure of embarrassment, Mr. Teufel." The admiral paused.

Many thoughts ran through Peter's head. Did the admiral think that he took Eva there? Had he seen the two of them dance at the party? Did he blame Peter for her getting roughed up the way she did? What had she said to him?

"It is fortunate for all involved that the police arrived when they did. My understanding is that upon their arrival, a Mr. Joseph … uh …" The admiral looked down at the paper on his desk before he continued. "A Mr. Joseph Kohler was giving you a pretty thorough beating."

"I am not much of a fighter, sir."

The admiral sat back in his chair and chuckled. "On the contrary—Peter, is it? You are an honest man who fought a battle in defense of my daughter against two men, both sizable men—for a girl you hardly know. Some, including me, would say that is an honorable fight. It says a lot about you as a man, young Teufel."

Peter let out a sigh but held his tongue.

"Being the Chief of the *Abwehr* allows me a certain level of access to information in this country. I have read all of the reports. The bartender at the *Der Dunkle Ort* stated that my daughter had an altercation at the bar with the two men. He also relayed how you followed them outside in a hurry. The police, though a distance away, saw how you came to my daughter's defense."

"I felt compelled to help, sir," Peter murmured.

"And I am grateful that you did, Peter," Canaris replied. "This is not the first difficulty that Eva's mother and I have had with her, although this is the most serious. I am afraid that we will be handling our daughter a little differently from now on. But that is a family matter."

Peter felt compelled to speak. "Admiral, I did what I did because it was the right thing to do. It was only happenstance that I knew who the young lady was."

"Your German is excellent for an American," Canaris stated "I believe that you mean what you say. You are an honorable young man who came to my daughter's aid. For this, I would like to offer a small gesture of my appreciation."

"That won't be necessary, sir," Peter protested. "I just want to put this affair behind me and get back to school. Of course, if I must return to Berlin for any proceedings, I will do so."

"That will not be necessary. I have dealt with the matter," said Canaris with a smile that showed no real happiness. "Yet, I feel that I must do something to repay your courage and chivalry. It is not wise for a man in my position to be indebted to anyone, you must understand."

Peter thought for a moment. Here was the head of German military intelligence asking to level the field between them. While some would think this was a good thing, Peter did not. It would not be wise to have a powerful man like this feeling as if he owed you something. Peter thought quickly about what he could ask for. Dinner ... tuition ... a car ... Nothing felt right.

Then Peter, remembering his recent issues riding the trains, said, "Can you keep me from being delayed at train stations?"

The admiral looked at Peter. He was an American and all Americans were in a hurry. Current directives from the *Führer* prescribed checkpoints at all rail stations, no exceptions. Still, Canaris was indebted to this young American, and rank did have its privileges.

Canaris turned in his chair to a filing cabinet behind him. He opened the middle drawer of the cabinet and removed a small piece of paper about the size of a cigarette case and, setting it on his desk, jotted something on it. Then he opened his desk drawer and pulled out a leather sheath and slid the piece of paper into it and handed the paper to Peter.

"Present this document to anyone who asks for your papers. You will be allowed to travel within the Third Reich without further question," Canaris said.

Peter opened the sheath and read the document inside.

~

The bearer of this document, Peter Teufel, is traveling under the direction of, and with the authority granted by, the Chief of the Abwehr. As such, all assistance and courtesy will be facilitated by you to assist this person. The bearer is allowed to travel at the greatest of speed within the bounds of the Third Reich from this day, 30 December 1938, forward.

Wilhelm F. Canaris

Wilhelm F. Canaris
Konteradmiral – Kriegsmarine
Abwehr Chief

~

Canaris added a caveat: "This document will allow you to travel, without delay, within all of Germany. It does not allow you to travel internationally under the same directive. For that, you will have to wait in line with everyone else. As the head of military intelligence, it is my prerogative to expedite travel of some individuals, no questions asked. You are now one of those individuals."

"Thank you, sir."

"I will also have a German passport made for you. That will take a couple of days. I will have it delivered to your parent's apartment. That should solve all of your travel troubles in Germany."

Peter smiled and placed the travel memo into his pocket.

"Now, Peter," Canaris said. "I am a busy man. Not too busy to thank a man who has minimized the embarrassment to my family, of course, but busy none the less. I will have you escorted back to your home."

Peter nodded.

"No thanks are required from you. I only ask that you never speak of the events that occurred this week or the small gift that I have given in recompense. Agreed?"

With that, the double doors to Canaris's office opened, revealing the two men who had escorted Peter to the admiral's office. Peter gave Canaris a handshake, a thank you, and headed out of the room.

Wilhelm Canaris sat back down in his chair and smiled. He had evened a debt to someone who had done him and his family a good deed. Peter Teufel was an interesting young man, an American, an engineering student at Stuttgart Institute of Technology with very good grades. Still a young man, but one who was honest, had values and courage. He could use a man like that someday.

Canaris turned and opened the bottom file drawer behind his desk. He removed a folder and from within the folder, a piece of paper. It was a file of foreign contacts and the Chief of the *Abwehr* had another foreign contact that he wanted to document. In his line of work, you could never have too many contacts.

Chapter Three: Rendezvous

Peter sat alone in his dorm room. He had returned earlier that day from his Christmas holiday in Berlin. It was a Sunday night and the new semester started the following morning. He was sorting through his books, preparing for his classes. He stacked the textbooks on his desk: *Applied Physical Metallurgy and Design*, *Kinematics and Dynamics of Machinery*, *Power Plant Systems Design*, *Computational Heat Transfer and Fluid Flow*, and *Honors Poetry*. It was a full load of classes that should keep him busy.

He paused and pondered his Christmas break. The whole Eva Canaris affair had been quite an experience, one that he hoped to never repeat. Yet meeting her at the embassy's Christmas party had actually been a good thing. For it was there that he also met Marilyn, such a beautiful woman, unlike any he had ever known. Those eyes, those piercing blue eyes, they had melted Peter's heart every time he looked into them. Saying goodbye to her had been difficult. He missed her already.

Yet it was the argument with his father, the last night that he was in Berlin, that had upset him the most. His father had again drawn him into the study at the Teufel apartment to discuss the future of the family. They had argued for thirty minutes, each man stating that he knew what was best. They didn't agree and harsh words were spoken. In the end, Peter had walked out of the study, his mind made up: He was finishing school in Germany and that was that.

What could his father possibly know that Peter didn't know already? There was no war in Europe and there would not be one, in his estimation. The repatriation of the *Sudetenland* was merely Germany standing up for Germans. If war were to come, it would be to the south, in Yugoslavia. If Germany actually did have eyes on expansion, as his father had insisted, it would be to establish a link to the Mediterranean where Germany would have unfettered access to that sea. It just made sense to Peter, if the Germans did become aggressive.

Done sorting his books, Peter pulled a sheet of paper out of his desk and began to pen a letter to Marilyn.

August 25, 1939 21:07
Stuttgart, Germany
Stuttgart Institute of Technology

Peter finished his last class of the day and headed to his dorm to study. Walking along *Kreigsbergstrasse* in the warm summer sun, he was happy to have started his final semester of college. He only had three required classes to go before he graduated and then he could get on with his life. He walked into the lobby of his residence hall and turned to the right to the bank of mailboxes.

Peter recognized the writing on the front of the envelope in his box. It was from Marilyn. He ran up the two flights of stairs and flew down the hallway to his dorm room.

Marilyn was coming back to Europe for a few days and had invited him to come see her. She had been back to the States and spent some time in England and Ireland, but she had not been back to Germany or even close. Now she was traveling to Poland for the Associated Press to photograph a ceremony being conducted by the Polish government. This was his chance to see her again and he would do everything within his power to be with her.

Peter grabbed his teapot, filled it with water, and set it on his electric hotplate. He had built the hotplate in one of his engineering labs and he had kept it for his personal use. They had been studying Ohm's law, voltage was equal to current multiplied by resistance, and Joule's law, which calculated the power involved. In this case, the power was the amount of heat generated by an electrical resistor as a current passed through it. These things interested him almost as much as the thought of Marilyn did. Almost.

He sat back waiting for the water to boil and looked at the calendar. Today was the twenty-fifth and she would be arriving in Danzig, Poland on the thirtieth, but only for four days. *Four days were better than nothing.*

It took a very long time for Peter to fall asleep that night.

August 29, 1939 18:15
Berlin, Germany
Berlin Central Train Station

Peter stepped off of the train into the crowded Berlin Central Station and stretched his arms and legs. It had been a long ride from Stuttgart and now he needed a bite to eat. His next train didn't leave for just over an hour. That train would take him to see Marilyn and he didn't want to miss it. He decided to buy his ticket before he got something to eat.

He walked off of the train platform and proceeded to the ticket counter. He queued up in line with the other travelers and waited to speak to the agent. The line slowly moved ahead, testing Peter's patience. Finally, he reached the agent. "One ticket to Danzig, please."

"The 19:19 eastbound is full. Sorry. Next." The agent called over Peter's head for the next customer.

"Wait. I really need to get to Danzig."

"Son, the train is full. There is nothing I can do."

Peter reached into his wallet and pulled out the travel pass that Admiral Canaris had given him. It did say *all assistance and courtesy,* and now he could certainly use exactly that. He handed the agent the paper.

"Here."

The agent read the paper and stiffened upon reading the name of the signatory. "Wait here."

The agent turned away from the ticket window and walked back to a German officer sitting at a desk in the office. Peter watched as he handed the travel pass to the military man. The officer read it and snapped at the agent. The agent hurried back to the window and handed Peter a ticket.

Peter sat quietly in his seat on the train as it pulled slowly out of the station in Berlin. It had already been a long day traveling from Stuttgart and it would be a long night proceeding to Danzig. He had noted many people, mostly soldiers, boarding the train to Berlin and the station where he switched trains had been teeming with military personnel. He tried to get some sleep with only limited success.

He awoke as the train whistle sounded. He could feel the train slowing down. Peter sat up straight and looked out the window. He could see that the train was stopping in a small town. The sign hanging from the station said *"Tantow."* Looking at his railway map, he determined that he was in a small town on the German border with Poland. As the train came to a stop, several of the passengers in his car stood up and made their way to the exit. They were all soldiers.

Peter looked again out of his window and he could see that hundreds of soldiers were disembarking the train. The soldiers, in their green uniforms, assembled into columns. Each carried a rifle and a field pack. Peter figured that a base must be nearby.

After a few minutes, the train again began chugging its way eastward towards Danzig. Peter, able to stretch out in the near empty car, returned to sleep. Nine more hours until he was to arrive at his destination. Then he could see Marilyn.

August 30, 1939 16:04
Danzig, Poland
Danzig Hauptbahnhof

Peter waited under the large clock in the Danzig station. He was tired. It had been a long trip from Stuttgart with only a few hours of sleep on the train. Suitcase by his side, he scanned the station to see if he could spot Marilyn. People were coming and going in a continuous flow of humanity, but there was still no sign of her. Then he felt a tap on his shoulder. "Looking for someone?"

He spun around and saw her standing there. Her long dark hair was perfectly combed, her lips were a deep luscious red and her eyes ... those beautiful blue eyes. He no longer felt tired.

"Let's get out of here, shall we? I have a room at the *Kasino Hotel*."

They rode a bus to Sopot, just up the coast, on the Gulf of Danzig. It seemed to Peter, now that they were together again, that they had never been apart. Marilyn was easy to talk to. He was as happy as he could ever remember being when she was at his side. He was glad that he had made the trip to Poland to see her.

They spent the evening walking along the beach in front of their hotel, holding hands, at ease with each other's presence. They walked along the wooden pier that jutted far out into the bay. It was the longest wooden pier in Europe, at least that was what the hotel concierge had told them. They watched as the sun set, and at the end of the pier they kissed as the gloaming engulfed them.

"I have to work tomorrow," Marilyn said. "I need to be in Danzig to photograph the proceedings, but the day after that I should be free. We can spend the day however we want to."

"When do you have to leave?"

"My ship will leave on the second at 10:00."

"Not much time, but we will make the most of it."

September 1, 1939 05:51
Sopot, Poland
Kasino Hotel

Marilyn Miller awoke to the sound of thunder. She looked next to her to see if Peter was awake, but he was sleeping soundly. She got out of bed, naked as the day she was born, picked up her robe from the chair in the corner and wrapped herself. She made her way to the open fourth-floor window and looked out over the bay. She saw flashes of light and heard the subsequent rumble of thunder a few seconds later.

Still drowsy, she focused on the lightning. It was so close to the water and it looked a little strange. It was not white bolts of lightning that she saw, but, rather, large flashes of orange. Then she heard another sound—the hum of an airplane, or rather, airplanes.

With the sun starting to peek over the horizon, Marilyn looked towards the sky. There she could see formations of airplanes heading out into the bay. They were flying in clear skies. Then it became clear to her that it was not thunder she heard; these were explosions!

From her window, she looked down the coast towards Danzig. Then she ran to her suitcase, pulled out one of her cameras and raced back to the window. She began taking pictures of the airplanes and of the smoke rising above Danzig.

With daylight advancing, she was now able to see a ship out in the bay. It was a warship, firing salvos into Danzig. She could see the flashes of the guns and hear their roar. She photographed the ship as well.

Peter rolled over in bed and looked at Marilyn standing in the window.

"What are you doing?"

"There is something going on. An attack, I think."

"What?" Peter rose out of bed. He stood next to Marilyn

and gazed out into the bay. He, too, could see the ship firing shells towards the city to the southeast.

"I'm almost out of film. I have only one more roll."

"What do you think this means?"

"I'm not sure, but I think that this means that Poland is at war … and I might be the only person with pictures of it."

She put her camera down and whipped off her robe. Peter looked at her with amazement. She dressed quickly and started packing her bag. "I have to go. I have to get these pictures to my editor."

"But you don't leave until tomorrow."

"I have to leave now. I have pictures of real news, not photos of garden parties and diplomatic handshakes. Real news. This is a big deal for my career. I need to get these photos back to New York."

"What about us? What about me?"

"You should get back to Germany, and quickly. I don't think that Poland is the place to be right now. I'll write you when I get back. Don't worry."

"I could come with you."

"No Peter, you most certainly cannot. This is work, my work, and I work best alone. Besides, you need to get back to Germany."

Peter watched as she picked up her suitcase and a bag of photographic equipment and turned to him. He was not at all pleased by this turn of events. She set the bags back down and raised one of her cameras, snapped a picture of him and collected her things again.

"I love you Peter, but I must go. I promise that I'll write to you. Be careful heading back to Stuttgart, ok?"

He could only nod. She scurried out the door and was gone. Peter stood there looking at the door that had closed behind her. All he could hear was the sound of naval gunfire in the distance.

September 4, 1939 12:30
Stuttgart Germany
Stuttgart Institute of Technology

Peter dropped his suitcase on the floor of his dorm room with a thud and let out a long sigh. He collapsed down on his bed and dropped his face into his hands. It had been a very long three days.

After Marilyn had left, he had packed his things and left the *Kasino Hotel*. He had walked several blocks to the train station and booked a ticket to Berlin. On the train, he found out that Germany was invading Poland. A German radio station had been attacked a few days before by the Poles. Now, the Germans were striking back.

At the Polish border, the train was halted and all of the passengers were told to get out of the cars. They were delayed most of the day. Standing beside the train, he had seen columns of German soldiers marching into Poland. Tanks and trucks were also moving to the east. Overhead, he had witnessed planes, many planes.

Using his travel pass from Canaris had again paid dividends. He was finally allowed to reboard the train when many others were not. He had seen people being arrested and hauled away by the German Army. The train had then traveled on to Berlin where he experienced more delays. He was forced to spend a day and a half in the city before he could get a train to Stuttgart.

Now he sat quietly in his dorm room. His thoughts shifted to Marilyn. Was she safe? Had she made it out of Danzig? He lay down on his bed, resigned to the fact that all he could do was wait for a message from her letting him know that she had made it out alive. He anticipated that it would be a long wait.

Chapter Four: Holiday

Anne sat in silence across the table from her husband Erik in the dining room of their house in Omaha. After returning from Germany in February, they had purchased a home in the upscale district of the city known as the "Gold Coast" near where Anne's mother lived. Erik had retired from his job with the State Department and had given in to her wish to live close to her only living relative, Gerta Tanzer.

The Teufels settled back in Nebraska in the spring of 1939, leaving their only son, Peter, in Germany. A decision that Anne now regretted. She had let her husband persuade her into letting the boy "sow his oats" and now that decision weighed upon her. She was positive, in retrospect, that the decision had been a mistake. War had come to Europe and her only child was there—in harm's way, she was sure of it.

"You are quiet tonight, Anne."

"Just thinking about Peter."

"He is fine. His letters say so, right?"

"Yes, that is what he says." She looked down at her uneaten dinner. She used her fork to push and prod the food on her plate this way and that.

Erik noticed. It was a sign that she was upset. Years of marriage had taught him that.

Erik, too, was concerned about Peter, but he hid his worries from his wife. After all, it was his inability to convince Peter to return to the States that led to his staying in Germany to finish college. He proceeded carefully. "He graduates in a month. Then he will return home. I am sure of it."

"Are you sure, Erik?"

"Yes dear, I am sure. The boy just wanted to make a statement, to push us a bit. He will come running home after graduation, I am positive."

Erik Teufel was almost convinced by what he had said, but it appeared to him that Anne needed more reassurance. Mothers always worried about their children and it must be worse for the mother of an only child.

"This was our first holiday without Peter. Some Thanksgiving ..."

"Oh, honey. So, Peter wasn't with us this year. He will be next year. Besides, Nebraska beat Oklahoma 13-7 yesterday, so everything is right in the world, right?"

His attempt to distract her with football results was a complete disaster. She immediately burst into tears. Erik wondered how he could recover from his misstep. *Why do women act the way that they do?* He sat silently, gazed upon his distraught wife, and waited for her to say something, anything.

"Well, *this* has been a wonderful holiday." She slammed her fork down on the table. "Happy Thanksgiving! Our son is in Europe! War-torn Europe, while you listen to football on the radio. Don't you think that we should do something, Erik?"

Erik knew that the conversation had rapidly digressed to a place that he never intended it to go. He realized that he was dancing on eggshells at this point. Years of diplomatic training kicked in. *Find common ground.*

"I agree with you. I do think that we should do something, Anne, so I want to understand what it is that you think that we should do."

"I think that we should bring him home. I think that we should call your contacts at the State Department and have them put Peter on a ship heading home. That's what I think."

"I will get on it first thing tomorrow Anne. I promise."

But Erik would wait. He knew his son would surely stay until graduation in December. He would get in touch with the embassy staff in Berlin through the State Department and inform Peter that he should come home after graduation. Erik would contact them in a couple of weeks.

December 22, 1939 09:30
Berlin, Germany
US Embassy, Chancery on Pariser Platz

Richard Gunderson hung up the telephone and cursed under his breath. It was three days before Christmas, and he was a busy man. He had to complete his normal paperwork and then prepare for the embassy Christmas party. Now, he was even busier.

The call was from the Alexander C. Kirk, the chargé d'affaires at the embassy. Kirk was the top US diplomat in Berlin and ultimately Gunderson's boss. The call was for him to make a trip to Stuttgart to find Peter Teufel and to give him a message. The young man was to return to the States after his graduation. *Not exactly the kind of diplomatic assignment I was hoping to get when I took this job.*

Gunderson didn't need a trip to track down some college kid, especially not at this time of the year. But as the junior man in the embassy on his first overseas assignment, he certainly couldn't say no. He would get his things in order and head to Stuttgart first thing in the morning. With any luck, he would be back in Berlin in time for the party.

December 24, 1939 18:20
Stuttgart, Germany
Stuttgart Institute of Technology

Peter moved about his small dorm room, deciding what to keep and what to dispose of. The room had been his home for the last four years, but, happily, it was time to move on. He had graduated from the Institute with a degree in mechanical engineering, finishing fifth in his class.

He looked down at his diploma and thought of the work that he had put in to earn it. Hours of studying, hours of lab work, all of that effort providing him with a solid background in a field that he loved. He wondered if his father would be proud of him. Peter believed that his father was a little disappointed that he had matriculated into engineering instead of medicine, but that course of study held no interest.

Peter was interested in how things worked, not in how people worked. As he'd come to realize the first summer that he worked for his Grandpa Tanzer in the train yard, solving problems and understanding the interrelationships of complex machinery were the things that interested him.

He had written his mother twice in the last year. She had written him thirteen letters, each more beseeching than the last, pleading for him to return home to the States. His father had not written at all. His mother still treated him like a little boy which chafed at him a bit. He was a man, a twenty-one-year-old man. He could take care of himself, even now that Europe was at war.

After the Germans invaded Poland, everything had quieted down. Sure, England had declared war on Germany, as had the French, but nothing had really happened after that. Peter figured that appeasement would continue to rule the day, as it had in the past, and the declaration of war was just to get Germany's attention. In his mind, Germany's next move, if there were a next move, had to be into Yugoslavia. Surely the British and the French would not throw their military into the defense of the Slavic people? The word around campus was that this whole thing would die down in a few weeks and Peter believed exactly that.

Today was Christmas Eve. His first Christmas away from his family. No holiday dinners, no festivals, no gifts under the tree. He suddenly felt sad. He was alone. Most of his friends had left school in time to be home for Christmas, but Peter did not have any place to go. He decided that he would give himself a Christmas present. He would travel Europe before he headed back to the United States. He had money left over in his trust, quite a bit of money, and now he could spend it on a different kind of education. Where should he go?

Switzerland would be nice with all of its skiing, dining, and sightseeing. Or maybe Italy. There was so much to see in Italy, the leaning tower of Pisa, Venice, Rome, it all seemed good to him. Perhaps Amsterdam. He had never been to the Netherlands. What about the lights of Paris? He had heard stories of how beautiful the city of Paris was. What if he could get Marilyn to meet him in romantic Paris? His mind raced with the possibilities.

First things first, he needed to finish cleaning out his dorm room. He took several loads of junk to the dumpster outside of the dorm. Papers, books, pencils, a protractor, and even his self-built hot plate were taken out for disposal. He dumped it all into the vessel. Reconsidering, he retrieved the hot plate and returned it to his room. He would leave it for the next occupant. A legacy of sorts.

He had two suitcases of things that he was going to keep, mostly clothes, but amongst the things he was keeping were the letters that he had received from Marilyn. He had been very relieved to receive one from her following their rendezvous in Poland. He had found it in his mailbox towards the end of October. She had indeed escaped Poland on a liner headed for Portsmouth, England and had sent her photos of the attack on Danzig to her home office in New York. The photos appeared in almost every major newspaper in the country. More importantly to Peter, she was safe and sound and heading back to the States at the time.

She had sent him a second letter that he received in early December that informed him that with the "war" going on in Europe, her boss wanted to keep her stateside for her own good. She was upset about the restrictions he put on her. He let her know emphatically that "war correspondent" was a man's job. She wrote Peter that she was pushing to get back to Europe, but in a non-warring country, such as Switzerland, or, more likely, Portugal.

Rereading the letters in his dorm room cemented the idea of the Christmas present he had decided to give himself. If Marilyn was likely to go to Portugal, then he would go to France. From there it was just a hop, skip, and a jump to Lisbon or wherever she talked her way into going.

He sat down at his dorm room desk for one last time to pen two letters. The first letter was to his parents. He let them know that he was fine and that he was going to travel around Europe as his Christmas present to himself. It was a short letter and he attached it to a cylinder that contained his rolled-up diploma from the Institute. The second letter was to Marilyn. This letter was much more voluminous. He outlined his plan to tour France, taking his time, in hopes that she would be able to join him there, or that he would join her in Portugal, if that came to pass. He also expressed his thoughts and feelings for her. He concluded the letter with his sentiments and sealed the letter in an envelope addressed to her in New York.

The next morning, Christmas Day, Peter moved out of his dorm room. He checked his mailbox one last time and then dropped the room key off with the student manning the desk in the lobby. He left the building and headed to the campus *Reichspost* with his two suitcases in hand. There, he purchased stamps for both deliveries. Each stamp was printed with a likeness of the *Führer*.

Leaving the post office, Peter then proceeded to the *Deutsche* Bank. There he withdrew the remaining funds in his college trust. It was a considerable sum, one which would afford him a fine holiday in France.

After leaving the bank, he walked to the *Hauptbahnhof* to get his ticket from Stuttgart to Basel, Switzerland, a neutral country. Crossing into Switzerland would be easier than crossing into France, he assumed, as, technically, France was at war with Germany. Once in Switzerland, he planned to travel on to Paris and, after that, he would tour France.

Crossing the border into Basel turned out to be relatively easy. He didn't even need to show his Canaris travel pass in order to cross. Security was high and there was a bit of a wait, but he was eventually allowed to make the crossing. Once in Basel, he purchased a ticket to Paris and in a few short hours he was on his way.

December 25, 1939 15:31
Stuttgart, Germany
Stuttgart Hauptbahnhof

Richard Gunderson got off of the train in Stuttgart. After a long train ride from Berlin, he was tired and still a bit hungover. He'd had a few too many with his compatriots from the embassy the night before, and he was less than pleased to be on a mission to find an American college student so far from Berlin.

Leaving the train station, Gunderson walked down *Kreigsbergstrasse* looking for the address. After two blocks, he found his destination. He went up the steps and into the lobby. He approached the desk, where a student sat reading a book. He wrapped his knuckles on the desk to get the attention of the student.

"I am looking for Peter Teufel."

"You are late. He checked out this morning."

"Really? Do you know where he went?"

The kid at the desk just shook his head and returned to his book.

Realizing that further discussion with this college kid would be a waste of his time, Gunderson headed back out onto the street. He paused on the sidewalk, trying to decide his next move. Should he search Stuttgart for this kid? He could be anywhere. He checked his watch. If he left now, he could still make it back to Berlin in time for the party. *It isn't my kid.*

Chapter Five: Oenophile

Peter peddled his bicycle down the country lane. He was riding north out of the city of Bordeaux on an unseasonably warm day. So far, his holiday had been completely enjoyable. After leaving Stuttgart, he'd made his way to Paris, where he spent two weeks seeing the "City of Light" and tried to experience all that it had to offer, including the Eiffel Tower, the Louvre, and Harry's New York Bar. Following his stay in Paris, he had traveled to the French Riviera, staying a week in Saint Raphael and then a few days in Toulon. Two days ago, he took a train to Bordeaux. After nearly a month of touring France, he had decided to make France's famous wine country his temporary home.

His plan was to get an apartment in Bordeaux. There he would write to Marilyn and give her his address. Once he had rented a place, he would then travel some more while periodically returning to Bordeaux to see if she had written him. He wanted to visit the Netherlands and perhaps see more of Switzerland. He was not sure where he would go next. For now, he was content to see the wine country along the Gironde estuary.

He felt the warm sun on his cheek as he peddled up a small rise in the road. Pumping harder, he cycled up to the crest of the hill and saw a sight that caused him to coast. Up ahead, on the side of the road sat a tractor. Jutting out from underneath the tractor were two boots, the toes of which were pointing at the sky. As he got closer to the tractor, Peter could see that a man was lying under the tractor working on something.

Peter rode up to the green tractor, the word "Renault" inscribed in white letters on the side of the engine cowling. Parking his bike, he lay down on his back and shimmied under the tractor next to the man, who was attempting to fix the steering mechanism. Peter studied the problem.

On the ground next to the man were a few tools: an adjustable wrench, a wire cutter, and a hammer. The man turned to look at Peter, but said nothing. The man continued to work with his hands, trying to reassemble the mechanism which connected the steering wheel shaft to the shaft that ran to the front of the tractor to turn the wheels. A pin, smaller than a pencil, was missing from the pinion, and the man was trying to use a small screwdriver as a replacement. The screwdriver was too large and did not fit.

Peter grabbed the wire cutter and slid out from under the tractor. He walked over to his bicycle and knelt down at the front tire. He used the wire cutter to snip one of the spokes near the rim and then he snipped the same spoke near the axle. He took the metal spoke and crawled back under the tractor next to the man and offered him the spoke. The man took the spoke from Peter's hand and nodded. Aligning the steering shaft to the gear, he slipped the spoke into the hole. It was a little smaller in diameter than the original pin, but it would do for a temporary repair.

Peter then handed the man the wire cutter. The man took the tool and cut the spoke to the desired length, leaving two centimeters of the spoke sticking out of the joint on each side. The man used the adjustable wrench to bend the ends of the spoke so that it would not fall out of the gear assembly.

The two men wiggled out from underneath the Renault tractor and stood in the road. The man offered his hand. "*Merci beaucoup*. Remi Gagne."

Peter shook the man's hand and responded in French, "Peter Teufel. You are welcome, sir." With that, Peter turned and mounted his bicycle.

"Wait, have you had lunch? The least I can do to repay your assistance is to provide you with lunch. The farm where I work is only a few kilometers away."

Remi climbed up onto the tractor seat and started the engine. He shifted the tractor into gear and headed back to the south, the way that Peter had come. Peter followed the slow-moving tractor on his bike. They headed south down the lane for a short way and then turned to the east.

Traveling along the road, Peter noticed that they were passing row after row of grape vines. The vines were brown and looked like wires tangled around each other, but the rows were perfectly aligned, each parallel to the next. After a short distance, the tractor turned into a long drive and Peter followed.

Trees lined the path on each side of the straight, gravel driveway. At the end of the lane, Peter could see a large, white stone building. A broad stone stairway led up to the entrance where four large pillars, two on either side of the door, stood in front of the façade. *This couldn't be "the farm."*

It was.

The tractor slowed to a stop and Remi shut down the engine. He hopped off of the Renault and raised both of his arms as he announced, "Welcome to my farm, the Chateau Margaux."

Peter followed Remi up the steps and through the double oak doors into the chateau. The interior of the building was nicely appointed but not opulent. The two men walked through the entry, through a dining room, and into a large kitchen. In the kitchen were two cooks dressed in white tunics with puffy white hats on their heads. Remi greeted them both as he led Peter into a small room with a table and four chairs, where they each took a seat.

As lunch was served, Remi explained that Chateau Margaux was more than a farm. It was a vineyard. He explained how they grew the grapes, pressed the fruit, and fermented the juice. He also told Peter how they made their own oak barrels for aging the wine. The older man explained that this was his primary job at the vineyard, barrel-making. He was a cooper, although he did other things here as well. Remi assured Peter that Chateau Margaux made the finest wine in all of France. As proof, he retrieved a bottle for them to share with their meal. Peter had to admit that the red wine was indeed very good.

Remi finished the last bite of his lunch, wiped his lips with his napkin, and then took a small drink of wine. Setting the glass down, he looked at Peter. "So enough about me. What are you doing here, Peter?"

"I am on holiday, traveling around France. I just graduated from college and I am taking a tour before I return to America."

"American, eh? Your French is pretty good for an American. What did you study at the university?"

"Mechanical Engineering."

"That explains how you sized up the way to fix my tractor so quickly. Using the spoke as a pin was a good idea."

"It won't last too long. You will have to replace it with another pin, but it will hold for now."

"You know, this is a large vineyard with a lot of equipment, tractors, pumps, crushers, and the like. I could use a guy like you around here."

"I appreciate the offer, but I am not really looking for a job, Mr. Gagne, I am really just looking for a place to stay for a few months. A place to put my things and to get any mail, while I do a bit more traveling."

"Where are you staying now?"

"I have a room in Bordeaux, but that is temporary."

Remi poured each of them a little more wine, and then spoke. "How about this? We have a small apartment above the fermentation building. It is quiet and you can come and go as you please. You could stay there. If I need your services, when you are around, I could call on you. What would you say to that?"

Peter thought about the offer. Access to really good wine and a nice place like this as a sort of home base for travel might be a good fit.

"I accept your offer, Mr. Gagne."

"Please, call me Remi. Let me show you around."

February 18, 1940 17:59
Margaux, France
Chateau Margaux

Peter sat in his apartment above the fermentation building. In the preceding month he had settled into life on the vineyard. Remi had introduced Peter to Mr. Gravois, who was in charge of making the wine. He had also met the owner of the estate, a man named LeBlonde, whom Peter was told spent very little time there.

After accepting Remi's offer to move onto the estate, Peter had cleared out his room in Bordeaux and set about making the little apartment his new, if temporary, home. The apartment had a bedroom, a living room, and a small kitchen with a dining table. It was small but cozy, a perfect place for a young man like Peter. An old radio in the living room kept him up-to-date on world events.

The first night in the apartment, Peter had written a long letter to Marilyn, letting her know that he was in France and that she could write to him there. He often thought of her, how she was, where she was, and whether she was thinking of him. He asked if she had any travel plans back to Europe. He hoped that she did.

During his stay at the Chateau Margaux, Peter was free to come and go as he pleased. He had made a few day trips around the area, visiting other vineyards and spending some time in Bordeaux as well. For his part of the agreement, he had also fixed a few items for Remi. Peter had replaced the mechanical seal on a pump in the fermentation house and he had made a permanent repair to the steering mechanism on the Renault.

Peter found that the operation of the vineyard was interesting. He had watched Remi and learned how wine barrels were made. Barrel-making was a labor-intensive effort, just as much artistry as it was craftsmanship. Remi had shown him the whole operation of the farm, from how the harvest was conducted to crushing the grapes and collecting the juice to fermentation, aging, and bottling. There was even a small laboratory where the grapes were tested for ripeness by analyzing the degree of *Brix* in the juice to ensure that the fruit was right for picking. It was quite an undertaking that went into the making of one bottle of wine.

A knock on the door drew Peter's attention. "Peter, are you there?" It was Remi.

"Just a minute." Peter opened the door for the Frenchman. "Come on in."

"I brought you a gift." Remi held up a bottle of clear liquid. The bottle had no label or markings of any kind. It was just a clear glass bottle with what Peter surmised was alcohol in it. "Pomace brandy, *marc* we call it in France. I made it myself. The Italians call it *grappa*, but my *marc* is superior to their swill."

"Well then, you may enter."

"I figured after a long day of helping me build barrels that you could use a good drink."

Remi made his way into the apartment's small living room. He sat down as Peter retrieved two glasses from the kitchen. Peter sat across from his friend and set the glasses on the coffee table between them. Remi poured the brandy into the glasses and raised his in a toast.

"*Vive la France! Vive la République! Vive la liberté!*"

With his guest, Peter toasted the fortunes of France. Taking a sip of his brandy he noted that it was strong, burning his throat as it went down. "Why the show of patriotism Remi?"

"My country is at war, even if it is a *phony* war."

"*Phony* war?"

"Five months have passed since war with the *Boche* was declared and nothing has happened. The Germans are afraid of us. They sit on the other side of the Maginot Line and wait for the peace talks to commence. This is not a war. It is nothing but an armed nap."

"The Germans don't really want a war with the French. They only wanted to obtain the lands that were rightfully theirs in Poland and Czechoslovakia."

"I think that you are right, young man. We gave the *Boche* a bloody nose in the Great War. They want no part of the French fighting man in this war."

Another round of brandy was decanted and the two men again raised their glasses to France.

"Did you serve in the Great War?"

"I did indeed, but luckily for the *Boche*, I arrived at the front only days before the armistice was signed in November of 1918. This time the Germans know that they better come to the table and seek a peaceful settlement."

"I suspect that will be the case."

Remi took a final pull from his glass and stood up. He headed for the door, turning around just as he reached it. "I better get to bed early. Tomorrow, we begin pruning the vines. A truckload of laborers will arrive early in the morning to begin the work. Will you be around tomorrow if something breaks?"

"I will be here. Let me know if you need anything."

"Good. Thanks. Oh, and don't forget the poker next Saturday night. Phillipe wants a chance to win his money back from you." Remi had a smile on his face as he left.

February 19, 1940 12:13
Margaux, France
Chateau Margaux

Peter sat on a stool in the work shed adjacent to the fermentation building. On the ground in front of him lay a reassembled bearing for a wagon wheel. Remi had rousted him out of bed at around 08:00 to fix a wagon wheel that wouldn't turn easily. Towed behind the tractor, the left rear wagon wheel dragged along the ground rather than rolling on the gravel.

Peter had disassembled the bearing, noting that it had very little grease, and cleaned the dirt and gravel from the internals. The clean bearing surfaces packed with fresh grease now spun easily when turned. All that was left to do was replace the bearing on the shaft and attach the wheel. He made a note to himself that the other bearings were probably in a similar condition. He would advise Remi to have them all cleaned and repacked with grease.

One of the cooks rang the lunch bell. Peter stood up and walked out of the shed and headed out into the noon sunshine. Walking over to the row of tables alongside the fermentation building, he could see the workers coming in from the field. Men and women who had been pruning the vines by hand all morning now headed to the tables for lunch. He sat down among the workers.

Remi joined Peter's table as the soup and fresh-baked bread were served. "What is the story with the wagon?"

Peter explained what he had found and recommended that every bearing on the vineyard be checked. He explained to Remi that routine maintenance on the equipment would save him a lot of grief in the future. The old barrel-maker asked what other equipment or components would benefit from this type of care and attention. Peter told him that he would make a list of any equipment that might need such maintenance.

Peter put in a full day of work in the vineyard. He spent the majority of his time performing preventative maintenance on the winery equipment. Remi had agreed that maintaining the equipment in that manner was a good idea. Peter felt a real sense of accomplishment when the work was through. He felt good as he headed towards his apartment at the end of the day. On the way, one of the cooks told him that he had received a letter. It was from Marilyn.

After reading the letter, in which Marilyn expressed how much she missed him and wished that he would return to the

States, he suddenly felt very alone. All along, he had just wanted to prove to his parents that he was an adult. That he was in charge of his own destiny. The argument with his father had been a turning point. Now even Marilyn doubted his resolve. Peter believed that he still had a point to prove.

March 18, 1940 13:21
New York, New York
Rockefeller Center, Associated Press Headquarters

Marilyn sorted through the proofs on her desk. Each photograph was labeled with her name and that of the Associated Press. The pictures were of the Saint Patrick's Day Parade. They were good, but it wasn't real news.

She looked up from her desk and stared at a frame hanging from her wall: the picture of Peter that she'd taken in Danzig. He was smiling, but his eyes showed sadness.

In the six months since she'd taken that picture, she had thought about Peter a lot. Although she had only spent a small amount of time with him, he was special. He made her feel loved. He made her feel like she was the only woman in the world. So much so, that she had written him a dozen letters, each letter asking him to return to the States.

His replies were encouraging. He had expressed his feelings about her. However, he was adamant about staying in Europe a while longer to prove something to his parents. She didn't quite understand that, but she knew that he sincerely believed that he needed to finish what he had started.

Marilyn looked back at the proofs. She selected four of the best ones and placed them in a folder for the copy desk. Then she sat back and thought about how she could persuade Peter to come home.

She realized if letters did not work, then she must meet with him directly. Face-to-face was always the best way to communicate. She would have to go see Peter and tell him that she wanted him to come to New York to be with her. Her biggest problem was how to get to France. A trip like that would cost money. Money that she did not have.

A thought occurred to her: *If the Associated Press sent me to France, it would not cost me a thing!*

She decided at that moment that she would meet with her boss, Mr. Benkleman, and ask for an assignment to France. Marilyn knew that the AP was short of reporters on the ground in Europe and she could certainly do the job. She would meet with her boss as soon as she could and would continue to ask him week after week until he relented.

She had to get to Peter and get him back into her life. She didn't want to let this love of hers get away.

Chapter Six: Harvest

Peter sat in the warm morning sun as he worked on a gear assembly for a crushing machine. The crusher would be needed for the upcoming fall harvest and he wanted to make sure that it was in tip-top shape. One of the gears had several broken teeth and he had replaced it with a new one. All that was left to do was to reinstall the gear mechanism into the machine and it should work perfectly.

Life around the vineyard had been an enjoyable experience for Peter all through the spring and early summer. He had settled into a comfortable pattern of making day trips around France and one week-long trip to Spain with stays at the Chateau Margaux in between. That had all changed in May, when word came that the German Army had invaded France, Belgium and the Netherlands. Peter had heard of the invasion upon returning from Spain and, by the end of June, France had collapsed. Just last week, the Germans arrived in Bordeaux. Things had changed.

Peter set down the gear mechanism and wondered what he should do next. The war that his father had warned him about had actually arrived. He had seen tanks on the road not far from the vineyard and that had concerned him. Remi had been absolutely stunned at the rapid demise of the French Army and he told Peter that, as a Frenchman, he was honor-bound to resist the *Boche*. For his part, Peter wasn't sure what he should do. Should he try to get back to the United States? Should he stay put until things settled down? Should he get to Spain or Switzerland and hole up until the inevitable peace treaty was signed? He wasn't at all sure what he should do.

He had planned to take a yearlong holiday after college to see more of Europe. The first six months had been exactly what he had dreamed of, traveling around France and Spain. He had wanted to see more of Switzerland and perhaps Italy or Greece, too, but with a true European war at hand, it might not be possible or wise. He now wondered if he should have heeded his father's advice.

Peter's thoughts were interrupted by the sounds of engines rumbling in the distance. He could hear the vehicles driving along the road in front of the vineyard. He walked around the chateau in time to see a German staff car, followed by a line of trucks, turning into the lane that led to the winery.

Peter saw one of the winery workers run into the chateau. Shortly, Mr. Gravois, the wine maker, exited the building and walked down the stairs to greet the unwelcome visitors. Peter made his way to Gravois' side. Remi also found his way to the front of the chateau from where he had been working in the coopery. The three men waited as the procession of military vehicles made its way down the lane.

The staff car came to a halt near where Peter, Remi, and Mr. Gravois were standing. A German Army officer stepped out of the car and approached the men.

"*Sind Sie der Inhaber?*" the officer asked.

Neither of the two Frenchmen spoke German, so Peter translated. "He asked if you are the proprietor."

Mr. Gravois replied to Peter, "Tell him who I am, please."

Peter informed the officer that Mr. Gravois, as the wine maker, was in charge of the operation of the winery and that the owner, Mr. LeBlonde, was not currently in France.

"Very well. Please inform Mr. Gravois that the Reich is confiscating the wine to be used or sold by the Reich to fund the war effort against the aggressors in France."

Peter noticed that as he explained what was going on, Remi bristled with anger.

"Also inform him that any attempt to prevent our rightful acquisition of the wine will be dealt with severely. Now, show me the wine cellar."

Again, Peter relayed the message and, as he did, the officer waived on the trucks. Mr. Gravois pointed in the direction of the storage cellar where the majority of the wine was stored in oak barrels. The trucks began to roll towards the cellar.

It was then that Remi made his move and rushed the German officer. Peter could do nothing to stop it. He was just as surprised as the German officer was when Remi lunged at the German with his cooper's knife. The officer dodged the thrust at the last second and spun Remi past him. Remi's momentum carried him crashing into the grill of the staff car, head-first. There Remi fell to the ground. By the time Remi rolled over to sit up, he was staring down the barrel of the officer's pistol. The two men exchanged looks of hate.

"Please don't shoot him, sir. He is an old fool," Peter pleaded.

"Fool or not, he assaulted an officer of the *Wehrmacht*. You are under arrest. In the coming days you will wish that I had shot you."

With that, Remi was led away and placed into one of the trucks. Peter would never see Remi Gagne again.

July 6, 1940 14:54
New York, New York
Rockefeller Center, Associated Press Headquarters

Harvey Benkleman sat in his office on the seventh floor of the fifteen-story Associated Press Building in the heart of Manhattan. He was a tired man of fifty-four with thinning hair, a paunch, and a three-pack-a-day Chesterfield habit. He had been in the news business since he'd started hawking newspapers on the streets of New York City as a boy. He had worked his way up to management through hard work and determination. Now he was in charge of the international desk and he faced a problem: he was running out of reporters at a time when the news was international news.

Just then he heard a knock at his office door. He looked up and through the glass could see a woman. He motioned for her to enter and sighed as the door opened. He had no choice.

"Come in, Miss Miller." Benkleman waved toward the chairs in front of his desk. "Miss Miller, I have given this a lot of thought. For months now, you have requested a European assignment and each time I have denied it. But things have changed, and I need a good photographer on the Continent."

Marilyn tried to hold her jubilation in check. She was finally going to get a chance to be a part of the action, to cover the war in Europe. She would also be closer to Peter. This was the day that she had prayed for.

"The shots that you brought back from Danzig made this company a lot of money. How you got out of there was a miracle. I am unwilling to send you in to cover combat, but I am willing to let you cover other European political events in order to free up our other assets to cover the war. I am posting you to Zurich."

"Yes, Mr. Benkleman." While it wasn't combat coverage, she would at least be back in Europe where the real news was.

"You will be working for Bob Pennington over there. Oh, and I have a few rules. You will always travel with a man. No solo photo shoots. You will only cover what Bob assigns to you, no freelancing. Got it?"

"When do I leave?"

"Monday. See the travel desk for your itinerary."

On the way downstairs, Marilyn made a note to herself to write to Peter in France, letting him know that she would be in Switzerland. She imagined that she should arrive about the time that her letter would. She had prayed that he was safe in Bordeaux now that the Germans had occupied France. His last letter said that he was doing well, but that was six weeks ago.

July 23, 1940 20:00
Margaux, France
Chateau Margaux

Things had changed rapidly in Western France and in particular at the Chateau Margaux. The Germans had taken a week to move the thousands of barrels of wine out of the cellar. During that time, Mr. Gravois disappeared, along with many of the workers at the winery. A German Major named Bauer had moved into the chateau, making it his headquarters. In his first act, he had informed the remaining staff that they were now "workers for the Reich" and that wine production would continue as before. Bauer had replaced both Gravois and Gagne with a former apprentice. Work progressed at the winery, but at a slower pace.

Two days before, Peter had been questioned by Bauer about his role at the winery. While Bauer spoke passable French, the conversation was conducted in German. Peter informed him that he was the mechanic at the winery and offered Bauer little else. Peter felt that he was better served by holding his cards close to his vest.

That afternoon, Peter sat in his apartment over the fermentation building wondering what he should do. His holiday had taken a turn for the worse now that a real war had broken out in Europe. He listened to the radio every night to keep tabs on the events of the day. He listened as the reporters told of great air battles between the Germans and the British that were being conducted over the English Channel. He also learned that German submarines were attempting to blockade shipping to and from England. The sinking of ships bound for the island nation grew by the day. The new Prime Minister of the United Kingdom, Winston Churchill, had given a speech shortly after the fall of France, announcing: "If the British Empire and its Commonwealth last for a thousand years, men will still say, this was their finest hour." Peter wondered what would happen if the British were defeated or sued for peace.

Peter took in all of these events as he sorted through his next course of action. He could try to flee to Spain and make his way back to the United States. He could cross into Switzerland and find a way back to America. Or he could travel back into Germany proper and wait out the war. After all, the Germans were clearly winning the conflict. Once Britain capitulated, which surely would happen, everything would return to normal. At least, he believed it would.

Peter left his apartment and went to check on the mail. He walked over to the chateau and proceeded into the servant's entrance. He sorted through the letters, some of which were addressed to the recently arrested Remi Gagne. The last letter that Peter thumbed through was addressed to him. It was from Marilyn.

Peter snatched up his letter and headed back to his apartment. Closing the door to his loft above the fermentation house, he settled at the small dining table and tore open the letter. After reading that she was being stationed in Switzerland, arriving in early August, he no longer wondered what his next move would be. Marilyn had written that once she was settled in the country, she would write to him to let him know when and where they could meet. Peter now knew that he had to stay put until her next letter arrived. In the meantime, he would prepare to make his exit from France as soon as she informed him of her plans.

September 17, 1940 09:31
Margaux, France
Chateau Margaux

Peter was working in the fermentation house coupling hoses in preparation for the fall harvest when he was summoned by a German soldier. Major Bauer wanted to see him in front of the chateau. Peter put his work aside and walked to the front of the major's residence. There stood Bauer alongside a brown military *Kübelwagen*. The rear hatch of the car was open, exposing the access to the engine. As Peter approached, Bauer spoke. "I need this fixed. It is running very rough."

"Yes, sir."

Peter hopped into the driver's seat and started the engine. It started, but the engine was sputtering and shaking. He shut the engine down with a turn of the key and told the major that he needed to grab a few tools. He set off to the fermentation building and returned a few minutes later.

In his mind, Peter went over the three things that he knew were true about the internal combustion engine. It needed fuel, air, and an ignition source to run. This *Kübelwagen* appeared to be getting fuel and air, so he reasoned that it may not be getting the spark that it needed to run properly.

Peter knelt down behind the vehicle and removed each of the four spark plugs, one at a time. He noticed that each one was dirtier than the last. He cleaned the plugs with a brush and checked the gap on each one. He reinstalled the plugs and started the car again. It purred like a kitten. The whole process took less than twenty minutes.

"There you go, Major. It should be fine now. Just dirty plugs."

"You are a good mechanic, *Herr* Teufel. Where did you learn your craft?"

Peter hesitated before responding. Again, he did not want to provide too much information about himself. Less was better in his mind.

"I worked for my grandfather as a boy at a railroad repair yard. The rest I picked up in college at the Stuttgart Institute of Technology. I majored in mechanical engineering."

"What is an educated young German such as yourself doing working at a French vineyard? You would be better serving the Reich back in Germany."

It was not a question. It was a statement. Peter didn't correct Bauer's assumption that he was German. "After graduation, I wanted to see a little bit of Europe and wound up here."

"Given the current circumstances, the Fatherland could

benefit from a man of your skill."

"Am I not serving the Reich by helping to harvest such a valuable crop?"

"You are an underutilized resource. You are a worker for the Reich, my worker, and I have decided that you are needed elsewhere. You will gather your belongings and accompany me into Bordeaux, where you will be reassigned in Germany to something more suited to your abilities."

Peter tried again to persuade the Major. "What about the fall harvest? It is critical to ensure that the equipment works properly to make the wine."

"The new *Weinführer* Heinz Boemers will ensure that the entire Bordeaux region is productive. He will ensure that the harvest is completed. You, on the other hand, will be serving your country in a more productive capacity as is your duty to the Reich. Now, go, gather your things."

Peter recognized that he was being ordered to leave the winery and that he was being relocated back to Germany. For what purpose he was being relocated back to Germany, Peter did not know. He gathered his belongings and packed his suitcase. As he did so, he considered making a run for it. He had planned on getting Marilyn's letter and heading to Switzerland in a week or so, but that wasn't in the cards. He decided to follow the orders from Bauer and not make any waves.

Peter rode with Major Bauer and his driver into Bordeaux. He was assembled with a group of other workers being sent back to Germany to work in the wartime industries. There were French, German, and people of other nationalities being loaded onto a train bound for Germany.

Four days later, a letter addressed to Peter Teufel arrived at the Chateau Margaux. The letter would have informed Peter that Marilyn would meet him in Basel, Switzerland on Saturday September 29. The letter was never opened. By then, Peter was in Kiel, Germany.

Chapter Seven: Construction

October 1, 1940 07:00
Kiel, Germany
Germaniawerft Shipyard

Peter arrived for his shift along with his fellow workers at the *Friedrich Krupp Germaniawerft*. The short walk from his compound to the shipyard in the cool fall air had been a nice way to start a dreary day. He was assigned to the construction of a type X U-boat in yard number 615. The submarine was destined to be the *U-116* and designed to lay mines. He entered the hull of the submarine and reported to his supervisor, an older man named Kohl.

In the few weeks that he had been back in Germany, Peter had determined that he was more of a prisoner than anything else. At the Bordeaux train station, he had been given papers that stated he was a German being returned to the Reich for service in the war industries. Major Bauer had vouched for his credentials *mistakenly*, along with his engineering background. He had been transported on a train with others who were being forced to work for the German war machine. The journey had led them from Bordeaux to Paris and then onto Bonn in Germany.

In Bonn, the passengers on the train were segregated into various ethnic classes and further divided by skill sets. Peter was placed with other Germans with "technical-engineer" stamped on his papers. Other Germans in his group were carpenters, farmers, bricklayers, and even a doctor. After a long night in Bonn, Peter was placed on a train to Kiel. He had been assigned to work at the shipyard.

Upon his arrival in Kiel, he was given a room in the labor camp. He learned that the camp was divided into sectors based on the country of origin and worker classification, in accordance with the *Organisation Todt* directives. The Nazi government had established an organization to obtain, organize, and assign forced labor in support of the war effort. People from Germany and from occupied nations were rounded up and sent to work replacing the men who were fighting the war. Peter had been assigned to help construct U-boats.

Peter spent the day helping a crew of men install one of the two *Germaniawerft* Type 46 supercharged diesel engines. He was tasked with helping to assemble the supercharger. The work was difficult and dirty. A submarine was a cramped place in which to work.

But the U-boat was a technological marvel to Peter. It was a long tube filled with interrelated systems and components all designed to operate the submarine. Wires and pipes ran everywhere. Pumps and motors were crammed into the hull. Valves, switches, compressors, tanks, dials, and indicators were strategically located throughout the boat.

Peter finished his twelve-hour shift and walked back to his living quarters in the compound. He had a small room to himself, with a bed, a small table, and a couch. The communal bathroom was down the hall along with the showers. Meals were taken in a cafeteria and the food was decent. He learned from Kohl that the Germans were separated from the other races within the work camp. Kohl also mentioned that the foreigners did not have it nearly as good.

Some of the Poles and Slavs were piled into bunkhouses built for forty that were now required to house nearly twice that number. Their food was not nearly of the quality or quantity that was given to Peter. They were even paid less for the same work and, in some cases, were not paid at all.

Peter's mindset had changed considerably after being conscripted into the labor force. He had enjoyed his time in France, but now everything had changed. Even though he was "German," he was rarely allowed outside of the compound, except to go to the shipyard. He worked six days a week for what was really very little pay. The few times that he was allowed to venture out into Kiel, he was forbidden to travel outside of the city. The train station would not allow conscripted workers to buy tickets for travel beyond the city limits. For all intents and purposes, he was trapped.

Peter rested upon his bed that night, considering his options. He was in a place that he really did not want to be. He was an American whom everyone in Kiel believed was German. He had been conscripted to work in the shipyard and it would be difficult to get back to his homeland.

He considered going to the *Organisation Todt* leader and letting him know that Peter Teufel was an American, but *would that be a good idea*? His treatment as a "German" was better than what the other people from Europe were receiving. Would an American be treated like the Poles and Slavs? He decided that, at least for now, pretending to be a German was the best course until he could figure a way to get out of Kiel.

Peter figured that his best bet was to find a way to Berlin, to get to the American embassy. The United States was not a part of this war, and if he could make it there, he could get home. He would have to make a plan.

December 23, 1940 18:47
Kiel, Germany
Germaniawerft Shipyard

After another seemingly endless day, Peter's shift was soon coming to an end. Every time that he looked at his watch, the hands had hardly moved. Minutes felt like hours. He waited for the end-of-shift whistle to blow so that he could make his run to Berlin.

Over two months of planning had gone into this effort. He had obtained all of the schedules of the compound guards, befriending those who would most likely be on shift during his departure. He had gathered all of the train schedules and selected a late-night train from Kiel to Berlin. *Fewer prying eyes during the night.*

Peter had assumed that the Monday before Christmas would be a high-volume travel day. Workers trying to get home for Christmas would clog the train station, making it easier for him to blend in and go unnoticed. Yes, tonight was the night that he would make his way to Berlin.

He looked at his watch, 18:51 ... an eternity until 19:00! Two and a half months he had planned, and now he had to wait nine more agonizing minutes.

He had spent the months helping to build *U-116*, and he actually enjoyed building the submarine. He tried to use his time wisely, working hard installing mechanical components. It helped pass the time until he could make his escape to Berlin. He even went so far as to read the operating manuals for the equipment onboard the boat. He knew how to start the diesel engines and had even done so during testing. He knew how to run the air compressors and the ship's main propulsion motors, all in an effort to pass the time until tonight.

At 18:58 by Peter's watch the whistle sounded to end the shift. *Two minutes early, thank God.*

Peter stepped off of the U-boat along with the rest of the workers making their way back to the compound. He contained his excitement as best as he could, keeping pace with the other workers on the trek. Peter returned to his room, changed out of his work clothes, and went down to the cafeteria for dinner. He ate his dinner of pork, cabbage, and potato soup as slowly as he could. He had time.

He returned to his room and gathered his things. No suitcase, just his documents, including the Canaris travel pass and his money. He did not want to draw any attention to himself by carrying a suitcase out of the compound. He waited, checking his watch. Only an hour to go.

At 21:30 he put on his coat and left his room. He walked to the gate where he believed that Fritz Grohl would be on duty. Over the past two months he had befriended Grohl, an enlisted man in the *Heer,* with conversations and by bringing the soldier hot coffee during the cold fall nights. Peter made his way to the guardhouse slowly and saw that Grohl was indeed on watch.

"Good evening, *Herr* Grohl."

"Hey, Peter. What brings you out on a cold night?"

"*Ach du lieber*! I had to work late so I missed supper. Heading to town to get a bite to eat."

"A man has to eat, now doesn't he? *Auf wiedersehen.*"

Peter waived to the soldier as he made his way onto the streets of Kiel.

He walked south out of the compound along the harbor front, heading for the Kiel *Hauptbahnhof* only a few kilometers away. Relief coursed through him as he walked along on the winter night. He was leaving the labor camp behind and that suited him just fine.

He made his way to *Gablenzbrüke* street and turned west. After a short distance, he turned north on *Sophienblatt,* proceeding the to the train station. He entered the main station and stepped up to a café. He was early. He had walked faster than he had planned. His plan was to wait until close to midnight to buy his ticket. The station personnel would be changing shifts at midnight. His train departed at 00:26 for Berlin. He could wait.

At five minutes to midnight, Peter queued up in the line at the ticket counter.

"One ticket to Berlin, please."

"Your papers please, sir."

Peter had planned for this. Now was the time to pull out all of the stops. He did not offer the agent his papers. Instead, he handed the man his travel pass from Canaris. The agent took the document and read it. The agent paused, sizing up the young man.

Peter was getting nervous. If he could just get on this train, he was 90% of the way home. "I am going to see my *opa* and *oma* for Christmas."

Peter watched as the agent looked suspiciously at the travel pass. He wondered if the agent noticed that the date on the pass was two years old. It appeared as if something just didn't seem right to the agent but still, Canaris was a powerful man. After a long moment, he issued Peter a ticket.

Peter took the stub from the agent and boarded the train to Berlin. He sat down with relief, knowing that in a few hours he would be in Berlin and only a few kilometers away from the American embassy. He was going home and, when he got there, he would contact Marilyn. They would be able to see each other. *Who knows, maybe she is the one.*

Peter was jostled out of his thoughts by a man nudging his shoulder.

"Your papers, please."

Peter stared at the man, who was wearing a dark overcoat and a dark hat. The man had a serious look on his face. *Police? Gestapo?* Peter had to think fast. He retrieved Canaris's travel pass and handed it to the man. The man looked at it briefly and again asked for Peter's papers.

Apparently, this man was not impressed with his "get out of jail free" card from Canaris. Peter had no choice but to hand the man his worker's documents. The man took his documents and read them.

"Technical-engineer assigned to the shipyard, eh? You are not allowed to leave Kiel under these documents."

"But my travel pass from the *Abwehr* allows it."

"The date on your pass is two years old. Your conscription papers are from a few months ago. They supersede your pass, which I am confiscating. Stand up, you are under arrest."

December 24, 1940 13:31
Omaha, Nebraska
Gold Coast District

Anne Teufel was preparing for Christmas Eve when she noticed the mail carrier pass in front of her house. She finished setting the table. They had family coming tonight for dinner and she wanted everything to be just right … except it wouldn't be right. Peter was still in Europe.

She took off her apron and laid it on the kitchen counter. She walked into the living room only to find that Erik was asleep on the couch. She grabbed her coat out of the closet and went out to get the mail. She returned to the house and sorted the stack of envelopes.

Bills, a couple of Christmas cards, and an advertisement for soap were in the pile. Then she noticed a letter addressed to "Ambassador and Mrs. Erik Teufel." That was odd, Erik was never actually the Ambassador. She noticed that the letter had been mailed from Zurich, Switzerland, but the return address was the Associated Press headquarters in New York. She opened the letter.

~

November 29, 1940

Dear Ambassador and Mrs. Teufel,

My name is Marilyn Miller and I am writing you concerning your son Peter. I met Peter at the US embassy Christmas party in Berlin in 1938. I believe that I was introduced to you both, briefly, that evening. I have stayed in touch with Peter over the last couple of years. I know that he stayed in Germany to finish college, while you returned to the States. I last saw Peter in Poland in September of 1939 and we have exchanged letters in the interim. When last I heard from Peter, he was in Bordeaux, France. We had plans to meet in Basel, Switzerland but he never arrived. That was in the fall of this year.

I do not intend to worry you. I am only seeking to find out that he is indeed ok. Has he returned to you? Have you heard from him? With the European war going on, I just wanted to verify that your son was safe and sound. Please let me know if you can verify that he is safe by responding to my address on the envelope.

Sincerely,

Marilyn Miller

~

Erik Teufel was awakened from his nap by the sound of his wife crying. He arose from the couch and headed into the kitchen where he heard her sobbing. As he entered, she did not speak. She only continued to sob as she handed him the letter.

Chapter Eight: Launch

Peter lay upon an iron cot in the city jail. He had been confined there early on the morning of Christmas Eve. *Merry Christmas*, he lamented. This was his reward for trying to get back home, not to Berlin, but to the United States. Fortunately, it appeared that the Gestapo thought only that he was fleeing to Berlin. After four days in the Kiel jail and being questioned by the Gestapo, he hoped that he would not get any more presents like this for Christmas.

The Gestapo had taken all of his papers at the train station and cuffed him like a common prisoner. They had questioned him on and off for two days. Peter figured that with the Christmas holiday, they were short on staff and really didn't want to spend a lot of time questioning a "German" worker who just wanted to see his grandma and grandpa during Christmas.

Finally, a guard summoned him from his cell. At the front desk, Peter was told to stand in front of the officer on duty.

The man before Peter was a police officer, not Gestapo. Peter attempted to look contrite as the officer spoke. "It is the duty of all Germans to serve the Reich, *Herr* Teufel."

Peter nodded.

"Your work is vital to the war effort. Even one day away from your duty could harm this nation. Do you understand?"

Peter nodded again.

"I have been ordered by the Gestapo to return you to the shipyard so that you can continue to support the Reich. Your papers will be stamped as a flight risk and as such, you will no longer be allowed to leave the labor compound. Do you understand, *Herr* Teufel?"

"Yes, sir."

Peter was escorted back to the shipyard compound. He no longer had his travel pass from Admiral Canaris and now he was prevented from leaving the compound except to report to work. He was tired, disparaged, and out of ideas to get home.

April 13, 1941 10:15
Kiel, Germany
Germaniawerft Shipyard

Udo Kohl was pleased with the progress that his workers had made on the construction of *U-116*. The submarine would be ready to launch in a few weeks and, shortly thereafter, it would be commissioned to serve in the Kriegsmarine. As a former U-boat sailor in the Great War, this gave him a tremendous sense of pride.

Born in the small farming village of Aidlingen, Udo had served Germany aboard U-boats in his youth. Learning all that there was to know in the engine room of his WWI boat, he was now a master at building underwater vessels. A badly broken leg during a routine torpedo loading exercise had led to his dismissal from the *Kaiserliche Marine* in 1917. He had been working for *Krupp,* building U-boats since 1920.

In his estimation, the U-116 was a fine engineering achievement. His crew of laborers had built an excellent undersea vessel for the Reich and that made him proud. He supervised men, technical men, from all over Europe. Some were only fit to carry tools; some were adept machinists; but one had caught his eye, Peter Teufel.

In all of his years building sailing vessels, Udo Kohl had never had a worker who was as inquisitive, talented, knowledgeable, and handy as Teufel. He had learned that the kid had been to college for mechanical engineering, but it was more than that. The young man had a knack for solving problems. He could work on any piece of equipment set before him. Most of all, Kohl liked Peter. Never complained, always got his work done. He was a fine German lad.

"Peter, come here."

"Yes, sir, *Herr* Kohl."

"There is an easier way to remove that bearing Peter. Let me show you."

Peter stepped back from the lubricating oil pump that he had been working on. The pump had failed its flowrate test and Peter had been assigned to disassemble it to determine the cause of the failure. He had been using a pry bar to force the bearing off of the pump shaft, but to no avail.

"Be my guest," Peter said, handing the pry bar to Kohl.

"This is not the tool to use. You must always use the right tool for the job, makes a man's life much easier."

The older man reached into a nearby tool cabinet and removed an odd-looking tool. The tool had three arms with ninety-degree hooks at the end. The arms were threaded on a shaft with very fine threads, with the shaft ending in a hexagonal bolt. Kohl took the tool and placed the shaft of the tool in line with the shaft of the pump. He then slipped the three ninety-degree hooks behind the bearing and twisted the hexagonal end to tighten up the arms of the tool against the bearing.

Peter could see right away that the tool that Kohl was using would apply significantly more mechanical advantage than his pry bar would. He stood back and watched the more experienced man work.

Kohl took a wrench and placed it over the hexagonal end of the shaft. Then he began to turn the shaft with relative ease. The bearing slid down the pump shaft until the tool loosened and fell to the deck. From there, Kohl removed the bearing from the shaft. "You see, the right tool for the right application, that is all it takes."

"That is pretty amazing."

"Not amazing. It's mechanics. You should have learned that at your school—what was it, Frankfurt?"

"No, Stuttgart."

"Well, you should have learned it there," Kohl said with a smile. "Now, finish disassembling that pump and let me know what you find."

Udo Kohl sat back and watched as Peter took the pump apart. He noticed that the young man was not intimidated by the work. In fact, he tackled it with gusto. His current observation of the kid only reinforced the impression he'd developed over the last six months or so. This guy had a good mind. He could fix things. Udo believed that Teufel would make a good submariner. He noticed that Peter not only read the technical manuals for each piece of equipment that he worked on, but he also read the operational manuals to understand how the piece of equipment was supposed to work. *That is the making of a true U-boat sailor.*

If only he were Peter's age, he would gladly join the *Kriegsmarine* today.

May 3, 1941 12:05
Kiel, Germany
Germaniawerft Shipyard

Peter lined up with the other shipyard workers under the warm May sun. Next to him stood his supervisor, Udo Kohl. Before the workers stood a wooden stage, shrouded in ceremonial Nazi banners. The workers had all been summoned for the launching of *U-116*.

On the deck of the newly built submarine stood several *Kriegsmarine* sailors adorned in their dress uniforms. The newly appointed captain was perched up on the conning tower. Several shipyard workers also scurried around the topside of the boat, readying themselves for launch.

Peter listened as a vice president of the *Krupp Germaniawerft* spoke about the glorious support that the shipyard had provided to the war effort. He went on and on about how the workers had gifted the Reich with such a wonderful and deadly minelaying submarine. Peter had to agree with that. The boat was indeed a lethal weapon of war.

The next speaker was an admiral of the *Kriegsmarine* who vowed to utilize the *U-116* to destroy the aggressors in the West. To Peter, it all sounded like propaganda, but he knew that the boat was lethal. He had helped to build it.

When the admiral had finished speaking, the band struck up the German national anthem, *Das Lied der Deutschen*—"the "Song of Germany." As the band played, the large craft slipped into the bay creating quite a wave then floated, bobbing momentarily in front of the shipyard. The crowd cheered exuberantly as the boat came to rest majestically on the water.

The dignitaries and the civilians began to leave. Following their orders, Peter and the other workers stayed where they were. As the stage cleared and the crowd thinned, Peter wondered how long he would have to stand before the empty dais, waiting on the signal to return to work. Now that the *U-116* had been launched, he wasn't sure what he would be working on next.

A German officer of the *Kriegsmarine* took the stage. He approached the podium and waived to the workers lined up along the waterfront. Reaching into his pocket, he removed a piece of paper and laid it upon the wooden podium. Adjusting his hat, he spoke: "Attention workers of the Reich. I am *Kommodore Sandhoefener.* I am here to congratulate you on your exemplary work on the *U-116*. Your hard work has not gone unnoticed by the *Kriegsmarine*, the Reich, and by our *Führer. Heil Hitler!*"

The workers standing by Peter returned the salute with a modicum of joy. Peter noticed that Udo Kohl was happy to return the salute, more so than the rest of the contingent of workers.

"The work that you have performed here at the *Krupp Germaniawerft* shipyard, like other shipyards throughout the Fatherland, has surpassed the production quotas expected. Each and every day Germany launches new and better fighting ships to combat those who threaten the Reich."

Peter wondered how long that he would have to stand here and listen to this back-slapping, self-aggrandizing speech. He just wanted to know what his next project was so that he could get to work building another engineering marvel.

"It has come to my attention, however, that our current rate of building German warships has outrun our ability to man such ships, which is a nice problem to have, although a problem that is difficult to address."

Sandhoefener paused and received a smattering of applause. "As chief of manning for the U-boat fleet, I am obliged to ensure that every sea-going U-boat is manned with capable and rightminded Germans to carry out the missions assigned by the *Führer*. To that end, I will be assigning every third man present today to duty within the *Kriegsmarine*."

None of the workers clapped at this announcement. Peter, who had not really been paying attention to the speech, was now fully intent upon every word that the *Kommodore* spoke.

"You, the workers of the Reich, are the ones most familiar with the design and construction of the U-boats. It is you who could best serve the *Führer* by manning the U-boat fleet. I can't take you all, as more boats need to be constructed, but I can offer some of you the glory of serving in the *Kriegsmarine*. Now, count off!"

The *Kommodore* pointed to the left side of the rows of assembled men. Each man in turn counted out *one, two,* or *three,* and every third man was pulled out of line for duty in the *Kriegsmarine*.

Peter was in the second row, so he had time to think. He quickly counted the number of men in the front row and then the second row; ascertaining his number quickly, he realized that it was two. He would stay with the shipyard and not be assigned to the *Kriegsmarine*.

Udo Kohl counted the number of men as well. He was a "three," a candidate for U-boat service. His mind quickly raced back to his heady days on a submarine during the Great War. And just as quickly, he realized that he was forty-four years old with a feeble leg. He would be a hindrance to any operational U-boat. Proud though he was, he could not risk the lives of sixty other sailors who would have to compensate for a crippled old man.

As the count came down the second row, Peter was content. He knew where he stood. He watched as a man a few bodies down from him screamed *Heil Hitler!* as he learned that he was a "three." The other workers clapped and cheered for the man, for he was obviously delighted to be in the *Kriegsmarine*.

During the commotion, Udo Kohl made his move to best serve the Reich. He slipped behind Peter and assumed the number "two "position, making Peter a number "three". *It was best for the Fatherland.*

The count progressed rapidly and Peter only figured out what had happened when it was his turn to call out the number. Before him, Udo said "Two," and Peter was forced to say, "Three."

"*Gott verdammt es!*" Peter cursed under his breath.

Udo had heard him and quietly responded. "You can damn the Gods now, young Teufel, but I have done you a great favor."

Peter was quickly pulled out of line and forced to gather with the growing group of new *Kriegsmarine* conscripts. He was now joining the German Navy.

Chapter Nine: Sailor

August 22, 1941 05:15
Kiel, Germany
Kriegsmarine Enlisted Indoctrination Center

Peter sat quietly at a table in the mess facility along with the other *Kriegsmarine* recruits eating his breakfast. Today was Friday and his birthday. He had just turned twenty-three years old, but none of the other sailors knew that. As always, he had just fifteen minutes to eat his breakfast. Three months after his conscription into the German Navy, life as a recruit in training had become a never-changing routine.

The first week had been a blur. He was given a stack of paperwork to fill out, poked and prodded by doctors, subjected to various inoculations, and given uniforms, a sea bag, and a bad haircut. What followed this indoctrination period was daily instruction on how to be a sailor. He was taught various knots, how to read signal flags, how to march, how to salute, and how to say "*Yes, sir.*" He learned many things as a recruit, but what struck him most was that being a sailor in the *Kriegsmarine* was even worse than being a forced labor worker in the shipyard.

The days began at 04:30 and ended at 21:00 each night. There was no time for relaxation; every minute of the day was scheduled. Physical training, breakfast, classroom instruction, marching drills, lunch, seamanship training, damage control training, dinner, weapons instruction, and so on and so on, until the day was done.

Peter had done all that he was told to do. He received excellent marks in each phase of his indoctrination. He had even been appointed recruit squad leader, which he supposed was an honor, although it came with added responsibility. If any sailor in his squad made a mistake, it was his job to get it corrected. At the end of each day, he was tired and sleep almost always came easily to him.

As he ate his boiled eggs, bacon, hard cheese, and toast, he was consoled by the fact that today was his last day of recruit training. It would finally be over. Tomorrow, Saturday, was graduation day, and early next week he would be assigned to a ship as a *Matrose*, just another seaman recruit. Ordinary in all ways except his country of origin.

At exactly 05:30 *Bootsmann* Abel, Peter's company commander, ordered the men to cease eating breakfast and to muster in the classroom in ten minutes. Peter picked up his tray and silverware and quickly set them in the window entrance to the scullery. Donning his cap as he headed out the door, he walked swiftly to the classroom.

Peter's company assembled in the classroom and each man took his assigned seat. The men were seated by squad. Idle chatter filled the room until *Bootsmann* Abel entered.

"Quiet down. You are not yet sailors of the *Kriegsmarine*. Now listen up. Your training is nearly complete. You have made it this far and you will soon be proud members of our fleet. After graduation, I will be glad to call you my comrades and shipmates. I have in my hands your orders. Next week, you will all transfer to your respective commands."

There was a buzz of excitement amongst the men in the classroom. Each sailor present had a wish list of where exactly he wished to serve in the Navy and now was the time that each man would find out if his wish had been granted. The room went silent as Abel continued. "*Matrose* Adenauer, Western Fleet, motor torpedo boat T-26. *Matrose* Arbeit, Baltic Fleet, supply and logistics. Tough luck Arbeit, you won't be going to sea."

Peter listened as dozens of other names were called off in alphabetical order. Teufel would be near the end. He waited as each man before him received their assignment. Some went to destroyers, others to submarines; one man was even assigned to a weather station in Norway.

"*Matrose* Teufel, you get to walk across the street, Northern Fleet, *U-216*, right here in Kiel."

Peter wasn't really surprised. It made sense for him to be assigned to a submarine as he had previously worked in the shipyard building them. Still, this did not please him. It was one thing to help build a submarine, but it must be a completely different animal to actually submerge in one.

Peter drifted off into thought as the remaining few names were read from the list. He was certainly in a pickle. How was he ever going to get back to the United States while assigned to a German U-boat?

August 22, 1941 15:23
Baden, Switzerland
Stein Castle

Marilyn Miller stood atop the rocky promontory jutting over Baden gorge. In the valley far below, the river Limmat flowed along its course under a clear sky, its blue waters meandering through the sleepy little village of Baden. The view from the ruins of Stein Castle were spectacular. Although the structure had been abandoned several centuries before, one stone tower still stood. Remnants of the castle walls lined the crest of the mountain and adjoined the lone spire. The Swiss flag, a white cross on a red field, flew from the upper most point on the tower.

Marilyn snapped picture after picture. This was her last assignment in Europe for the Associated Press. She was being recalled to the United States for a new assignment.

As beautiful as the vista before her was, she could not seem to truly enjoy the day. Her mind was on Peter Teufel. It was his birthday today and she had not heard from him in a year. Her letters to France had received no response and she worried more and more as time passed that something had happened to him. She had received two letters from Peter's mother, but his parents had not heard from him either.

She was now losing hope that she would ever see Peter again. There was a time when she had thought that he might be "the one," the man that she would marry. Their time together, though limited, had been so enjoyable. He had stolen her heart the first time that they had met in Berlin, and their few days together in Danzig had only confirmed that she was in love with him. He was kind, gentle, intelligent, and handsome, the kind of man she could introduce to her parents. She missed him greatly.

In the year that followed his last letter, she had spent her time immersing herself in her work. She had been assigned to various news-making events in Switzerland and even spent time in Liechtenstein, covering the annual wine festival in Vaduz. She received mail on a regular basis, but never a letter from Peter.

Marilyn continued taking pictures of the castle ruins until the current roll of film ran out. She sat down on a step in front of the tower and started to change the film. It was then that she began to weep uncontrollably, for it dawned on her that she may never see him again. *Better to have loved and lost than to never have loved at all*, but the cliché did not console her in the least. Maybe it was time for her to move on and let her broken heart mend.

August 23, 1941 19:51
Kiel, Germany
Das Beir Haus

Matrose Peter Teufel sat alone at the bar in *Das Beir Haus*, the closest bar he could find to the Navy base in Kiel. For Peter, unlike most of his fellow classmates, graduating from recruit training was something that he really did not feel like celebrating.

The pass-and-review ceremony had been executed to perfection, which pleased *Bootsmann* Abel to no end. As a reward for good performance, the non-commissioned officer had given every man in the company liberty until 21:00 Sunday night.

A few other sailors were drinking in the bar, but Peter was drinking alone. He took a big gulp of the frothy brew and wiped his lips on his sleeve. His thoughts were on his predicament and how he could get out of it. Staying in Europe as long as he had was a mistake. Now he had to figure a way to get out of the country and get back to the States. He feared writing a letter home to his parents or to Marilyn, as someone might question the delivery address. If anyone found out that he was American, he could face serious consequences.

The United States was not in this war, but they certainly had been supporting Great Britain, a fact that was frowned upon by the Nazi government and the Wehrmacht, including the *Kriegsmarine*. German U-boats had already attacked ships from his home country, and the frequency of such attacks was on the rise. Now Peter was set to go to sea in the *U-216*. To that he drank, not in celebration but in resignation. He would have to find a way to get back to the States from aboard a submarine. *An impossible task.*

August 27, 1941 07:00
Kiel, Germany
Germaniawerft Shipyard

Peter walked past row after row of submarines under construction in the *Krupp Germaniawerft* Shipyard. He was very familiar with the facility, having worked there only months before. He searched for yard number 648, the construction number for the *U-216*. He was wearing his dress uniform with his sea bag slung over his shoulder.

He passed several boats under various stages of construction. Some were just steel skeletons, while others had a complete hull. Then he saw the number 648 over the door to a small wooden building, the construction foreman's office.

Not far from this building, Peter could see his new home. There, sitting upon chocks and cribbing, sat the *U-216*. While still under construction, her hull was complete. Above the deck of the submarine and high in the air above him, a crane lowered equipment on top of the boat.

Peter approached the door to the foreman's office and opened it. Inside, an older, bespectacled man sat behind a desk reviewing blueprints. Peter was sure that this was the job foreman.

"I am looking for the officer of the day for the *U-216*."

"That would be Goedel. He is on the boat. Head up the scaffolding stairs and you will find him."

Peter made his way up the temporary stairway. Climbing up and up, he reached the wooden walkway that joined the scaffold on the topside of the submarine. As he stepped onto the deck, an officer popped out of the hatch. Peter immediately came to attention and saluted.

"*Matrose* Teufel reporting for duty, sir."

The officer was wearing a dirty, grease-covered work uniform. He looked up at Peter and gave him a half-hearted salute. "Welcome aboard, sailor. You are number seventeen to report, only about forty more men to go and we will be ready to go to sea."

"Sir?"

"Never mind. I am *Oberleutnant zur See* Goedel, your new executive officer. You should head down to barracks number sixteen and speak to the chief. He will assign you to a bunk. Then change into your work uniform and report back here. We just got a delivery of deck plates for the engine room. You can help carry them below."

"Yes, sir!" Peter turned to cross back over the walkway on his way to barracks sixteen.

December 17, 1941 05:07
Kiel, Germany
U-216

Oberleutnant zur See Karl-Otto Schultz stood on the bridge of the *U-216* as the boat pulled away from the pier. Having been launched in October and only commissioned a few days before, the newest submarine in the *Kriegsmarine* was now departing on a training mission. A potentially dangerous training mission.

The *U-216* had performed well during sea trials and testing after her launch. The crew had put her through her paces in the Baltic Sea. Multiple dives, tests, and drills soon followed, and the boat and her crew had answered them all. There was, of course, still room for improvement, and Schultz would ensure that the crew's performance would meet his high standards.

Now that all of the testing was complete, Schultz had been ordered to take the boat to sea for a final training mission; however, the country was at war, so the mission was more than just training. He had been ordered by *Vizeadmiral* Dönitz to deliver badly needed diesel engine parts to the *U-86* operating in the Atlantic. That boat, under the command of *Kapitänleutnant* Walter Schug, had been operating on one diesel engine and needed the spare parts to stay on station. After the rendezvous, Schultz was to proceed to France for an inspection by Dönitz himself.

"All ahead two thirds," Schultz commanded.

The order was repeated by the officer in the control room, who relayed the order to the engine room. The word was relayed back to the bridge that the boat was answering ahead two thirds.

"Very well."

Down below, in the engine room, Peter was standing his watch under the instruction of *Oberbootsmann* Hans Rupp. The old salt knew little of Peter's past experience building U-boats, or his mechanical engineering education. What Rupp did know was that the young sailor had quickly taken to the ship's qualification process. The kid was able to draw the systems from memory and state the purpose of each systems' components. As qualifications went, he was ahead of the rest of the new seamen in the engineering department.

Rupp had recognized quickly that the young sailor had a good aptitude for mechanics, and Rupp was a hard man to please. Rupp also believed that a young college kid like Teufel had a hell of a lot to learn about submarines before he would meet Rupp's standards for qualifying in the engine room. He figured it was time to test the new sailor.

"Well, Teufel ..." Rupp yelled over the noise of the diesel engines. "We are now at ahead two thirds. What do we need to do?"

Peter thought about the chief's question. Falling back on his studies on heat transfer and fluid flow, he mentally dissected what was different now as opposed to a few minutes ago. He reasoned that the diesel engines were working harder now that they were under load, and that would result in an increase in the amount of heat that the engines produced.

"Cut in more cooling water to the jacket cooling water heat exchanger for the engines, and the oil coolers will need more flow, too, Chief."

Rupp tried very hard not to show his surprise. This young seaman was pretty sharp. Rupp considered his position for a minute. He couldn't let this kid think that he knew everything. "Yes, but you forgot to check the bearing temperatures. Any time that you change the load on the diesel or any time that you adjust cooling, you must check the results. You have a lot to learn, *Matrosengefreiter.*"

Rupp commended himself for his own quick thinking. It wouldn't do his reputation any good as the engineering chief to have Teufel going to the others and letting them know that he had answered the question correctly. Rupp had to put him in his place. But still, the kid was pretty sharp.

"I will check them right after I adjust the cooling water flow. Is that acceptable, Chief?"

"That will be fine."

The *U-216* sailed out into the Baltic Sea on the surface. The seas were unusually calm for that time of year, with the winds from the west at only a few knots and the skies overcast. When Schultz reached the one-hundred-meter curve on the map, he ordered the boat to submerge.

"Dive, dive, dive," the captain called down to the control room.

Back in the engine room, the diving alarm sounded. Peter glanced at Chief Rupp. The crusty old salt looked back at Peter with a mocking *What do we do?* expression on his face.

Peter ran for the air induction valve controls. He had to shut down the diesels, secure the air flow to the engines, shift propulsion to the electric motors, and "check the results," as Chief Rupp had just instructed him.

For his part, Rupp kept hounding Peter to hurry up, get it done faster. That was the way a qualified submarine sailor trained, and Rupp was a good trainer. Rupp appreciated that Teufel didn't do anything wrong, but he knew that the young sailor should do it quicker.

After his six hours on watch, Peter crawled into his tiny bunk in hopes of getting some much-needed sleep. He, along with the rest of the crew, had been working eighteen-hour days to get the *U-216* ready for sea. Yet sleep would not come to him.

Less than a week ago, the captain had announced that the *Führer* had declared war on the United States. This weighed heavily on Peter's mind. He was now at war, fighting against his own country. The fact was unacceptable. It was one thing to man a U-boat in a war against the British, but against his fellow Americans was too much. It was treasonous.

He tossed and turned in his bunk, unable to get the thought of his predicament out of his mind. *Should I go to the captain and explain my situation? Maybe he would understand?*

Maybe they would turn me over to the US embassy? Or, more likely, I would be arrested as a spy, shot even. I have to find a way out of this.

Sleep finally came, but answers did not.

December 22, 1941 00:53
Atlantic Ocean, 700 Kilometers West of Galway, Ireland
U-216

Oberleutnant zur See Johann Goedel was the officer of the deck when the *U-86* was identified. The night was dreadfully clear with the stars shining overhead. He knew that it would be easy for the enemy to spot two surfaced U-boats on a night like this.

"Notify the captain that the *U-86* has been sighted."

The *U-216* slowly approached Captain Schug's boat in the dark. Signals were exchanged as Goedel piloted his vessel along the starboard side of the crippled submarine. Transferring the needed parts would restore this boat to full combat readiness, he assured himself. Still, it was a tricky maneuver to make such an approach and transfer at sea.

"Transfer party topside," Goedel called down to the men below.

Six men scrambled topside, each carrying a bag of parts for the stricken submarine's diesel engine. The transfer was made quickly and without incident. The transfer party quickly returned below decks and, when they did, Goedel ordered the dive. Thirty-six seconds later, the *U-216* disappeared into the sea.

Chapter Ten: Metallurgy

January 23, 1942 01:04
Atlantic Ocean, 380 kilometers
West-Southwest of Dingle Bay, Ireland
U-216

The *U-216* was in trouble and at that moment only *Oberleutnant zur See* Johann Goedel was fully aware of just how much. As the Executive Officer, or simply XO, he was responsible for overseeing the repairs to the submarine after the destroyer attack from the night before. All of the damage had been fixed or compensated for, with the exception of the high-pressure air leak near the entrance to the forward battery compartment. The leak was small initially, but worsened when they surfaced after the attack. A small crack in the pipe had propagated. The leak prevented the *U-216* from fully charging the forward bank of air receivers with air from the compressors. Without air in the receiving tanks, there would be no air for filling the forward ballast tanks when the submarine wanted to surface.

Under his supervision, the men had tried every trick that they could think of to repair the pipe. Assisted by Chief Machinist Rupp and the apprentice Teufel, they had exhausted their options. Rubber patches, wooden plugs, and even canvas wraps were attempted, but they could not hold the pressure. Goedel was fresh out of ideas. Frustrated, he knew that he must now inform Captain Schultz that the boat would have to make it to France on the surface under skies dominated by the RAF. He turned to the two enlisted men. "Well, do you have any ideas, Chief?"

Rupp looked down at the floor and shook his head no.

"How about you, Teufel?"

Chief Rupp chimed in before Peter could respond, "*Ach, ole Two Pair here is still a kleiner Junge.*"

"Young boy or not, what do you think, Teufel?"

"We could weld it, sir."

Chief Rupp blurted out: "We don't have a welder, son."

"We could still weld it. I've seen things like this done before, studied it a bit in college as well."

"Go on," Goedel prodded.

"We could use aluminum and iron oxide, sir. Thermite, it's called. I have seen it used to repair broken railroad tracks when I worked with my grandfather during the summer. When aluminum and iron oxide are heated together, the resulting thermite generates a lot of heat, enough to weld steel."

"And you have done this before?" Goedel asked.

"I helped, sir. The railroad men did the repairs. I watched and fetched tools. But I've seen how it's done. I'll need some aluminum dust, and some rust, sir. Chief Rupp, do we have any magnesium onboard?"

Goedel wondered if the sailor could really do this. But what choice did he have? Without a repair, the chances of making their return to France safely were slim.

"Wait here," Goedel told the two enlisted men. "I need to speak to the captain."

At twenty-nine years of age, Johann Goedel was an experienced submarine officer. He was born and raised in Wilhelmshaven, Germany and enlisted in the *Reichsmarine*, the predecessor to the *Kriegsmarine*, in 1929. Proving himself an able seaman, he worked his way up the enlisted ranks quickly as a quartermaster. Navigation was his specialty, but like all experienced submariners, he was familiar with all aspects of an operating submarine. With the advent of the *Kriegsmarine* in 1935 and the rearmament policies of the Nazi party, officers were needed to man the growing U-boat fleet. So, at twenty-two Goedel was advanced to *Leutnant zur See*. Now, after seven years serving aboard U-boats, he found himself the XO going to the captain who was actually a year younger than himself, with a risky plan.

Goedel headed towards the captain's stateroom. Knocking on the bulkhead next to the curtain strung across the doorway, he announced himself. "Captain, damage report for you, sir."

"Come in, Johann. What is the news?"

"We have tried everything, sir, but with little luck. Every time we start the compressor, our repair blows out."

"Johann, without that repair, we are in grave danger, unable to submerge. We ran on the surface all day and we were lucky with the low overcast and fog, but the weather is clearing. We are still four days from Lorient!"

The captain rubbed his eyes. He looked very tired to Johann, and rightly so. Being the captain of a U-boat was a demanding task. The lives of fifty men were in his hands.

Goedel had expected to be given his own boat when he departed his last submarine, but had instead been assigned as an experienced XO to Shultz on the *U-216*. The *Kriegsmarine* tried to pair new captains with experienced officers on their crew. Goedel's time for his own command would have to wait.

"There is one idea that we haven't tried, sir." Goedel explained the thermite repair option to Schultz. Ten minutes later, the XO returned to the repair site where Peter and the chief patiently waited. The two men were discussing Peter's repair idea in more detail.

"You really think that you can do it, Peter?" Goedel asked.

"Yes, sir. It is not without risk, but I know that it can work."

"Can we run a small test?"

"Sure, but it will take some time."

"Listen, we have only a few hours till the sun comes up, and by then we'd better be able to submerge. You have all the resources of the boat. Whatever you need, ask," Goedel said.

An hour later, Peter was sitting on the deck plates in the engine room between the two rumbling diesel generators. With him were the XO and the chief. Peter sat with a bucket of water in front of him, and next to it, a steel plate. On top of the plate there sat two steel bolts end to end. Where the two bolts touched, Peter poured a little pile of thermite—one part of fine aluminum filings, and three parts iron oxide rust.

Peter then grabbed a flare from the aft signal locker and cut the paper casing. Inside of the flair were small gray pellets, magnesium pellets. Peter took one pellet and placed it carefully on top of the pile of thermite. He was ready, at least as ready as he could be. He hoped that this would work, as he had only seen it done but had never done this himself.

"Ready?" Peter hollered over the noise of the diesels.

The XO nodded as Peter continued. "Keep the fire extinguishers handy. When this lights, it will continue to burn until the reaction is complete. There is no stopping it. If anything else catches on fire, put it out, got it?"

Again, the XO nodded. Peter stood up and placed the flare back into the locker. He then picked up a small, handheld gas torch. He lit the torch and walked back to the bucket. With one more nod from the XO, he held the tip of the flame to the magnesium pellet. For a few seconds, nothing happened. Then a white glow grew quickly as the magnesium began to burn. The intensity of the light caused everyone to look away. Then the light intensified more! Peter knew that this was the thermite burning. An acrid smoke began to billow up from the reaction. For about seven seconds, the light illuminated the engine room like the noonday sun. Then it quickly faded away as the reaction completed.

Peter took a pair of pliers out of a nearby toolbox. With the tool he knocked the bolts into the bucket of water. They hissed loudly as steam rose from the water. After a minute, he reached into the bucket with the pliers and removed the bolts. They were indeed welded together.

Peter swung the pliers like a hammer against the deck once, then twice. On the second swing, the bolts separated, much to his dismay. Both the chief and the XO stepped forward for a closer look.

"There were gaps in the weld ... but it does work," Peter said.

"It separated with a few smacks on the floor!" exclaimed the Chief.

"We need to change just a few things. The aluminum must be finer, a powder if possible. We will need the smallest file that we have. Same for the rust. Also, the bolts were not completely clean. The metal surfaces must be clean. And I need some plaster. Is there some in the medical kit?"

January 23, 1942 04:48
Atlantic Ocean, 352 kilometers
West-Southwest of Dingle Bay, Ireland
U-216

Four men sat around the officer's dinner table. Karl-Otto Schultz wanted to make sure that he understood the risks that he alone would be responsible for. With him sat Goedel, Rupp, and Teufel. Schultz had questions and wanted answers.

"We have about three hours until first light. By then, we better be ready to dive. This weld ... explain this to me again, *Herr Goedel.*"

"It's risky, sir, but our test was promising. With your permission, sir, I would like *Matrosengefreiter* Teufel to explain the details."

The CO nodded at Peter.

"Sir, the mixture of iron oxide and aluminum burns at a very high temperature. Hot enough to weld steel. Our test showed that it will weld, and we have made adjustments based on what we learned during the test."

Peter went on to explain the plan to repair the air line. The pipe to the air receiver was a 76mm pipe with a longitudinal crack of about 70mm. In order to patch the pipe, they intended to weld a 90mm pipe over the crack in the air line. The 90mm pipe had been scrounged from a non-vital piece of equipment. Cut to 13cm in length and quartered lengthwise, the patch would fit over the existing crack in the air line. The inside diameter of the 90mm pipe was exactly the outside diameter of the 76mm pipe, which would result in sufficient surface area contact between the pipe and the patch.

Peter then described how they had manufactured the aluminum dust and iron oxide using a fine file. Since the crack was on a vertical run of pipe, the thermite needed to adhere in place. He explained how he would mix a little plaster of Paris and water into the thermite mixture to make a putty. "Applied to the patch and ignited with magnesium from the flair, burning at nearly 2500C, the thermite *should* weld the patch to the pipe."

"Where did you learn this, Seaman Teufel?" the CO asked.

"I worked for my grandfather in the railyard during the summers. We sometimes had to repair railroad tracks. I saw it done there. When I was in college, we studied the reaction in chemistry."

"You went to college?" the CO asked.

"Yes, sir. Stuttgart Institute of Technology. I graduated with a degree in mechanical engineering, sir."

The CO sat back in his seat, sighed and shook his head. He turned to the XO. "What are the chances of this working?"

"Fifty-fifty, sir. Maybe less. But what other choice do we have?"

"Goddamn it, Goedel, I know that," the CO spat. "Tell me the worst thing that can happen."

The XO looked at Teufel. "Well, Two Pair, what can go wrong?"

While Peter didn't really like the nickname that much, there was nothing he could do about it. Then he thought about the question. He considered lying and saying that nothing could possibly ever go wrong, but he reconsidered. Truth here might be the best course.

"There is going to be a lot of heat and smoke produced. We plan to have the ventilation on with all of the hatches open. Still, if we use too much thermite and it falls onto the deck ... well, sir, fire is our biggest concern."

"We'll have men standing by with extinguishers, Captain," Goedel added.

The CO sat for a long time just thinking. He pulled out a cigarette and lit it. He drew in a large puff of smoke, savored it, and then exhaled. Then, consciously, he offered a cigarette to the other three as he spoke. "Give it a try, gentlemen. If it does not work, we will all be shooting at British bombers with *Maschinenpistole 40s* as we run to Lorient!"

Twenty minutes later, the repair team was staged at the entrance to the forward battery compartment. It was do-or-die time. If the repair did not work, they would be in a great deal of danger from British air attacks. Peter had done all that he could think to do, checked everything that he could think of, but now was the time to see if this would work. His life quite literally depended on it.

The crack on the air line was on the backside of the pipe near the pressure hull. It was difficult to get to. Peter had to wedge himself between an electrical cabinet and some pipes just to get to the damaged pipe. Once there, he slathered the 90mm pipe patch with the thermite putty and affixed it over the crack. It fit pretty well in Peter's estimation. He then took the thermite putty and lined the edges of the patch with a liberal coating. Better to have too much than not enough. He applied a little more thermite.

Peter peeked around from his awkward position outboard of the pipe. He made eye contact with Chief Rupp. "Hand me a few magnesium pellets and the torch, Chief."

The chief did as Peter instructed and watched as Peter pushed a few pellets into the putty. Peter lit the torch a safe distance away from the thermite and looked at the XO. "Are you ready, sir?"

The XO nodded. "Ready, Two Pair. Get it lit and get your ass out from behind there, ok?"

Peter nodded and then turned to his work. He put the tip of the flame to the magnesium. He held it there for a few seconds … Nothing. He wondered if he had added too much water and plaster of Paris to the thermite? He continued to hold the flame to the patch and still … nothing.

Finally, the magnesium started to burn. Peter turned and smiled at the XO. The time it took to make that turn was too long.

Fitzzzzz Wooofffff! Once lit, the magnesium took off much quicker than the test in the engine room. The thermite lit as well. Peter struggled to get out from behind the pipe, but his shirt snagged on a bolt affixed to the electrical cabinet.

Peter dropped the lit torch as he struggled to free his shirt from the bolt and then he felt it. At first it just felt warm, like turning your face into the sunshine, but, in a split second, his face was hot. Surface-of-the-sun hot. Peter yanked at his shirt, but it was still snagged. The heat was intense. Peter turned his head away from the thermite.

Goedel stood mesmerized. In front of him was a bright flash of white light followed by billowing grayish-white smoke. He could feel the heat two meters away. The compartment quickly filled with smoke and the men next to him retreated through the hatch into the next compartment. But Goedel couldn't retreat. One of his men was in trouble.

Peter struggled again against the bolt. The heat was unbearable. He screamed as a piece of slag landed on his eyebrow. With a mighty jerk he ripped the shirt off of the bolt and tumbled away from the pipe.

Goedel raced to Peter and grabbed onto his arm and yanked Peter from between the pipe and the electrical cabinet.

"Ah, goddamn it! It burns, it fucking burns!" Peter screamed in perfect English.

It was slow motion for Goedel at that point. The young sailor stumbled and tripped, falling down heavily against the opposite bulkhead. He hit hard. His head slammed against the steel bulkhead and he crumpled to the deck. Goedel saw that the kid was on fire, his shirt was aflame.

Struggling against the smoke and heat, Goedel smothered the flames with a blanket. To his left, Goedel could feel that the reaction was coming to an end, but something else caught his attention. Another fire.

The heat from the thermite had caught the bulkhead insulation on fire. Flames were quickly spreading. Goedel turned and yelled into the forward compartment, "Chief, get your ass in here and put out this fire!"

The chief came rushing into the compartment, followed by two other sailors. They sprayed their extinguishers left and right. It all happened so fast, but the fire was out.

Goedel looked down at Teufel. He was unconscious. His face was already starting to redden and blisters were forming. The XO turned to look at the pipe. Smoke still filled the compartment. He could not see very well, but with the ventilation running, the air was beginning to clear. He looked back at Teufel. Had he heard what he thought that he heard?

The XO stood up and went to the repair. It was still smoking a bit, but the patch appeared to be firmly in place. Remembering how the bolts had snapped apart after the test, he could not be sure that the fix had worked but it looked like … maybe … just maybe, it had worked.

"Chief, station a man here with a charged extinguisher. You get Teufel to my bunk and get the pharmacist to see to him. I need to speak to the captain."

January 23, 1942 07:17
Atlantic Ocean, 325 kilometers
West-Southwest of Dingle Bay, Ireland
U-216

Johann Goedel stood by the entrance to the forward battery compartment. He was tired and troubled. He had been awake for nearly forty-six hours and it was beginning to show. He had stood by the repair as they started up the air compressor to fill the receiver. As per Teufel's previous instructions, they had only filled the air tank to just above the minimum pressure. The repair, almost unbelievably, had held the pressure. Now, the compressor stopped. He wanted to give it a couple of minutes at pressure to see if it held, but they were running out of time. He picked up the phone. "Control, this is the XO. The repair has held. We are able to dive."

Moments later, the command to dive came. Goedel turned and headed for the dinner table. He needed a bite to eat and then some rest. As he strode to the compartment, he couldn't shake what he had heard. Teufel had screamed in English. *Did I imagine it? I don't think so. I was tired, but when that thermite lit him up like a Roman candle, I was damned alert. Why would he do that?*

As Goedel sat down at the table, the CO entered.

"Nice job, Johann. I was not sure that it would work."

"I wasn't sure either, Karl, but that kid, Two Pair Teufel. He knows what he is doing."

"He is a bright young man, college-educated, too."

"Yeah, he is a pretty bright but … he is uh, different."

"What do you mean? He is a bright, educated German who has saved this boat for the Fatherland. He deserves a medal!" Shultz exclaimed.

"Maybe he does …" Goedel responded. "Maybe he does."

"And you Johann. A command is in the offing for you. You will have my endorsement."

"Thank you, sir. How is Teufel? Has the pharmacist looked at him?"

"He will make it. The burns are not too bad. Holtz says that he will be fine with just a little scarring here and there. He buttered him up with burn salve like a piece of pumpernickel toast. Teufel should be ok in a few days."

"Good. I need some sleep Karl. I have had it."

With that, Goedel fell asleep on the bench beside the table. As he fell into a deep sleep, he could hear the words in English, perfect English, "Ah, goddamn it! It burns, it fucking burns!"

January 27, 1942 10:18
Bay of Biscay, 34 kilometers South of Lorient, France
U-216

Peter opened his eyes, but something wasn't quite right. He vaguely remembered being awake a few times in the last few days, but he had been heavily sedated. This time, he looked around and realized that he was in the XO's bunk, but he couldn't see very well.

He reached his hand up to his face. It was bandaged. The thought quickly ran through his head, *Did I lose my eye?*

"Holtz says that you are going to be fine. A small scar above your eye maybe, but your eyes are fine."

Peter turned and saw the XO sitting next to him through his one, unbandaged eye.

"Did it work?" Peter asked. "Did the weld hold?"

"Yes, it sealed up tight. We dove the boat shortly after you tried to get out of standing watches by burning yourself."

Peter knew that the XO was teasing him so he smiled. He sat up in the bed. "Where are we?"

"Two hours from the barn. We will be in Lorient by noon. Then we will get a real doctor to look at you, just to be sure." Goedel paused for a moment. "Where did you learn to speak English?"

Peter stared at the XO with his one eye but did not respond. He had never spoken his native tongue on the boat. He believed that the *Kriegsmarine* would not look kindly on an American serving on one of their U-boats. *How did he know that I speak English?*

"When you ripped yourself out from behind the cabinet, you were screaming in English. Why?" Goedel pressed.

Peter thought quickly. He certainly could not tell him the truth, so decided to tell a partial truth. "I am the son of a diplomat. I speak several languages—English, Japanese, even a little French."

All of what Peter said was true, yet it didn't exactly answer the XO's question. He noticed that the XO looked a little surprised by this revelation. Peter hoped that his attempt to redirect the line of questioning would work.

"Four languages, an engineering degree? You are an interesting man, Two Pair. How does an educated son of a diplomat end up as a seaman on a U-boat?"

"I was working as an engineer in Kiel. I was conscripted by the *Kriegsmarine*. Just doing my part for the Fatherland."

All of that was true, but it certainly wasn't the whole story. He was an American who had gotten caught up in the war and was just trying to find a way back to the States. He wished that he had listened to his father's advice, but it was too late now.

Before Goedel could continue his line of questioning, word came to make preparations for pulling into port. The maneuvering watch was ordered to be manned and with that, Goedel left Peter to assume his watch station.

Peter lay back down. He was worried. He could tell by the look in the XO's eyes that the man suspected something. Did he suspect that Peter was not a German citizen? Or was he just intrigued by a man who is different than the average German naval conscript? The answers didn't matter much: Peter knew that it was time to get out.

Peter had enjoyed living overseas. He loved being in Europe. The culture, the food, the wine, it was all just a big adventure. Even the beginning of the war did not seem to change his lot in life very much, at least not a first. It had all been so much fun.

Now it was different. The war had come to him in a big way. Being depth charged and burned trying to save the boat had all made his European experience too dangerous, too personal. He must find a way off this boat and back to America … but how?

January 29, 1942 08:20
U-boat Bunker "Dom" – Lorient, France
U-216

Peter stood topside of the *U-216*. He lit a cigarette and savored the ocean air wafting through the U-boat pen. Any chance to be outside of the boat was a welcome occurrence. He requested permission to go ashore from the topside watch and gave the required salute. Down the gangplank and onto the concrete walkway of the bunker, he made his way down the length of the pen and headed up a stairway into the sunshine. It felt good to be in the sun. U-boat sailors could never get too much sun.

As he smoked the last of his cigarette, he field-dressed the butt and placed it in his pocket. It was then that he noticed the black Daimler-Benz staff car pulling into the bunker complex. The car rolled towards Peter and halted a few meters away. Out of the car stepped a *Kommodore* of the *Kriegsmarine*, an *Oberstleutnant* of the *Wehrmacht*, and two men in suits.

Peter came to attention and saluted as the officers passed by him and headed towards the stairwell. The only boat in the bunker was the *U-216* and Peter knew that they were heading towards it. Panic filled Peter. Could they be here for him? Had Goedel told the captain of his apparent suspicions?

Peter looked at the staff car. A driver sat in the driver's seat. Peter thought maybe he could overpower the driver and steal the car, but where would he go? You couldn't drive from France to America. He quickly dismissed the idea.

He was stuck for the time being.

Twenty minutes later, the four men emerged from the bunker and walked purposefully back to the staff car. The car pulled away from the curb and headed back the way that they had come. Peter turned and headed back down into the bunker. He transited the walkway and requested permission to board the *U-216*. The topside watch waived him aboard. As Peter walked up the gangplank, the topside watch spoke to him. "Hey, Two Pair, the captain wants to see you right away."

Peter nodded and headed towards the hatch. *Was this it?* He climbed down into the submarine and headed for the captain's cabin.

"*Matrosengefreiter* Teufel, sir," he announced at the door. "I was told that you wanted to see me, Captain."

With Captain Shultz was Goedel. Both men were smiling. Did they know?

"Get your dress uniform on Teufel. You are to meet with none other than *Vizeadmiral* Dönitz!" Schultz said. "A car will be here at noon. The three of us are heading for the town of Kernevel where the admiral will see us."

Chapter Eleven: Sicherheitsdienst

Vizeadmiral Karl Dönitz sat in the elegantly decorated library of the Villa Kerillon. Located on a point near the town of Lorient, this was his submarine headquarters in France. Across from him sat two of Germany's most influential officers, *Vizeadmiral* Wilhelm Canaris and *Obersturmbannführer* Walter Schellenberg. To trifle with these two men, the Chief of the *Abwehr* and a head of the *Sicherheitsdienst* (SD), would be an ill-advised course of action. Dönitz needed their help.

"Gentlemen, let us begin with the end in mind, shall we? *Großadmiral* Raeder has informed me that we are going to establish a submarine base in the Far East. I am tasked with establishing such a base." Dönitz took a sip of coffee before continuing. "My research staff tells me that while there are several potential sites, one in particular seems to have all that the *Kriegsmarine* needs to operate effectively. That site is Penang, Malaysia. A former British installation, now currently in the hands of our friends, the Japanese. I propose a scouting mission, if you will, to determine the feasibility of Penang."

Admiral Canaris commented, "My understanding is that the *Führer* wishes for this base to be operational quickly."

"True," replied Dönitz. "I can't waste a lot of time sending a ship around the Cape and back to inspect the facilities there. I need to expedite a scouting mission. That is where I need your help."

"As you are aware, Admiral, we have a means to get such a party, a small party, to Japan. I suspect that is why you requested my presence, isn't it?" said Canaris.

"It is," Dönitz replied. "Would the *Abwehr* be willing to arrange transportation for such a group?"

"In support of the Fatherland, the *Abwehr* will provide the necessary accommodations. It will have to be a small group—four or maybe five men. We can fly them from Finland to Manchuria, and then on to Penang, if needed."

"My superiors in the SD have informed me that we will be sending a man with the group to further establish our intelligence networks in the area," Schellenberg added.

Canaris bristled. He believed that there really was no need for two intelligence organizations to be tied to this mission. Both Admirals looked at Schellenberg and nodded. Both of them knew that while only an *Obersturmbannführer*, this man was incredibly connected within the party. In Canaris's mind, this was not a hill to die on.

"Do you have a man in mind, Walter?" Dönitz asked.

"I have a man, a reliable officer named Lübeck. He will be representing the SD in this matter."

"And you, Wilhelm?" Dönitz queried Canaris.

"I have several candidates. I will provide you with the selected man when that has been decided."

Schellenberg ate a small bite of croissant. "Do any of your people speak Japanese, Admiral Canaris? Admiral Dönitz? Lübeck does not."

Each man replied in the negative.

"Good question Walter," Dönitz said. "We will need someone with this skill to help translate. While we are working with the Japanese, I would not completely trust one of theirs to act as our interpreter."

The three men spent the next thirty minutes discussing the mission. It was determined that the party would be briefed in Berlin and then travel by air to northern Finland, where the *Abwehr* had access to a remote airbase. There, a specially modified FW-200 Condor, provided by Canaris, would fly the men to Harbin, Manchuria. From there, the Japanese would transport the team to Tokyo for political purposes, and then on to Penang. This still needed to be coordinated with the Japanese, but the information Dönitz had received indicated that they would eagerly support such an endeavor.

Dönitz informed the others that he had selected a senior captain, *Kapitän zur See* Fritz Ackermann, to lead the group. Ackermann was a former U-boat captain who was now in charge of logistics at the German submarine base in Kiel. He was the perfect man to evaluate port facilities for submarines. Additionally, Ackermann would be supported by an officer with recent submarine operational experience. The admiral had selected *Oberleutnant zur See* Johann Goedel for the task. As the executive officer of *U-216*, Goedel was going to rotate off of his current boat and potentially assume command of his own submarine after this mission to Penang.

"You will get an opportunity to meet *Oberleutnant zur See* Goedel this afternoon, gentlemen. It seems that on his last patrol, he distinguished himself by leading repairs to his damaged submarine that reflect great credit upon himself and the *Kriegsmarine*," Dönitz said with pride.

"We are pinning a medal on a man who was party to allowing his boat to be damaged?" Schellenberg quipped.

Canaris interceded before Dönitz could respond, "Having never served on an operational U-boat, *Obersturmbannführer*, I can see how you might not have the full appreciation of the perils of submarine service."

It was Schellenberg's turn to bristle. He didn't trust Canaris and now he had been subtly rebuked by him. He was glad that his men were going to be a part of this mission, if only to keep an eye on the *Abwehr*.

Dönitz relayed the *U-216*'s patrol report, outlining the extraordinary repairs conducted by the crew and Goedel in particular. Along with Canaris's comments, it seemed to silence the SD head. "We will have a brief ceremony to award the medals after lunch. An emissary from the IJN, Imperial Japanese Navy, will be joining us for our afternoon meeting in order to finalize the mission to Penang."

"Splendid," said Canaris. "As I recall from my many years on submarines, the food should be excellent."

Canaris noted that Schellenberg did not miss the last little dig, but he let it go as the men stood and, led by Dönitz, proceeded to the dining room in the villa

January 29, 1942 12:00
U-boat Bunker "Dom" Lorient, France
U-216

Schultz, Goedel, and Teufel, each attired in their dress uniforms, stepped out of the U-boat bunker and headed towards the waiting staff car. The three men of the *U-216* climbed into the vehicle, the officers in the back and Peter next to the driver. As they headed out of the U-boat bunker compound and headed down the road towards Lorient, turning south and heading for the coast, it was Goedel who spoke first.

"Remember what I told you, Two Pair. We are meeting with Admiral Dönitz. Military protocol is a must. It is not like it is on the boat."

"Yes, sir."

Peter reached up to his face and touched the bandage that was still covering his right eye. It was held in place by gauze which wrapped around his head and obscured the right side of his face. He wished that he could take it off, but the doctor in Lorient said that it had to stay put for three more days. He adjusted the review mirror and looked at his face. The blisters were mostly reduced, but his face was still red in places. The skin was beginning to peel, and his "good eye" was still blood-shot. *I look like a fucking mess.*

Goedel turned to Schultz. "This should be interesting, eh, Captain?"

"I believe that it will be, Johann."

Peter wondered what "interesting" meant. Had Goedel divulged his obvious suspicions of him? Was this going to be an inquisition of the American U-boat sailor? Peter was nervous that his charade might all come to a disastrous end. But there was no time to think of the outcome as the car entered through a guarded gate that stood before a large three-story red brick French villa.

Armed men opened the car doors and let the three sailors of the *Kriegsmarine* out of the vehicle. Inside the villa, they were greeted by an assistant to Admiral Dönitz, who ushered them to a waiting area next to a grand spiral staircase that led to the upper floors. There they waited until they were summoned to an audience with the head of the submarine force.

The three men were led into the library of the villa and stood at attention. In front of them sat three German officers. Peter looked straight ahead, his good eye fixed on the far wall looking over the heads of the three officers before him. Military protocol demanded that he stand at attention.

"At ease gentlemen," Admiral Dönitz said.

With that, the three men of the *U-216* spread their feet with arms behind their backs and relaxed just a bit. It was then that Peter looked at the men who were seated before him. The man in the *Kriegsmarine* uniform was Dönitz, surely; the man next to him was an SS officer he didn't recognize, and the man next to him was … Canaris!

Panic paralyzed Peter. *Jesus H. Christ! What if he recognizes me?* He knew that if Canaris did recognize him, it could be the end of Peter Teufel.

"Gentlemen, I bring you here today to discuss a matter of great importance to the Reich," Dönitz began. "The men of our submarine force must be true Germans, dedicated to the Fatherland, and unwavering in their commitment to the *Führer*." He paused to pick up a box from the table next to him.

Peter wondered again if this was it. The words "true Germans" and "unwavering" spoken by Dönitz, could they be the preamble to "Peter Teufel is an American spy?"

Before Dönitz could continue, a door to the right of Peter opened and a short, round man entered the room. Dressed in a dark navy uniform of the Imperial Japanese Navy, the man marched into the room and saluted Admiral Dönitz as he spoke in adequate but stunted German. "I bring the greetings of the emperor to you admiral and I bring you the support of the empire."

Silence permeated the room. Then Admiral Dönitz stood up and saluted the Japanese officer. He moved to him and shook his hand. The Japanese officer made a bow and Dönitz returned it uncomfortably. Then Dönitz turned and spoke to the entire room. "Gentlemen, may I introduce our envoy from Japan, Captain Hideki Tomago."

Peter chuckled softly as the senior German officers stood to shake Captain Tomago's hand. Goedel looked at Peter with disapproval and asked quietly, "What is so funny?"

Peter stopped chuckling and whispered, "Tomago. It means *egg* in Japanese. Look at him."

With that Goedel, snickered, too, and then elbowed Peter firmly enough to end the exchange. They were traveling in very high circles and it would be severely frowned upon to be caught making light of a Japanese envoy's name, physical appearance, or both.

"Captain Tomago," Dönitz said. "Please be seated. I am honored that you have joined us. Our meeting will begin shortly. First, we must honor some brave sailors of our submarine service. It would be an honor for us all if you would witness these proceedings. Will you, sir?"

"It would be a pleasure, sir." Hideki took a seat next to Canaris.

Dönitz smiled as the portly Japanese officer took his chair. Dönitz would have a word after this with his aid about how this dunderhead was allowed to burst into this room prematurely. Not wanting to embarrass the man, or jeopardize the interests of the Reich, Dönitz made the best of the situation.

"*Oberleutnant zur See* Schultz, I bring you and the men responsible for restoring the *U-216* to full combat readiness before me today in order to honor them, commensurate with their bravery, in their service to the Fatherland," Dönitz proclaimed. "We are fortunate to have *Vizeadmiral* Canaris, *Obersturmbannführer* Schellenberg, and Captain Tomago with us here today to witness this."

Peter felt relieved. Goedel was going to get an award. This was not the unveiling of Peter's deception. But why was he here?

"*Oberleutnant zur See* Goedel," Dönitz announced. "It is with great pleasure that I bestow upon you, by authorization of the *Führer* Adolf Hitler, the Iron Cross 1st Class for actions demonstrated onboard the *U-216* while in enemy-controlled waters. Your actions to repair the submarine reflect great credit upon yourself, the *Kriegsmarine*, and the Reich."

Dönitz opened the box that he had picked up off of the table and removed a red, black, and white medal. Those in attendance applauded politely as Dönitz stepped forward and pinned the Iron Cross onto Goedel's uniform. The admiral stepped back from Goedel and saluted, which was returned in kind. Then the admiral retrieved another box off of the table and returned to the three men of *U-216*.

He stepped before Peter and spoke. "*Matrosengefreiter* ... eh ... Two Pair, is it?" Dönitz said with a smile. "That is what your shipmates call you isn't it. It is with great honor that I present to you the Iron Cross 2nd Class for actions demonstrated onboard the *U-216* while in enemy-controlled waters. Your actions to repair the submarine reflect great credit upon yourself, the *Kriegsmarine*, and the Reich."

Again, there was a round of polite applause from those witnessing the awards ceremony. With that, Dönitz turned to the other senior officers and spoke. "Gentlemen please, if you will, extend your congratulations to two heroes of the Reich."

Both Canaris and Schellenberg stood up from their chairs and walked forward to congratulate the two submariners. Extending their hands to each of the *U-216* sailors in turn, they congratulated the men on their resourcefulness in saving the submarine. When Canaris shook Peter's hand, thankfully, there was no recognition that Peter could see in Canaris' eyes.

Hideki Tomago, who was a little slower to respond, likely due to a linguistic barrier, followed the German officers to congratulate the submariners.

Hideki shook Peter's hand. "Well done, young man. You are a fine sailor and a credit to your country." Hideki must have realized he had defaulted to his native Japanese for he immediately blurted in German, "Good job, sailor."

You could ask Peter a thousand times why he did it, maybe it was to exercise his Japanese skills, maybe he felt sorry for the portly Japanese officer who was shaped like an egg, or maybe it was just to speak aloud after Goedel had told him to hold his tongue, but he just could not resist. "Thank you very much, Captain Tomago," he answered in perfect Japanese. "I am honored by your salutation. I only acted as any good sailor like yourself would act under the circumstances."

Hideki automatically replied in his own language, "You are welcome." And then he stared at Peter wide-eyed. It took a moment for the Japanese officer to register that someone else knew his native language, but when it did, he laughed out loud.

All of the Germans looked at the Japanese officer, except for Schellenberg. Peter noted that the SD officer was looking at him with interest. It was clear to Peter that Schellenberg was surprised by the exchange in Japanese.

"Is something wrong, Captain Tomago?" Dönitz asked.

Hideki paused and said in German, "No, no not at all. I just am pleased to be here in the service of the emperor, honoring men of such courage and culture."

Schellenberg gave Peter a very long look. *How would a simple seaman know Japanese?* the SD head wondered. Schellenberg made a mental note of this, as it was interesting, to say the least.

The ranking officers returned to their chairs. As poignant as the ceremony had been, they were anxious to commence the meeting concerning Japanese support of the Penang mission. Again, it was Dönitz who moved the proceedings forward.

"Gentlemen, may I again state that the *Kriegsmarine* is indebted to you for your service to the Fatherland. While your deeds will always be remembered, I must attend to pressing matters of the Reich. *Oberleutnant zur See* Schultz, you will return here tomorrow to discuss the results of your last patrol. Return to the *U-216*. I am sure that you are needed there. You are dismissed."

Schellenberg grinned. Having sunk no British shipping on the *U-216*'s last patrol and being damaged by depth charges, someone had to be held accountable. *Dönitz has recognized the men who had saved the boat, but he is going to address the man who was responsible for her damage tomorrow.* Schellenberg made a mental note that the Admiral was true and faithful to the Reich.

Schultz saluted the dais before him, turned and marched directly out of the library.

"*Oberleutnant zur See* Goedel," Dönitz continued. "We would like you to stay and discuss an opportunity with us. Please take a seat."

Peter stood in his place as the XO of the *U-216* walked over to an empty chair. Proper military protocol reminded him that until ordered to do so, he was to stand before his superiors. He wondered about the interchange that he had heard. His captain had essentially been reprimanded. Both he and Goedel had been given the knight's cross, but Schultz had been given nothing. *Military formality for the CO to be present when men below him received such adulations but not receive them himself?* He thought not.

"We have a mission that we think that your skill set is well suited to support," Dönitz said.

"Eh, hem ..." Schellenberg grunted and looked at Dönitz. When their eyes met, Schellenberg shifted his gaze at the bandaged *Matrosengefreiter*, still standing before them. His intent was clear: the enlisted man should not be privy to this conversation.

"Right. Please wait outside. *Oberleutnant zur See* Goedel will join you shortly."

Peter saluted and marched out of the room. *What was that all about?* Here he was being given a medal, while his XO was being called before a panel of officers. *What the hell was going on?*

When the door closed behind the sailor, Dönitz continued. "Johann, the Reich has a need for a man with your skills."

He went on to explain the need that the *Führer* had for establishing a base with access to the Pacific. And that how improved cooperation with the Japanese would be of great benefit to the Reich, leading to the defeat of the British in the Indian Ocean. He explained the need for an experienced submariner such as Johann Goedel to evaluate the viability of Penang to service U-boats. Upon completion of the assignment, Goedel would be given a new boat to command. While the assignment was expressed as an offer, it was ostensibly an order.

"I would gladly accept such an assignment, sir."

The five men spent another hour and a half agreeing on details of the mission. A tentative timetable that would please the *Führer* was decided upon. The mission would indeed depart from Finland and proceed to Manchuria, but from there the team would travel to Tokyo to meet with Japanese military officials before traveling to Penang. Once the port facilities had been evaluated the team would travel back to Germany to report their findings. A contingency plan was in place to inspect two other ports if Penang was unsuitable; however, it was hoped that this would not be necessary.

Goedel sat quietly as the senior officers discussed the details of the mission. He knew that the mission was important to the Reich, but at the same time he was a little disappointed. He had earned command of his own U-boat and now, once again, his appointment to a command was being delayed. He reminded himself as he sat there listening that he was an officer in the *Kriegsmarine* and as such it was his duty to follow orders.

"Well gentlemen, I believe that we are in agreement on how to proceed," Dönitz said. "Captain Tomago, you will contact me directly when you have confirmed your country's ability to support our mission, correct?

"Admiral I will personally see to it. Flights, accommodations, food will all be arranged. We will even provide an interpreter for your team."

"Very well then, Captain," Dönitz remarked. "You can return to Berlin to make the arrangements that we have agreed upon."

Goedel watched as the rotund Japanese officer stood, saluted, and exited the library. As the door closed behind him, the German officers looked at each other. Canaris broke the momentary silence. "I don't know about you, but I do not like the idea of having a Japanese interpreter from Japan. I think that we must have a German-born translator."

Schellenberg agreed with Canaris. "While they are our ally, I do not fully trust them. We need one of our men to go who understands their language in order to hear conversations meant only for Japanese ears."

Canaris replied, "My one man only speaks a few words in Japanese, but he cannot read or write the language. I am afraid that we need to find someone and quickly who meets our needs."

Goedel spoke for the first time during the conversation, other than when he was asked a direct question. Looking at Canaris, he said, "We have someone at hand who speaks, reads, and writes Japanese, sir. You just pinned a medal on him."

"You mean the enlisted man?" Schellenberg interjected. "I heard him speaking to Tomago in Japanese, but he is not an officer."

"Yes, sir, *Matrosengefreiter* Teufel. He speaks Japanese fluently," Goedel replied. "He is well educated, with an engineering degree, speaks four languages and, by my personal observation, is a very capable man."

Teufel ... Teufel, where had he heard that name before? Canaris thought to himself. He quickly ran through a mental list of Germans with that name but came up with nothing.

"We cannot possibly send a simple seaman as an envoy of the *Führer* to meet with the highest levels of the Japanese government!" Schellenberg exclaimed.

"You are absolutely right, Walter," Canaris agreed. "This man is not an officer. That we can fix. He is educated and his idea for the thermite weld repair on *U-216* demonstrates that he is resourceful. We should make him an officer and send him with the team."

Dönitz looked at Canaris. "I will start the paperwork immediately. Young Teufel will be *Leutnant zur See* Teufel by this time tomorrow. Agreed?"

The three senior officers present agreed, yet in his mind, Schellenberg did not like this development. He was leery of the young sailor, for reasons that he did not fully understand. He made a note to discuss this concern with Lübeck upon his return to Berlin.

January 30, 1942 14:00
Prinz-Albrecht-Strasse, Berlin
SS Main Security Office

Klaus Lübeck waited patiently outside of his superior's office on the fourth floor of the *Schutzstaffel* main security building. The building housed the offices of the SD—the *Sicherheitsdienst*—the Nazi intelligence organization. The SD was the Nazi Party's eyes and ears. It searched for information on those who threatened the Reich within Germany or anywhere around the globe. They differed from the *Abwehr*, which focused mainly on military intelligence, though sometimes the two worked together.

Lübeck was on time, for to be otherwise would bring the wrath of his boss, *SS Obersturmbannführer* Walter Schellenberg. Klaus was only an *Hauptsturmführer* in the SS, but he served Schellenberg as his right-hand man. He was a man who got things done. A man who could do the dirty work for Schellenberg. That suited Lübeck just fine. He liked to get his hands dirty.

The door finally opened and Lübeck marched into the office of Schellenberg, stood before his desk, and saluted. Schellenberg returned the salute and motioned for Lübeck to take a seat. "I have another assignment for you, Klaus, one that I think you will enjoy."

"I am willing to serve the *Führer*, the party, and the Fatherland in any manner."

"I know that you are, Klaus. That is why I chose you for this one. The *Führer* has decided that we need to support our Japanese allies with improved relations as well as military intelligence. The *Führer* even wishes to conduct joint military operations with them."

He continued after a nod from Lübeck. "It seems that *Großadmiral* Raeder has convinced the *Führer* to establish a naval base in the Pacific region in support of this strategy. Primarily, it will be a submarine base and Admiral Dönitz is being tasked with sending experienced officers from the submarine force to scout the location. Along with them, Admiral Canaris is sending one of his men to accompany them in order to gain military intelligence connections, to protect our interests of course."

"Who is leading this scouting mission, sir?"

"A senior captain, *Kapitän zur See* Fritz Ackermann, is to lead the group. Ackermann is a former U-boat captain now in charge of logistics at our submarine base in Kiel. He is the perfect man to evaluate port facilities for submarines. Ackermann will be supported by an officer with recent submarine operational experience. Dönitz has selected *Oberleutnant zur See* Johann Goedel for the task."

"How may I assist, *Obersturmbannführer*?"

"The *Abwehr* serves the military, but the SD serves the Reich. I will tell you in confidence that trust in Admiral Canaris has eroded a bit within the top levels of the party. His handling of Franco in Spain was abysmal and there are some who suggest that he is sympathetic to our enemies."

"And my orders are, sir?"

"Your task is two-fold: First, travel with the contingent to the proposed submarine base to establish our own intelligence network and, second, keep an eye on what Canaris' men are doing."

"Yes, sir. May I ask where and when I am going?"

"Penang, in Malaysia," Schellenberg said. "It lies on the west coast of the Malay Peninsula in the Strait of Malacca with access to the Indian Ocean and the Pacific. You will depart Berlin for Finland in a few days. From our airfield near Petsamo, you will fly to Manchuria and then on to Penang."

"Yes, sir."

"Remember, you are to keep an eye on the *Abwehr*, but you will also be representing the Reich on behalf of the *Führer* when you meet our Japanese friends. Dress uniform at all times, understood?"

"I am honored to be chosen. You can count on me."

"I know that I can," Schellenberg affirmed. "Oh, Klaus, just one more thing. Have you taken care of the matter that we discussed last week?"

"Not yet, sir. I have been surveilling the ... problem."

"You should take care of that before you leave for Penang. You will be gone for quite a while. We wouldn't want that problem to fester, would we?"

"I will handle it directly, sir." Lübeck said with a wicked little smile.

January 31, 1942 21:17
Rudour Allee, Berlin
Vogelhaus Apartments

Klaus Lübeck felt good after taking a long shower. He stood before the bathroom mirror in his boxer shorts gazing at his own face. He was still fit and trim for a man of thirty-seven, yet his body showed the scars of a lifetime of fighting. Life had brought him many battles and he had faced them all.

Born and raised in Hamburg, the son of a dockworker, he had spent much of his youth kicking about the waterfront. It was there that he learned to fight. From a young age he routinely found himself coming to blows with anyone who crossed him. He had become very capable with his fists.

Dropping out of school, he went to work alongside his father, loading and unloading freight from the ships that traded in the harbor. He was well suited to the work, broad shoulders, muscular arms; he could hold his own working the docks at fifteen years of age. After six years of working the waterfront, he had moved to Berlin where he found his calling.

He became a member of the *Sturmabteilung,* the "Brownshirts." During this time, he functioned as a low-level enforcer for the Nazi Party. He was allowed to remove the rabble from the street with the support of the party. It was work that he enjoyed. He, too, joined the party, like many others, and slowly but surely made a name for himself as a man who could get things done.

In 1933 he had joined the SS as an enlisted man. Not from an aristocratic background and not well educated, he had started at the bottom. What he lacked in education he made up for in efficiency and brutality. He was decisive and dependable and slowly worked his way up to become a non-commissioned officer.

It was during 1939 that Lübeck began working for Schellenberg and the SD. He provided the muscle for Schellenberg during several operations, earning the trust of the SD. He remembered the incident in the Dutch city of Venlo, where the capture of two British agents had only been accomplished with timely intervention of brute force by Lübeck. One Dutchman had been killed, but the British agents were captured. For this, Schellenberg had promoted him to the officer ranks in the SD, reporting directly to the head of SD.

As he stood before the mirror, reflecting back upon his career, Lübeck quickly dressed in civilian clothes. Tonight was going to be like the old days, the Brownshirt days. He was tasked with dealing with a physicist with Jewish sympathies. The man was an enemy of the Reich. It was an assignment that he would enjoy.

Lübeck finished dressing and exited his apartment, went down the stairs and out into the cold Berlin night air. He made his way to the nearest Berlin *Stadtbahn* station to catch the city train. He rode the city train unnoticed by other passengers towards *Unter den Linden* boulevard in the *Mitte* district of Berlin. There, he stepped off of the train and walked purposefully towards the Berlin State Opera.

Standing across the street from the opera house, Lübeck looked like any other man waiting on the street, perhaps for a friend or a ride. He was skilled at looking like he belonged wherever he was without sticking out in the crowd. After ten minutes, people began to exit the opera. He waited until he saw the target.

Ernst Scheinberg exited the Berlin State Opera into the frigid night air. His overcoat was warm enough but the back of his neck was cold. He wrapped a wool scarf around his neck to stave off the chill. He had just seen Wagner's *Der fliegende Holländer* and it was quite a moving experience. Standing under the Greek-inspired stone colonnade in front of the opera house, he felt refreshed and reenergized. The opera always made him feel that way. It took his mind off of his work in theoretical physics, which he did in support of the Nazi special weapons program. He was proud of his contribution to the building of a greater Germany and he was loyal to the Reich. No one could question that.

Ernst stepped down to the street and made his way south towards his home. He was humming one of Wagner's pieces softly to himself, moving with the crowd and unaware that someone was following him.

Lübeck crossed the street and merged into the crowd exiting the opera. He took up a position a few meters behind his mark. The Jewish sympathizer would help him send a message to others and that was a good thing. Men like Scheinberg were a threat to the Reich and Lübeck enjoyed dealing with such threats. There was no need for discussion, no need to lecture the traitor; his fate was sealed. No, this man would serve as a message to others. It was time to act.

Four blocks further south, Lübeck watched as Earnst turned east down a side street. The SD man knew that it was only two more blocks and the traitor to the *Reich* would be inside his warm home. Earnst was still humming as Lübeck silently but swiftly shoved an icepick into the physicist's temple. The instantaneous sharp pain was the last thing Earnst Scheinberg ever felt.

Lübeck stood over the fallen physicist. His blood pumped vigorously through his heart. The thrill of the kill invigorated him.

The killer reached into his own pocket and pulled out a note. Whoever found Scheinberg would know that this was what happened to Jewish collaborators. Lübeck pinned the note on the man' s lapel. Then with a swift pull, he removed the bloody icepick from the man's head. He wiped the blood off on the dead man's coat, stood up, turned and walked away. Lübeck was a man who got things done.

February 1, 1942 21:20
Lorient, France
Rouge Vin Maison

Peter sat at a worn wooden table in the back of the dimly lit French bar. He felt slightly uncomfortable in his new *Krieg-*

smarine uniform. It was stiff and itchy. At least he no longer had to wear bandages on his face, he mused as he sipped his glass of wine. It was a nice Bordeaux and that suited him just fine.

The last few days had been a whirlwind for the newly minted officer. Both Peter and his XO had been detached from the *U-216*, at which time they were placed on temporary duty—special assignment. Upon leaving the boat, they were both delivered back to Admiral Dönitz's headquarters, where Peter had been sworn in as a *Leutnant zur See* and informed that he would be part of a mission to Penang.

Sitting in the quiet bar in Lorient, he knew how precarious his position was and that he wanted to escape the war and German-occupied France. Would Japan provide a potential escape? He doubted it. He would be further from home and that thought did not improve his spirits.

Johann Goedel returned to the table with another bottle of Bordeaux and sat down across from Peter. He, too, looked a little down in the mouth, but for a different reason. He had to wait yet again to get his command. They shared a somber moment as they drank the wine.

"Everything ok, *Oberleutnant*?"

"Two Pair, yes, I'm ok and out here, please call me Johann. You are an officer now."

Peter was still getting used to his new title. "Yes, sir. I mean, yes. You just looked troubled."

"I was hoping for a command, my own U-boat, one of those new sleek Type IX's rolling off of the ways in Kiel. Not some grand tour of the Far East."

"I don't exactly want to go either, sir … uh, Johann, but orders are orders, right?"

"Yes, they are." Goedel took a drink. "Submarines are all that I have, all that I know. I started in this outfit as an enlisted man and worked my way up the hard way, no offense, Two Pair."

"None taken."

"I have been busting my ass trying to get a command. I

should have had it last refit, but they wanted me to stay on for one more patrol and now that it is done, they push it back again with this boondoggle."

"You will get a command."

"Before the war ends? I doubt it."

"What do you mean, before the war ends?"

"Our thrust into Russia has been halted. Word is that the *Wehrmacht* is bogged down and stretched thin. Opening a second front like that was pure folly and a mistake and now … now that the Americans are in the war …"

That can only mean that Germany's prospects for winning the war have been diminished."

Peter realized that he was an American again serving in a war against his own country. Ever since he had been conscripted, he was merely biding his time until he could figure out a way out of this mess. Fighting the British was one thing, even though it didn't sit well with him, but serving the *Kriegsmarine* against the United States, that was intolerable. He should have left Germany as his father had implored him to do.

"So, what's your story, Two Pair? You got family back home?"

Peter hesitated. It was again time to weave truth and deceit. Do not reveal too much, but don't appear to be evasive. He told Johann that he was the son of a diplomat, educated in Stuttgart, adding just a few details to flesh out a plausible background.

"We lived in Japan for several years when I was a kid. My dad was stationed there. But they are both dead now. Car accident. A drunken *Wehrmacht* Major, two years ago. I have no living relatives."

Of course, as far as he knew, his parents were alive and well living in Virginia or Nebraska again. But Peter could never reveal the truth.

"We share that, Two Pair. I lost my parents when I was young, to the flu pandemic in 1919." Goedel lifted his glass to Peter in a toast to their departed parents. "Time to get to sleep.

We have to catch a train to Berlin tomorrow."

Chapter Twelve: Condor

February 3, 1942 11:45
Berlin, Germany
Kriegsmarine Headquarters

Peter sat uncomfortably in his chair in the expansive briefing room in the basement of the *Kriegsmarine* headquarters. The room was filled with maps and photographs associated with the mission to Penang. The team of five officers had been assembled here at 06:00 to be briefed by several members of Admiral Dönitz's staff. As he looked around the room, he sized up the other members of the team.

In command was *Kapitän zur See* Fritz Ackermann. He appeared to be a no-nonsense career officer—efficient, competent, and all business. When he spoke, he had an air of command about him. He was Dönitz's man.

Then there was *Fregattenkapitän* Gerhard Klopp, Canaris' man from the *Abwehr*. Tall, thin, quiet, and introspective, he spoke rarely but was obviously listening at all times. To Peter, he appeared to be a competent intelligence officer.

Next to Klopp sat *SS Hauptsturmführer* Klaus Lübeck. Peter had learned that this was Schellenberg's man from the SD. He was tall and athletic with sandy brown hair and a large scar over his right eye that curved down to his right cheek. He looked menacing and capable. Like Klopp, Lübeck rarely spoke during the briefing. Peter wondered if that was common amongst the intelligence types.

To Peter's left sat *Oberleutnant zur See* Johann Goedel. He liked Goedel. He was a good officer and a decent man in Peter's estimation. Seemingly all alone in this world, he was married to the sea. Peter believed that Goedel would make a good U-boat captain someday.

The last member of the team was of course *Leutnant zur See* Peter Teufel. Peter marveled at how he'd wound up here. The son of an American diplomat, an American citizen, now an officer in the *Kriegsmarine*, assigned to a special mission to scout a submarine base for Germany in the Pacific theatre.

Peter recognized early in the briefing that he was just a small part of the mission. He was there to translate for the senior German officers in their dealings with the Japanese. With two intelligence officers on the mission, he vowed to maintain a low profile at all times. He was going to stay in the background and keep to himself whenever possible. No need to draw excess attention to himself. If he ever wanted to escape back to the United States, he had to get past this assignment first.

"We have confirmed your travel plans to Penang with our Japanese allies. When your work is done you will return to Berlin by the most expeditious means available. Any questions?" said *Kapitän zur See* Horst Baddenberg, the man in charge of briefing the mission on behalf of Dönitz.

"What if the Japanese want something in return for the use of this base?" asked Ackermann. "Are we authorized to make concessions on behalf of the Reich?"

"Our information suggests that this will not be the case," replied Baddenberg. "However, you are trusted to use your best judgment, Captain. Remember, the *Führer* has personally expressed his desire to support the establishment of a German base in the region. Do not disappoint him."

"If there are no further questions, your plane leaves in two days, gentlemen," Baddenberg said sharply.

That evening Peter sat at the bar of the *Der Dunkle Ort* with Johann Goedel drinking beer. He had taken Goedel there to listen to music and to get a bite to eat. The place was nearly empty on a Tuesday night, which suited the two sub-mariners just fine.

"What do you think of our team, Peter?"

"Ackermann seems sharp, competent I suppose. Klopp is quiet, a thinker, not sure what to make of him."

"And Lübeck?"

"He looks like a prize fighter."

"He is a dangerous man," Goedel said. "He is SS. The word is that he is Schellenberg's heavy."

"Heavy?"

"If Schellenberg has a problem, he sends in Lübeck to fix it."

"I see. Ackermann is in command, so there is nothing to worry about, right, Johann?"

Goedel laughed out loud and took another long pull from his beer. He looked at the naive young *Leutnant* and smiled. "You have a lot to learn, Two Pair. We report to Ackermann. Klopp and Lübeck are on solo missions. Each is trying to establish intelligence networks in the Far East. One serves the *Abwehr*, military intelligence, and the other serves the SD, Nazi party intelligence. It is a competition. It also wouldn't surprise me if they were also keeping an eye on the three of us U-boaters."

"Why would they do that?"

"The *Kriegsmarine* is the least 'Nazi' of the military branches, and the U-boat fleet in particular. There is no love lost between us and the rest of the *Wehrmacht*. I would be careful around those two."

February 5, 1942 18:33
Petsamo, Finland
Petsamo Flugplatz

The *Heinkel 111* slowly circled the airfield before lining up with the runway on its final approach. Onboard, the five German officers waited in the cramped passenger compartment for the moment that they could get out of the plane and stretch their legs. The plane touched down smoothly and taxied over to one of the three hangars next to the runway, their rounded roofs piled high with snow. The door to one of the hangars was open and the grounds crew, dressed in winter gear, pulled the plane into the wooden structure.

Peter was the last of the five to exit the plane. He stepped down into the bay and immediately felt the blast of cold arctic air. He could see that a light snow was falling outside the building. *So, this is Finland.*

After eight hours of flying time from Berlin, with only one stop to refuel near Helsinki, Peter was ready to get out of the plane. At least on a submarine you could move around a bit, but on the plane he was stuck in his seat for the duration of the flight. He followed the others out of the bay and proceeded down a path to a nearby hut. Nearly a half meter of snow lay piled up next to the walkway. He entered the hut, which was heated by a stove in the corner, and stomped the snow from his boots.

Peter realized that the hut was actually the base dining hall. Around the room, rough tables and benches lined up in rows. In the back corner was a man busy at a stove, stirring a pot. The five travelers were summoned to help themselves to some venison stew and bread. Coffee was poured for the men as they sat at a table.

"Man, that was a long flight," Peter said to Goedel, who was sitting across from him at the table.

"That was nothing. The next leg will take nearly twenty hours."

Peter was not looking forward to being trapped inside an airplane for a flight of that length, but there wasn't much that he could do about it. He ate his stew and finished his meal with a shot of Schnapps and a cigarette.

After an hour's wait, the Penang party was led from the mess hall back out into the cold night air. The light snow had stopped falling and the moon was peeking out from the clouds. They walked the cleared path back to the airfield. In front of the hangars sat a large four-engine aircraft with *Luftwaffe* markings. The engines idled as the men boarded the plane.

Peter stepped up into the large plane and quickly found his seat. In the center of the fuselage rested two fuel tanks. He learned from Klopp that this was a specially modified *Focke-Wulf* FW-200 Condor assigned to the *Abwehr* for long-range missions. It was one of the few planes with the range to make the 5800-kilometer flight to Manchuria.

With the boarding door shut, the big plane taxied to the end of the runway and sat stationary for a few moments. Then the four engines began to rev up to take-off power, its propellers chopping into the cold, dense arctic air. The big plane, loaded with fuel, slowly began lumbering down the runway. As the speed built, the pilot deftly lifted the nose of the plane and it leapt into the night.

Peter sat quietly in his seat thinking to himself. The trip was 5800 kilometers. The plane would cruise at approximately 300 kilometers per hour. In his head he determined that the flight would be 19.3 hours. Well, might as well try to get some sleep, he thought. It was going to be a very long day.

The FW-200 Condor touched down just outside of Harbin, Manchuria and rolled out onto a taxiway. Peter looked at his watch. It was 22:00 local time. The flight had been 19 hours and 27 minutes. He was glad that it was over.

February 12, 1942 08:20
Harbin, Manchuria
Pingfang District

Peter lay upon his cot in the quarters that had been set aside for the Penang party. He was reading a book on diesel engine technology that he had brought with him. Having spent the last week translating for the team, he had learned that the Japanese hadn't exactly planned this mission as well as Captain Tomago had promised. There was much confusion and many delays in getting the party on to Penang. A trip to Tokyo was in line first for a "meet and greet" with the Japanese naval command.

Once the travel arrangements had finalized yesterday, it was Lübeck who delayed them again by informing the party that he must inspect one of the Japanese facilities in Harbin. Lübeck would be making the inspection with Peter as his translator.

Peter continued to read and was startled when the door to the living quarters burst open. It was Lübeck.

"On your feet, Teufel. You have work to do."

"Yes, sir."

Peter hopped out of bed and donned his uniform cap and coat and followed the SD agent to an awaiting car that made its way south through Harbin.

"Your job is to translate, *Leutnant* Teufel, understood?"

"I understand, sir."

"What you see, what you hear today is absolutely never to be repeated. Is that understood, *Leutnant*?"

Peter replied in the affirmative.

"The information that I am seeking today is to be considered a secret of the Reich and discussing it with anyone other than me is a serious offense. An offense with serious consequences."

"Yes, *Hauptsturmführer*."

They did not speak for the remainder of the drive south. Peter didn't like the thought of being privy to any secrets of the Reich and he was extremely uncomfortable having to translate for Lübeck under such circumstances. He did not like the man and the more time he spent with him, the more his dislike grew.

The car pulled up to a large, gated compound. Peter read the sign on the gate, which said in Japanese, "Epidemic Prevention and Water Purification Department - Unit 731." The two German officers exited the car and were escorted into the facility.

Entering the compound, they were shown to the nearest building and upon entering were introduced to Surgeon General Shirō Ishii of the Imperial Japanese Army and Captain Choki Ito of the *Kempeitai*, the Japanese Secret Police.

Peter began translating as Surgeon General Shirō Ishii spoke first. "Welcome, *Hauptsturmführer* Lübeck. I am pleased to welcome you to Unit 731. My understanding is that some of the experimental work that we are doing here may be of some interest to the Reich. Captain Ito will show you our facility. Captain, please provide these men with access to everything here that they want to see."

"Yes, sir," replied Ito.

With that, the *Kempeitai* captain gave Peter and Lübeck a tour of the huge facility.

As they moved about the complex, Peter began to realize that the Epidemic Prevention and Water Purification Department was not what it seemed.

In one building Peter witnessed the dissection of a prisoner who was not sedated. The woman being dissected screamed in agony. In a courtyard, the Japanese were detonating hand grenades at various distances from prisoners tied to posts to determine mortality rates and kill radiuses. Peter watched as several Chinese prisoners died in front of his eyes, while others, who were only wounded, were led back to theirs cells, untreated. He witnessed prisoners whose limbs were frozen solid by the "doctors." The Japanese "doctor" then swung a wooden mallet as hard as he could, smashing the frozen appendage to see the damage that it would cause. Peter would never forget that sound. When one of the arms snapped, Peter couldn't stomach the scene. He turned around, bent at the waist and vomited. This facility was a prison where experiments were conducted on Chinese prisoners. Horrific experiments.

Lübeck smirked at Peter and ordered him to translate: "Tell the captain that you are from the navy and just don't have the stomach for doing this kind of work."

Peter translated, word for word.

Captain Ito laughed. "Follow me, *Hauptsturmführer*. This is something that you may be interested in."

Ito lead the two Germans away from the building. As they proceeded into the next building, Peter could see that it contained a series of cells. Within most of the cells were prisoners awaiting experimentation. Ito informed Lübeck that the prisoners were referred to as "logs." The Japanese would tally how many "logs" were cut down each day. He pointed to a row of cells and spoke to his guests. "This is where we keep the prisoners for the venereal disease experiments. We breed one of the infected logs with a non-infected one to determine transmission probabilities."

"What if they refuse to perform?"

"We exterminate them. This one over here refuses to participate,'" Ito said, pointing to a Chinese man in a cell. "He will be shot this evening."

"May I save you the trouble?" Lübeck asked.

Peter's mind was in a fog. He was trying to process all that he had seen. Before he translated the request, he looked at Lübeck, slowly realizing exactly what the SD officer was asking.

Lübeck nodded at Peter and said, "Go on. Translate."

Peter did.

"Be my guest."

Lübeck withdrew his 9X19mm Luger P08 pistol from his holster and quickly fired a bullet into the prisoner's forehead. Blood sprayed the cell wall as the man dropped to the floor.

Peter turned to look at the shooter. Lübeck's expression was unchanged. There was no joy, no excitement, nor was there any remorse. There was no expression at all to indicate how Lübeck felt about killing an unarmed man in cold blood. Lübeck holstered the Luger and turned towards Ito.

"There. I saved you a bullet."

Ito looked very pleased as he led them out of the cell complex.

The three met again with Surgeon General Shirō Ishii at the completion of the tour, where Lübeck asked questions for about thirty minutes. The SD officer scribbled a few notes for future reference and thanked his hosts for their hospitality. They were then escorted out of the compound to an awaiting car for transport back to their barracks.

Peter sat in silence next to Lübeck as the car slowly made its way back to Harbin. His mind replayed the murder of the Chinese man over and over. Nor could he stop thinking about the horrific treatment of the prisoners that he had witnessed at Unit 731. He knew that war was hellish, but this was more than that. This was truly man's inhumanity to man.

Peter had heard rumors that the Germans had treated non-Germans, especially the Jews, harshly, but the discussions that Lübeck had with the Japanese indicated that this behavior was widespread throughout the Reich. It was clear to Peter that torture and extermination were tools being used by the Nazis to ensure the purity of the German race.

Something changed in Peter. "Why, *Hauptsturmführer*?"

"Why what, Teufel?"

"Why did you shoot that man?"

"To curry favor with our hosts."

"The man was unarmed, a prisoner."

Lübeck turned and looked at Peter. His eyes revealed disdain for the young officer.

"He was an *untermensch*, not a man but a subhuman, a dog, and a disobedient dog at that. I removed him from this life as a favor to Ito. I saved him the trouble."

"The man did nothing to you."

"I have my mission here and my orders come from the highest halls of the Party. You will not question my actions, *Leutnant*. Is that clear?"

"Yes, sir."

Lübeck looked away from Peter. "You are weak, Teufel. You have no guts. I don't believe that you are fit to be an officer. I will be keeping my eyes on you and I will certainly report what I see to *Obersturmbannführer* Schellenberg."

Peter lay awake in bed that night, failing to fall asleep. His brain was still trying to wrap itself around everything that he had seen at Unit 731. *What kind of people can do that to another human being?* As Goedel had told him, Lübeck was a dangerous man indeed.

His need to escape back to the States had intensified. Now, more than ever, he deeply regretted his decision to stay in Europe when his father and mother had moved back to the US in early 1939. He was so sure back then that he was making the right decision for himself and that his father had been so wrong. Now, in hindsight, he had been foolish and his prospects for repatriation were very dim. He had to figure out how to get back to the United States. There had to be a way.

Chapter Thirteen: Photograph

February 28, 1942 09:30
Harbin, Manchuria
Pingfang District

The Penang party eagerly boarded the Kawasaki Ki-56 twin-engine transport plane. The five German officers had been stranded in Manchuria for nearly a month. A lack of coordination between Berlin and Tokyo had been part of the delay; however, Lübeck's desire to learn more about Unit 731 had also extended their stay. No one had questioned Lübeck, not even Captain Ackermann. Even the *Abwehr* man, Klopp, avoided confronting "Schellenberg's man."

Peter sat in his seat on the plane next to Goedel, happy to leave Harbin, the sooner the better. He had escorted Lübeck on two more trips back to the compound, but, thankfully, there were no further tours of the facility. The meeting's objectives were to speak with Surgeon General Shirō Ishii and Captain Choki Ito in order to gather more information "useful to the Reich." Even those discussions were sickening to Peter. Lübeck had asked about termination rates, efficiencies, results of experiments, and disposal procedures. Peter did not look forward to being ordered by Lübeck to accompany him on any further intelligence gathering trips.

Now Peter was more at ease, knowing that he was leaving Harbin and returning to Tokyo for the first time since he was a boy. He wondered if he would recognize any of the people or places. He doubted if he would see the US embassy, since their countries were now at war. He also wondered if he would see anyone who might recognize him, but he reasoned that the odds were in his favor.

The five-hour flight to Japan was uneventful. The plane landed at *Atsugi* Naval Air Station, where the Germans were met by a Japanese naval contingent. Peter and the rest of the Penang party were driven from the airfield to Tokyo, where they were quartered near the German embassy. The next morning, Peter and the other four German officers were scheduled to attend a luncheon at the German embassy to be hosted by the German Ambassador to Japan, Eugen Ott. The men, in full dress uniforms, were escorted to the embassy in the heart of Tokyo where they were greeted by Ambassador Ott.

Peter followed the rest of the men into the dining room and took his seat at the far end of the table. His translation skills would not be necessary for this conversation. He listened to the discussion as he ate.

"Captain, I have been briefed by Berlin on the purpose of your mission. Establishing a base in the East is of supreme importance to the *Führer*. Understand that I am here to assist you by any means possible to accomplish your task."

"Thank you, *Herr* Ambassador."

Ott continued, "Call me Eugen, please. I trust that you understand that your mission is greater than just scouting for such a base. It is a mission that improves the relationship between our country and the Empire of Japan. Your party has an opportunity to greatly strengthen the military cooperation between Germany and the Empire. You are ambassadors in your own right."

"We understand the importance of our assignment," Ackermann said. "Any assistance that you can provide us would be appreciated. We spent nearly a month in Harbin, making connections, but we really need to get to Penang to accomplish our primary objective."

"Your time in Manchuria was spent wisely," Ott congratulated them. "You must understand the Japanese culture. They wish to afford you every opportunity to see how accomplished they are with respect to their military might."

"This sounds like further delays in getting a German base established in this region of the world," Ackerman observed.

Gerhard Klopp injected himself into the conversation, turning to Ackermann. "Fritz, our time spent in Harbin was of significant value. We made valuable intelligence connections. I suspect that the time here in Japan will also be in the best interest of the Reich. We would be wise to follow Eugen's advice. "

Ott continued with the point. "The culture here dictates that our Japanese friends be good hosts. They will want to parade you all around their island country to show you their military might. They consider themselves equal to us Germans and they will wish to demonstrate this. Isn't that so, *Herr* Teufel?"

Peter had been listening to the discussion but not really paying attention. Now the Ambassador had directed a question directly at him. "I am told that you spent time in Japan with your father, a diplomat. I have been here since 1934 but I do not recall meeting a Teufel. Who did your father work for?"

Peter felt his heart pumping a little faster. Was this the moment that his deception would be uncovered?

"I was a young schoolboy when I lived here in the twenties. I do not recall who my father worked for. Apparently, we returned to Germany before you arrived here."

Peter looked around the table. All eyes were on him. Everyone seemed to accept the answer, although Peter noted that Lübeck seemed to be making a mental note of the conversation.

March 4, 1942 18:45
Tokyo, Japan
Shinjuku District

Klaus Lübeck walked down the street, leaving *Shinjuku* Station. Captain Ito had given him a list of *Kempeitai* contacts that he should meet with in Tokyo. They were on their way to meet one of them. With him was *Leutnant zur See* Teufel, who would again serve as his interpreter. In Lübeck's mind there was something odd about the young German officer.

The young man didn't quite measure up to what Lübeck believed a good German officer should be. He had been unable to stomach what he had seen at Unit 731, but it was more than that. He spoke a strange dialect of German. It was sort of a blend between Northern Bavarian and Eastern Franconian, the likes of which he had never heard before.

How was it that Ott had never heard of Peter's father? The diplomatic corps of Nazi Germany was not a huge organization. Lübeck made a mental note to look into this matter upon his return to Berlin.

March 13, 1942 19:15
Tokyo, Japan
Chiyoda District

Peter stepped out of the embassy limousine in front of the *Meiji Seimei Kan* building in the *Chiyoda* district of Tokyo. With him were the four other German officers from the Penang party accompanied by Ambassador Ott and one of his aides. All of the officers had donned their full-dress uniforms, while the ambassador and his aide wore tuxedos with top hats. They were attending a dinner hosted by the Imperial Japanese Navy's Sixth Fleet, commanded by Vice Admiral Teruhisa Komatsu and his Chief of Staff, Vice-Admiral Hisashi Mito.

Peter carried a satchel with paper and pens for note taking, along with other supplies for the evening. As the junior officer, he was basically a servant for the others. This did not bother him in the least.

The German contingent left the sidewalk and entered the *Meiji Seimei Kan* building, escorted by an IJN officer to the second floor, where a large dining room had been readied for them. As instructed, Peter stayed with Captain Ackermann so that he could translate for him.

During the briefing at the German embassy, Ambassador Ott had reminded them that this meeting was crucial in bolstering the military relationship between the Reich and Japan. He encouraged the men to enjoy the hospitality of the Japanese. Their hosts would be greatly embarrassed if the Germans were rude in any way. If food was offered, eat some; if drinks were offered, drink some. He explained that the Japanese would be shamed or lose "face," if a gift were to be refused. They were to be on their best behavior, warned Ott.

They entered a receiving line of Japanese naval officers and government officials. On the other side of the room stood a line of reporters. Flash bulbs popped as pictures were taken. This was a media event for the Japanese government and a propaganda opportunity to show the Japanese people how the Germans had come here for their assistance.

Peter followed Ackermann through the line, making introductions to each Japanese representative. Hands were shaken and bows were exchanged. Finally, Peter reached the end of the receiving line where Vice Admiral Teruhisa Komatsu stood. The admiral bowed then extended his hand to Ackermann.

"*Willkommen, Kapitän Ackermann,*" Komatsu said in broken German.

Ackermann shook the admiral's hand and told Peter to inform the admiral that he was honored to meet him. Peter relayed Ackermann's sentiments to the admiral in nearly perfect Japanese.

The admiral responded in his native language. "Please enjoy our hospitality this evening, gentlemen. It is our honor to host you and Ambassador Ott. After we eat, we will have matters to discuss."

With the formalities of the receiving line complete, Admiral Komatsu gave a few brief words to those assembled. Peter translated for the Germans, informing them that the admiral was welcoming his allies from Germany and that the Greater East Asia Co-Prosperity Sphere would benefit tremendously from the alliance with Germany. He then called for the Japanese press to take pictures.

The event was well orchestrated by the admiral's staff. During the next ten minutes, the journalists took numerous photos, but they were not allowed to ask any questions. A statement would be issued to them all from the Sixth Fleet liaison officer on Monday. After the ten minutes were up, all of the media were escorted out of the dining room. The dinner would be for the Navy and government personnel only.

At the head table, Peter sat on one side of Ackermann while Admiral Komatsu sat on his other side. On Peter's left sat Goedel, Lübeck, and, finally, Klopp. Peter noticed that Lübeck and Klopp looked a little uncomfortable. He surmised that the two intelligence officers were not used to being photographed and being put on display. Their work was usually done covertly. Ambassador Ott and his aide sat at another table with the Japanese government officials.

All of the men in the room were served a traditional Japanese multi-course dinner. Peter informed his party that this was a *Kaiseki* held especially for them. The first course was a *miso* soup, followed by *sushi* and *sashimi*. Fine Japanese beer and *sake* were poured as well. Then several courses of Japanese delicacies were served. Peter explained each course. He informed his fellow officers that they were eating *Shirasu,* raw baby fish; *Kurage,* jellyfish; *Namako,* sea cucumber; and *Kusaya,* dried salted fish.

Peter was using his chopsticks to eat the dinner while the other Germans were using their forks. He had not used the traditional Japanese utensils in a very long time, but he was able to manage.

"Good God, Two Pair! This is different," Goedel whispered to Peter.

"It's good. It's an acquired taste," Peter smiled.

"I need more beer to wash this down," Goedel said. "I could sure use some *schnitzel* and *spätzle*, covered in dill gravy."

"Remember Ott's orders. Try a little of everything offered to you."

"Hell, I'll try anything once," Goedel responded. "All good submariners do."

Peter looked past Goedel to see Lübeck picking at his plate with his fork. The SD officer did not look very pleased with the offerings, but, as ordered to do so, he was trying a bit of everything.

"How is the jellyfish, *Hauptsturmführer*?" Peter said to Lübeck. "Served raw like this, it is quite an interesting texture, isn't it?"

Peter took his chopsticks lifted a piece of the raw jellyfish to his mouth and savored it.

Lübeck wondered if young Teufel was actually mocking him. Lübeck prided himself on being as tough as they came. He knew that he could stomach the grotesque Asian fare better than any man. Just to prove a point, Lübeck took a huge portion of jellyfish onto his fork and stuffed it into his mouth. He would show the young officer what he was made of.

Lübeck began to chew the mouthful of food. He had expected it to be, well, jelly-like, but it was not. It was slightly crunchy with a sour taste and not pleasant at all. He quickly swallowed the mass of *Kurage* and reached for his beer. His eyes were watering a bit as he swallowed three gulps of the brew. He vowed that he would never eat another bite of *Kurage* ever again.

Peter noticed a minute later when Lübeck excused himself from the table that the SD man looked a little green around the gills. Lübeck returned after a few minutes and sat back in his seat. Lübeck looked better, but Peter noticed that there was a small piece of chewed *Kurage* on his lapel. Had the SD officer been unable to stomach jellyfish?

Peter watched as the SD officer barely ate anything else placed before him. He picked and prodded with his fork, tasting a small portion now and then, but he never truly ate another bite that evening. Peter figured that this partially, in a very small way, made up for Harbin.

When dinner was completed, Admiral Komatsu gave another short speech. He thanked the members of the government and Ambassador Ott in particular for attending the dinner. He then notified the government officials that the Navy had military operations to discuss with the German visitors and that their presence was no longer needed.

Twenty minutes later, after many handshakes and bows, the Navy officers from Germany and Japan were alone in the dining hall. Admiral Komatsu spoke and Peter translated the conversation.

"Honored visitors of the Reich, I am informed by my government that you need our assistance in finding a suitable location to operate submarines in this region of the world. As commander of the Sixth Fleet of the Imperial Japanese Navy, I am able to offer assistance towards that end."

"We appreciate the gesture, Admiral," said Ackermann. "As you must know, we have mutual enemies operating in the Indian Ocean and the Pacific Ocean. With our interests in North Africa, our Navy wishes to pressure the British in the Indian Ocean. Forays into the Pacific will be a future possibility."

"Of course, we support such an arrangement. I am told that you are interested in several potential bases from which to operate. I am also told that Penang is at the top of your list. Is that true?"

"Yes, Admiral. Our information indicates that Penang would be the optimal site for an installation to support U-boat operations. And, to be blunt, Admiral, we are anxious to see the existing facilities in the harbor there."

"I understand your desire to get to Penang. I will ensure that your needs are met in a timely fashion. It will take a few days to arrange, but I can get you to Penang soon. In the meantime, I would appreciate it if you and your men would tour our submarine facilities here in Japan. We are quite proud of our fleet of submarines, as I am sure that you are proud of yours."

"We consider our submarines to be the finest in the world Admiral, but I have heard that the Japanese submarines are built with exceptional quality."

"Perhaps a short seagoing demonstration would improve your opinion of our underwater craft, Captain."

Ackermann, following the advice of Eugen Ott, accepted the admiral's offer. With any luck, they would be on to Penang in a few days.

March 16, 1942 10:09
Tokyo, Japan
Office of the Japan Times and Advertiser

Sutemi Nakano sat at his desk in the offices of the *Japan Times and Advertiser*, a Japanese newspaper published in the English language. The paper had been in existence for nearly fifty years and he had been a reporter for half of that time.

On his desk sat a media release from the Sixth Fleet as Admiral Komatsu had promised, and a stack of newly developed photographs. The details of the release were few. The document merely stated that representatives of the German Navy had come calling on the IJN for assistance, which the IJN was gladly providing. No names were given other than the admiral's and Ambassador Ott.

Sutemi had been at the dinner and had understood everything that was in the release. The document was not of any great assistance to him, as he knew that it wouldn't be. He had done his own investigation of the Germans after he left the dinner. He would have to write his article based on what he knew and what he had found out through his sources.

As a long-time reporter in Tokyo, Sutemi knew a lot of people. He knew government officials, military leaders, Yakuza members, and others. It paid in this business to get to know people. A source in the IJN told him that the Germans were looking for a base to operate submarines here in the Far East. He had also learned the names and ranks of the German contingent.

Sutemi set down the release and picked up the stack of photos. There were four dozen shots from the dinner at the *Meiji Seimei Kan.* He leafed through each picture in order to select one or two for his article. One in particular stood out. It was a photo of Admiral Komatsu shaking hands with Captain Ackermann, the remaining Germans stood on either side of the two men. The picture was clear and composed. This would be one of the photos for his article.

Sutemi set down the photos and adjusted the round glasses on his nose. He picked up a sheet of paper and rolled it into his typewriter. He started composing his article using the release and the information that he had received from his contact. When he finished, the caption under the photo listed all of the names and ranks of the officers in the picture. Satisfied, he sent the article to his editor.

Chapter Fourteen: Reconnaissance

April 13, 1942 06:51
Hiroshima, Japan
Hiroshima–Nishi Airport

The twin-engine *Nakajima* Navy Type 0 transport of the *Kure* Naval Air Group taxied to the end of the single runway at the Hiroshima-Nishi Airport. Onboard the aircraft sat the Penang party, all of whom were glad to finally be heading to Malaysia. The pilot pushed the throttles forward and the *Mitsubishi Kinsei* 43 radial engines roared as the plane began its take-off roll.

The Penang party had spent the last three weeks touring IJN naval facilities, submarine bases, and shipyards, including *Yokosuka, Kobe, Sasebo,* and *Kure.* The month-long stay in Japan had been a publicity tour, the IJN proudly showing off its naval facilities to their German visitors. Now the Germans were finally allowed to proceed in order to conduct the inspection of the port facilities in Penang.

Johann Goedel looked around inside the fuselage of the plane. Along with his four fellow German officers were fifteen members of the Japanese Imperial Navy. The transport plane was scheduled for a refueling stop in Manila and then it would proceed on to their desired destination. Goedel, more so than the others, wanted this trip to be over.

Goedel figured that when he returned, he would be given his own U-boat. A command of his own after twelve years of service. He had earned it. The sooner they completed their assessment of the facilities in Penang, the sooner that he could get on with his career. He would welcome the opportunity to captain his own submarine.

He wondered if he could get Two Pair assigned to his boat. The young man was likable, smart, resourceful, and educated. Teufel had handled himself very well during the last two months. He was even able to work with Lübeck, which Goedel was convinced was quite a task. Johann decided that he would ask for Teufel to be assigned to his new boat.

After a scheduled stop in the Philippines, where several of the Japanese naval personnel departed the flight for their duty assignments, the refueled plane took off for Penang. The flight from Manila was uneventful and their arrival was low key. Unlike in Tokyo and Harbin before, the Penang party arrived in Malaysia with very little fanfare. Goedel felt good about finally getting down to work.

April 22, 1942 17:05
Penang, Malaysia
Penang Harbor, George Town

Peter Teufel and Johann Goedel were aboard an eight-meter motor launch crewed by Japanese sailors, inspecting the port facilities from the water. The port was larger than Goedel expected, with plenty of room for the Japanese and the Germans to operate together.

The base was on the east side of the island located in George Town. Deep water access in the Penang Channel connecting to the Strait of Malacca made this an ideal location for a submarine base.

The temperature was warm, over 30 degrees Celcius as the launch maneuvered around the docks in the harbor. At the end of each pier, Goedel would motion for the launch to stop. Peter would then take a sounding of the water depth by dropping a weighted line, marked along its length in meters, and relaying the depth to Goedel. The senior officer would then note the depth on his map.

Peter was sweating as he labored in the boat but he didn't mind. It was nice to be out in the sun and getting a little work done. He wanted to shout "Mark Twain" every time that he took a sounding, but knew better than to reveal himself.

As they reached the northern-most pier, they repeated the sounding process yet again. Peter dropped the weighted rope, paused to let it reach the sandy bottom, and called out the depth.

"Twenty-two meters, *Oberleutnant*."

"Twenty-two meters. Got it. Tell our captain that we are done for the day. Time for a beer, don't you think, Two Pair?"

"I will take that as an order!"

The motor launch made its way back to its dock on the southern end of the harbor. Peter thanked the crew for their assistance and returned the salute of the Japanese crew as he departed the craft. Twenty minutes later, Peter and Goedel sat at a waterfront bar in George Town. Goedel picked up his beer and took a long pull before he spoke. "Only one more week of this and we will be headed back to Germany, thank God."

"It will be nice to get back home."

Peter knew that Germany was not truly his "home," but, as of yet, he couldn't see a way back to America from Penang. His odds were better in France. If he could get back to Lorient, he had a plan. For the last week he had been formulating how he might be able to sneak into Spain and try to make his way back to the United States.

"I want to ask you something, Two Pair." Peter waited. "You know when we return to Germany, I will be given my own boat. That has been my goal for a very long time now."

"You certainly have earned a command."

"I will have some say in who crews my boat. I was wondering if you would be interested in joining my crew?"

Peter had just assumed that he would be assigned back to the *U-216* when he returned to Europe. But an assignment with Goedel presented other challenges. "You want me on your boat?"

"Yes, I do. You are a bright guy, educated and resourceful. You qualified in the engine room faster than anyone that I have seen. I could use a man like you as my engineering officer."

Peter didn't know exactly what to say. He was taken aback by Goedel's offer. He liked Goedel and thought that he was a very good officer, but he wondered what Goedel would say when Peter slipped away on his run to Spain.

"What's the matter, Two Pair, don't you want to serve under me?"

"No. No. It's not that. I just hadn't thought about it. This is all new to me."

"Still think of yourself as a *Matrosengefreiter*, eh? Well, you are an officer now and I believe that you have the makings of a very good one."

"I don't know. I have never really thought about being an officer. What if the men don't respect me like they respect you?"

"You came up from the enlisted ranks, just as I did. They won't even know that, nor does it matter. You are an officer and rightly so. I could see that potential in you on the *U-216*."

Goedel waived down the waitress and ordered two more beers.

Peter considered the offer before him. He reasoned that, until he could make his break for Spain, serving under someone that he knew and trusted was better than rolling the dice with another captain. He took a long pull on his beer. "Count me in."

"Outstanding, Two Pair! We will have the hottest running boat in the whole *Kriegsmarine*!"

The two officers toasted their new alliance and drank liberally from their mugs. It was a sailor's tradition to do so. Peter felt himself relax a little after making up his mind to follow Goedel. While on this mission to Penang he had considered many alternatives for escape, he had never considered what they would entail. Now he had a plan. He would follow Goedel until he could make a break for Spain. He liked and respected Goedel; he was a good man.

"Good. That's settled. I have to say, you've really impressed me—our performance on the *U-216*, welding that air line, your education, but I realized that I greatly respected your abilities on this trip. Your ability to handle Lübeck sealed it." Goedel continued, "Lübeck is a killer. Fortunately, he is on our side. But he is an ass and I don't like him. I saw what you did to him at the dinner in Tokyo. You pulled one over on him and he wasn't quite sure if you were screwing with him. THAT is what a real submariner can do. You gained a lot of respect from me that night."

"I didn't do anything ..."

"And that is why I respect you. Lübeck did not know if you did anything, either. I would hesitate to try something like that again if I were you, but DAMN that was funny."

Peter gave Goedel a wry smile and they both drank to the dinner in Tokyo.

"We better drink up and get back to our quarters, Two Pair. We have a briefing with Ackermann tomorrow at seven."

"One more, *Oberleutnant*. I mean Johann. The night is young."

Peter watched as Goedel hesitated, mulling over the idea of another round. Ultimately, Goedel waived his hand in the air and shouted, "Barkeep! Two more beers."

April 22, 1942 15:00
Burke, Virginia

Anne Teufel was washing her breakfast dishes in her home outside of Washington, DC. Now that Erik was retired, the Teufels split their time between Omaha and Virginia. She kept busy with her task, but her mind was on other things. Her only son, Peter, had not been heard from in over a year. War had overtaken Europe and her little boy was somewhere in the fray.

It seemed like ten years since she had heard anything from Peter, and she was beyond worried. That young woman Marilyn Miller had let her know that Peter was in Bordeaux, France, but France had been overrun by the German Army. She had replied to Marilyn that she had not heard from Peter but that she would let her know as soon as she could.

Anne busied herself with the dishes. She didn't want to think about what was happening to her only son. The Teufels's retirement had been strained. She vigorously washed a plate as she stewed in her thoughts. Out of the corner of her eye, she saw a car nosing down the lane to their cottage. It was a government car. Anne's stomach tightened. She knew what a government car meant.

Anne recognized the man who stepped out of the 1938 Ford into the Teufels's driveway. Byron Schoenfeld had known Erik for many years at the State Department. The man had been a junior clerk in Berlin.

Anne led Byron around the cottage to the field behind the small house. There in the middle of the garden, planting seeds, was sixty-two-year-old Erik Teufel, dressed in overalls and a broad straw hat to ward off the sun. They exchanged pleasantries, and then Byron got to the point.

"I was hoping that we could talk in private Erik. It seems that your Government has a few questions that only a man with your background can answer."

Anne left the men and went into the house. She was not concerned about what Byron wanted to discuss. The progress of the war, diplomatic codes, shoeshines … None of that mattered to her. She only wanted to know about her son.

Out on the patio, Erik gestured to a chair and sat down. "What brings you out here to see an old retired diplomat Byron?"

"Erik, we have come into some information that puzzles us and alarms us at the same time."

"And what would that be?"

"Do you know where your son is, Erik?"

Erik Teufel's eyes widened as he sat back in his chair. He took a long drink of his bourbon. "We ... I ... left Peter in Germany to finish his education before Anne and I returned to the United States. I have not heard from him in months. Do you have news of him?"

"I have a picture that I want to show you. We got it from our British contacts in London. It is a copy of the *Japan Times and Advertiser* from March. Do you recognize anyone in this photo?"

Erik grabbed the paper from Schoenfeld and looked at the picture. There on the paper he saw a Japanese admiral and several German officers. He did not recognize anyone in the photograph.

"Not a single one. Why?"

"Look closely at the one on the left ... the German lieutenant. His name in the caption is given as *Teufel, Peter Teufel.*"

Erik shook the paper and gazed at the man on the left. His mind swirled as he realized that it was his son in the photo.

"Why is your son an officer in the German *Kriegsmarine*, Erik?"

"I ... I ... I ... don't know what this is about, Byron. I am shocked."

"A man by the name of Bill Donovan wishes to speak with you tomorrow. He is the head of the Office of the Coordinator of Information. He has the ear of the President. He has some questions that we at the State Department can't answer. You will be there won't you, Erik?"

All that Erik could do was nod. Schoenfeld emptied his drink and walked to his Ford. Erik watched him go. *Anne is going to be crushed.*

April 23, 1942 01:08
George Town, Penang, Malaysia
Lord Clive Hotel

Klaus Lübeck lay upon his bed in his room of the Lord Clive Hotel. The former British institution was now occupied by the Japanese. He had spent the day with his *Kenpeitai* contact who had made some inroads for him in the Far East. Schellenburg would be pleased. Lübeck now had channels that would allow the SD to track Japanese interests in this region. His contact was a Japanese national now residing in Penang, with the ability to speak a smattering of German. That suited Lübeck just fine. It eliminated his need for that gutless translator Teufel.

Klaus didn't like the young German *Kriegsmarine* officer. He was smug, too well educated, and a weakling. Teufel could not stomach the things that he had seen in Harbin. And besides, there was something about the young man that bothered Lübeck. His speech was … well, not quite German. His dialect was untraceable. Lübeck had made several notes about the young officer, and he was going to share them with Schellenburg when he returned to Berlin.

The "comfort girl" came out of the bathroom naked, and walked to the side of Lübeck's bed. He looked up at the Chinese woman and smiled. *She is pretty for one of the Untermensch*. He reached his hand up to the young woman and drew her into the bed.

The Chinese girl kissed Lübeck on the neck, the cheek, and the lips. This was not her first time, Lübeck thought. She mounted him smoothly, guiding his erection into her as she began to ride him slowly. She feigned delight as she rode up and down and he could tell that she was going through the motions. He would show her what it meant to be in bed with a member of the Aryan race.

Lübeck reached up to the Chinese girl's neck with his right hand as she ground her pelvis against his. He caressed her neck as she rode him, while with his left hand he pulled her long dark hair gently down her back. She moaned at this—in reality or in disguise, he didn't care. He became aware that he was about to finish and that excited him, so much so that he tightened his grip around the young woman's neck.

The woman began to struggle and gasp. With a surge of strength, Lübeck squeezed his grip even tighter. The young Chinese woman's eyes widened with shock and then horror. He stared at the girl as the light left her eyes. *Stupid woman, an Untermensch, she had it coming.*

April 23, 1942 14:00
Washington, DC
Office of the Coordinator of Information

Erik Teufel was escorted into the office of Bill Donovan. They had met once before at a function in the nation's capital, but he really didn't know the man. He knew who Donovan was by reputation, and that he was a confidant of Roosevelt, but that was about as much as Erik knew.

Donovan cut right to the chase. "You've seen the picture in the *Japan Times and Advertiser*?"

"Yes, I have but to be quite frank with you, I have no idea as to the circumstances that led to Peter being in that photo."

"Can you tell me why Peter remained in Germany when you and Anne returned in 1938?"

"He wanted to finish college there. We tried to talk him into returning to the States to finish school, but he was determined to finish there. We had a rather large argument about it and in the end, well, I guess that I gave in."

"Have you heard from him recently?"

"No, not for well over a year. He wanted to tour Europe after graduating. The war hadn't started yet and he had the funds to do it. We last heard from him when he was in France, living at a vineyard."

"That matches the information that we have. Our British contacts in MI6 have elements in Germany and in the Far East. I, of course, am not at liberty to divulge the nature of these connections but let me say that we get reliable information from them."

"Go on, Mr. Donovan, please."

"Your son Peter traveled Europe quite a bit before the war. Czechoslovakia, Switzerland, France ... Hell, he was in Poland when the Germans invaded. It seems that he was in Bordeaux in the summer of 1940 when the Germans occupied France."

"Jesus, really?"

"Apparently, he had plans to meet a woman in Switzerland that summer, but it never happened and we know why. He was rounded up and sent to Germany as forced labor and eventually conscripted into the German Navy, forced into service by the *Wehrmacht*."

"My God!"

"In your position in the State Department, you had access to some very sensitive information ... diplomatic codes, communication protocols, some intelligence on both Germany and Japan. Did you share any of this with Peter?"

"Absolutely not! I can assure you that my position and any information that was presented to me in the service of our nation was kept in strict confidence from Peter and even my wife."

"No need to be defensive, Erik. You can understand my concern. If Peter had such knowledge, he would be a security risk. The question now is ... what the hell are we going to do about your son?"

"What do you mean?"

"There are elements in our government that believe that he has voluntarily assumed allegiance to Germany. If that is the case, it bodes poorly for the young man."

"That is not the case! Peter is an American, just a misguided youth who got caught up in this war."

"I believe that is true Erik, and so do others in our government. If he is just a young American who got caught up in this war, he has certain knowledge that would benefit the United

States. He has been on German U-boats. He could be a wealth of intelligence for us. The real question is, how could we get him back here?"

Erik didn't have an answer to that question and neither did Bill Donovan.

Chapter Fifteen: J-30

Kapitän zur See Fritz Ackermann had gathered his men in the headquarters of the IJN Naval Base in Penang. The Penang party had spent the morning discussing their inspection results and, in Ackermann's mind, it was looking good. He was pleased with the progress that the team had made in the last week. The base had been analyzed and inspected for suitability as a U-boat base and all of the early reports looked promising. Penang would be the location for the Reich to operate submarines in this region of the globe.

"Goedel, give us an update on the mooring facilities."

"There are twenty-six piers, of various lengths, all with sufficient depth to operate our submarines. The Japanese currently use eighteen of them on a regular basis to support their surface and submarine needs. We will have access to the remaining piers, which should be more than enough space for our boats to operate."

"Very well. And what did your inspection of the shore facilities reveal? Do we have space to store fuel, food, parts, maintenance equipment, and munitions?"

"We do indeed, sir. With *Leutnant zur See* Teufel's help, I was able to inspect several empty warehouses on the waterfront that our Japanese friends are not using.

When the British abandoned them, they left the facilities in excellent shape."

"That is fortunate. I have met with the shipyard commander and arranged for our use of these facilities. He only asks that I let him know which locations the *Kriegsmarine* wishes to occupy, and he will make the arrangements."

Peter could see that Ackermann was pleased. This mission was an important one for the Reich and that of course boded well for the captain. Peter could also tell that Goedel was pleased, but for a different reason. With the Penang mission coming to a close, Goedel would get a crack at commanding his own boat.

Ackermann continued the de-brief. "*Hauptsturmführer* Lübeck, have you completed your duties here in Penang?"

"I have a few loose ends to tie up. They will be completed by the end of the week."

"And you, *Fregattenkapitän* Klopp, have you completed your mission here in Penang?"

"I have."

"Then I shall make arrangements for our return to Germany. Just one more ceremony that we must attend. I have received an invitation from Vice Admiral Teruhisa Komatsu for a dinner in our honor a week from tomorrow. It will be our last state function before our return."

Peter noticed that Goedel was not happy with this turn of events. He knew that Goedel was very anxious to return to Germany and even a week was a delay that he didn't like.

Ackermann continued, "I am told that Ambassador Ott will also be in attendance. In the meantime, take care of any last-minute details that you have here. I expect that we will depart Penang on the second or third of next month. Consider yourselves on leave until the dinner. I will ensure that you get the details. Dismissed."

April 24, 1942 17:28
New York, New York
Rockefeller Center, Associated Press Headquarters

Marilyn sat at her desk on the fourth floor of the AP headquarters. She had worked all week on a story about President Roosevelt, assembling photos from his recent visit to New York. Like all of her contemporaries, she wanted to ensure that the commander in chief was only shown in a good light. Some of her photos were not very flattering, but she eliminated those shots for a few that showed him as a strong, confident leader.

She finished her work and looked at the clock on the wall. Anxious to leave, she wanted to start the weekend off right. She had another date with her boyfriend David Hall and was excited to see him again. David was a copy editor at the AP and she had met him two months before. Two years older than Marilyn, he was a nice guy. He had tried to enlist in the Army after Pearl Harbor but was designated "4F" due to a knee injury suffered during an accident in high school. They were now an item in the office.

She got up from her desk and put on her coat. She retrieved her compact from her purse to make a quick check of her makeup. It was then that she thought about Peter. She had not seen him in over a year, but she couldn't keep him out of her mind. David Hall was nice, but there was something about Peter that connected with her deeply. She wished that he had shown up in Basel.

She looked at her face in the small mirror of the compact. *You are not getting any younger, Marilyn.* She snapped the compact closed and headed out her office door. On her office door hung the mail folder. She noticed that there were several interoffice deliveries and a couple of letters. She decided that she would check them next week and proceeded to the elevator. She wouldn't read Anne Teufel's letter until Monday.

May 1, 1942 19:00
George Town, Penang, Malaysia
IJN Headquarters

Peter sat at the dinner table next to Johann Goedel. The meal, hosted by Vice Admiral Teruhisa Komatsu, had been exceptional. Delicacies from the Far East lavished their table and Peter had enjoyed every bit of it. Rice wine had been poured liberally and the mood was festive. It seemed to Peter that Komatsu was very pleased with the German contingent and their assessment of the facilities at Penang.

Peter noticed that Goedel was not truly enjoying the evening. He watched as Johann ate his food, smiled when it was appropriate, and frequently looked at his watch. Peter could see he was fidgety. Goedel wanted the evening to be over.

"Are you ok, Johann?"

"Yeah ... I just want to get this night over with so that we can get on a plane tomorrow and head back home."

"Tomorrow will come. Don't worry. But you should enjoy tonight. After all, it has been one hell of a trip, right?"

"That it has but I am ready for it to be over. I just want to get back"

"I do know. A week from now, you will be conning your own boat and I will be covered in diesel oil making it run for you."

Goedel looked at Peter with kind eyes and smiled. It was his first true smile of the evening. It was then that Vice Admiral Komatsu stood up at the head table to speak. The room quieted down as the admiral lifted his glass of wine.

"Gentlemen, I give you my sincere appreciation and the appreciation of our emperor for your efforts to unite the Imperial Japanese Navy and the *Kriegsmarine* in order to defeat the Western aggressors. You have succeeded in your mission and I am sure that your efforts will contribute to a lasting cooperation between our navies and to the ultimate victory for our alliance. *Kanpai, otsukare-sama desu!*"

With that, every man present raised his glass and cheered. When the noise subsided, the admiral continued, "I would personally like to thank you, Captain Ackermann and your men, for indulging me and my countrymen for the last few weeks. Your presence has been a boost to our military forces and, more importantly, to our civilian population. The alliance that we have is now stronger due to your efforts."

Again, there was much cheering and glass raising by the attendees.

"I hope that our hospitality has been to your liking and I am sure that you have gained a greater appreciation of the power of the Imperial Japanese Navy." Komatsu paused. Peter could tell that the man was building up to something, but he was not sure what it was.

"Back in Tokyo, I wanted to arrange a voyage for you on one of our submarines. Unfortunately, operational priorities took precedence and such an excursion was not possible. However, with Ambassador Ott's assistance I have arranged for an even greater demonstration."

Peter looked at Goedel with a "Where is he going with this?" look on his face. Goedel shrugged and looked back at Komatsu.

"I have arranged with Admiral Dönitz for a resource-sharing opportunity. We will place a few *Kriegsmarine* officers on one of our boats and a few of our officers will go on patrol in your U-boats. This can only lead to better cooperation between our countries and hasten the annihilation of the enemy."

With that, the admiral lifted his glass again and all present drank to the prospect of improved Japanese and German cooperation. Then the admiral continued.

"Captain Ackermann, Admiral Dönitz has a need for your services back in Germany, but he was kind enough to provide the services of Lieutenants Goedel and Teufel to support our mutual agreement. I have orders, given to me by Ambassador Ott, that assigns them to return to Germany aboard the IJN submarine *I-30*."

Johann Goedel could not believe what he was hearing. Was the admiral saying that he was to return to Germany on a Japanese submarine? *That would take another goddamn month!*

"It is also my understanding that *Hauptsturmführer* Lübeck and Fregattenkapitän Klopp are required back in Berlin as soon as possible. They will fly with you Captain Ackerman on the third, leaving from Penang, to report for their next assignments."

Goedel looked at Peter. He was shocked. After two and a half months of traveling the Far East, they were now going to take a slow boat back to Germany.

"What the fuck?" Goedel whispered to Peter.

"The *I-30* is one of our finest submarines. *Oberleutnant zur See* Goedel and *Leutnant zur See* Teufel, you must be honored to be assigned to this mission. It is scheduled to leave Penang for France in mid-May and you will be its honored guests for the deployment. The *I-30* will be hauling much-needed cargo to Europe that has been requested by Adolph Hitler."

To Peter's surprise, Goedel filled his glass with rice wine and stood up from the table. Goedel knew that orders were orders. He raised his glass to the admiral. "We would be honored to accompany the *I-30* to Europe, Admiral!"

With that, Goedel drained his glass of wine to the cheers of all in attendance.

June 2, 1942 16:45
George Town, Penang, Malaysia
Lord Clive Hotel

Johann and Peter sat in the lobby of the Lord Clive Hotel. They had spent a month in Penang awaiting the arrival of the *I-30*, which, according to their Japanese advisors, had been delayed by operational priorities in the Indian Ocean. It had been a very long month for both men.

"Well, Two Pair, the Yard Master tells me that the *I-30* is supposed to arrive tomorrow. It's about goddamn time!"

"Does he know when the boat will leave for Europe?"

"He said that they would refit here for about ten days before sailing. Ten more damn days to wait before a month-long voyage to France. This whole trip has been nothing but delays."

"At least we're not getting depth charged sitting here. That is something, right?"

"Two Pair, you are an optimist. No one likes getting depth charged, but I want to get back into this war as a submarine commander. I have worked my whole life for this opportunity. I should have had a command over a year ago."

"The war will still be going on when we get back."

"I don't know about that. Goering's air force was unable to defeat the British and our foray into Russia has stalled. I wouldn't be surprised if *Herr* Hitler sues for peace to keep the occupied lands that Germany has attained. Hell, I could be out of a job by the time we get back!"

"Well, there isn't a whole lot that we can do about it here. We will just have to see what the situation is upon our return."

"Our return is going to be a pain in the ass, Two Pair."

"What do you mean?"

"We will be riding someone else's submarine."

"So?"

"The worst thing on a boat is a rider. A food-eating, air-breathing, non-qualified hotel load on the rest of the crew. Riders don't carry their own weight. All submariners hate riders."

"I never really thought about that ... We could make ourselves useful, couldn't we?"

"We could possibly stand lookout watches on the surface, but that would be about it. I can't read, write, or speak Japanese. It wouldn't do for me to try to qualify officer of the deck or anything like it."

"I could help you learn a few words of their language."

"Let's start with coffee, food, and the head, alright?"

Both men chuckled. Peter gave Goedel his first Japanese lesson but Goedel was not a good student. It took an hour for him to master the three words.

"Enough, Two Pair! I can't learn their language in one night. Let's grab a bite to eat. Tomorrow, we will meet the *I-30* when she pulls in."

June 14, 1942 06:00
George Town, Penang, Malaysia
Imperial Japanese Navy Submarine I-30

The *I-30* backed away from its mooring at Pier #7 in the Penang harbor. Commander Endo Shinobu stood in the conning tower of the huge submarine, giving orders to his crew. Once away from the pier a sufficient distance, he ordered a hard-left rudder and the starboard engine ahead one third. The large craft slowly began to turn south. Pushed by its two diesel engines, it headed down the Penang Channel and out into the Straits of Malacca. Once clear of the island of Penang, the boat headed for the western-most point of Sumatra, towards the Indian Ocean.

Below decks, Johann and Peter sat in the wardroom. The executive officer of the *I-30* was with them, explaining their bunk assignments. Peter translated. "He says that you are to take his bunk for the entirety of the patrol. He will hot rack with another officer. I, too, will hot rack with another officer."

"Absolutely not, Peter. I will sleep in the torpedo room. I will not be a load on this boat," Goedel said.

"Uh, *Oberleutnant*, remember, it is very important in the Japanese culture for them to not lose face. If such an offering is made and refused, it will be a great embarrassment for him. I strongly suggest that you accept his offer."

The *I-30*'s XO had watched Goedel's response and was looking a bit nervous.

"Alright. Tell him that the arrangements are acceptable, but tell him that we want to stand watches, or at least contribute something to the *I-30*'s day–to-day operation at sea."

Peter relayed the information to the XO, who was pleased that his offer had been accepted. The two Germans would be added to the lookout watch bill.

June 26, 1942 10:43
87 Kilometers East of Fort Dauphin, Madagascar
Imperial Japanese Navy Submarine I-30

Johann Goedel sat on a burlap sack of shellac in the forward torpedo room of the *I-30*. With a little more than an hour to go before he was to report topside for lookout watch, he sat thinking about his plight. By his calculations, the *I-30* still had at least thirty days to go before they reached Lorient. That meant at least another month before he would get his command.

Goedel had learned enough Japanese to say "plane" and "torpedo," words that any officer of the deck would want his lookouts to know. It made him feel like less of a rider, but the truth was ... he was still a rider. *After a dozen years on submarines, I am qualified to be a lookout on a Japanese boat.*

Through the torpedo room hatch stepped Two Pair, followed by one of the senior enlisted sailors on the boat. Peter was getting another check out on one of the submarines systems. Peter spoke to the man giving him the checkout. Goedel didn't understand the conversation, but he could tell by body language that Peter was explaining the trim and drain system to the man's satisfaction. When the conversation was done, the Japanese sailor took Peter's qualification card and signed it.

The Japanese sailor left the torpedo room and Peter walked over to Goedel. As the only two Germans onboard, they had decided to drop the military formalities.

"Hey, Johann, how are you doing this fine Navy day?"

"Jesus, Two Pair, are you really trying to qualify on this boat?"

"Sure, why not? I mean we are stuck here for the duration. I might as well learn something while I have the chance."

"You will be the only officer in the *Kriegsmarine* with a Japanese submarine qualification pin on your uniform. That will be worth a few free beers in Berlin, I bet."

"I just might be the only one. I am halfway done with my qualifications and we still have a month to go."

Goedel had to marvel at Two Pair. The kid was making the best of a bad situation. Qualifying on a foreign boat in a foreign language would be quite an accomplishment. It only supported Goedel's decision to have Peter assigned to his new command.

"This is one hell of a boat, eh, Two Pair? It is twenty meters longer than the *U-216* and the beam is half again as large."

"Yes, it is. It is faster than the *U-216* both on the surface and submerged. The diesels are extremely well made. I completed that checkout yesterday."

Goedel looked around the torpedo room and noticed the burlap bags of shellac like the one he was sitting on. There were also bags of mica. He wasn't sure why, but the Japanese were hauling hundreds of kilograms of both substances to France for use by the Reich.

"What the hell do you use shellac for, Two Pair? I mean, why are we hauling this stuff to France?"

"Shellac is found only in India and Thailand. We can't get it in Germany."

"What's it used for?"

"It has many uses but it makes for a good insulator on motor windings. It can be used in other electronic applications. It is lightweight and durable. We used a little of it in college for vibration studies on motors. It can also be used to make phonograph records."

Goedel shook his head. The kid knew practically everything. He was an interesting man, that Teufel. "Is there anything that you don't know when it comes to engineering?"

After a moment of thought, Peter gave an answer. "I don't know a lot about nuclear physics. It is a relatively new field of science and I have only had an overview course at Stuttgart. Some say that nuclear physics may lead to a breakthrough in propulsion systems for submarines, but I would have to read up on that."

"I should have known."

June 27, 1942 09:17
Berlin, Germany
Schutzstaffel Main Security Building

Klaus Lübeck sat in the office of the recently promoted *SS-Standartenführer* Walter Schellenberg. He was finishing up his debrief to his boss about the mission to Penang. Lübeck had been back in Germany for a month, but Schellenberg had been traveling at the behest of the *Führer*. This was their first chance to communicate directly.

"So, Klaus, you have established the necessary contacts in the East to support information gathering for the Reich. That is good. Have you had a chance to test and evaluate our communication channels from the region?"

"Courier deliveries are funneled into Berlin weekly via Manchuria. I have received several communiqués from my contacts. They are all being given to the analysis section downstairs for consolidation and interpretation."

"Excellent. All seems to be in order. I knew that I could count on you to get the job done."

"Thank you, *Standartenführer*."

"And what of Canaris's man Klopp? Was he as successful as we were in establishing an information network?"

"Not at all. Canaris sent the wrong man. Klopp is an academic, not a field man. He made a few contacts, but nothing of any consequence. He spent most of his time attending dinners and reading books."

"Well, the *Abwehr* has always taken a backseat to the *Sicherheitsdienst*. I am not surprised at all. And what of the others on the mission. Did you learn anything useful about Ackermann? Dönitz thinks highly of him."

"He is a straight shooter, a good loyal officer, as is Goedel. They were both all business. But ..."

"But what?"

"Well, sir, the other *Kriegsmarine* officer, Teufel, is a different matter. There is something strange about that *Leutnant*."

"How do you mean, Klaus?"

"Call it a gut feeling, sir. There is something not quite right about him. His dialect is unidentifiable. All Germans have a dialect, Dutch Low Saxon or Pomeranian, something, but his dialect is unusual."

"Speech impediment, maybe?"

"No, sir, it's just a dialect that I have never heard. And the kid was an enlisted man prior to the mission. An enlisted man with an engineering degree and the ability to speak French and Japanese. He is supposedly the son of a German diplomat, but I checked the records. There is no record of a German diplomat by the name of Teufel. Isn't that a bit odd, sir?"

"Yes. But he is just a *Leutnant* and he is a submarine *Leutnant* at that. His life expectancy is not very great. What harm can this man do?"

"That is the question, isn't it, sir? I think that the SD should keep an eye on him."

"Maybe we can do something about that, Klaus. I have been considering your next assignment. Perhaps this task would keep you in touch with this Teufel while accomplishing what it is that I need done."

"What do you need *Standartenführer*?"

"I need a backup plan, Klaus. You see, it is possible that we will not win this war."

"Sir?"

"The Russian fiasco has stretched our troops too thin. We are entangled in a two-front war, a dangerous thing. *Herr Hitler* will never sue for peace. He will fight to the bitter end and, if that end means that we lose the war, I need to have an exit strategy."

Lübeck nodded his head in agreement, but he knew that he did not have such a thing as a backup plan. All he wanted to do was to get things done for the Reich.

"How can I assist you?"

"My position in the SD has afforded me the opportunity to gather some wealth. I have done exactly that, in the form of gold coins. If we lose the war, our currency will be worthless. But gold, well, gold will hold its value. I need you to deliver a portion of my wealth to a bank in Singapore. I have an account there and access to safe deposit boxes."

"Certainly, *Standartenführer*. When does my plane leave?"

"No Klaus, no plane. This needs to be done with a little more discretion. You will transport my gold on a submarine."

Lübeck sat up straight in his chair. Did he hear Schellenberg correctly? He had loaded ships in his youth in Hamburg, but he had never actually been out to sea. Now his boss wanted him to go to sea on a craft that sinks on purpose?

"Uh, a submarine? I, uh, don't know if that would be the best method to accomplish your strategy."

"I do know, *Hauptsturmführer*. You will carry out this personal mission for me and, upon your return to Germany, I will provide you with an amount that will give you the means for a backup plan of your own. Besides, this will give you an opportunity to keep an eye on Teufel."

"How is that, sir?"

"The Penang mission was a success. The *Führer* is establishing a U-boat presence in the East. We are forming the *Monsun Gruppe*—a flotilla of U-boats—in Penang. The first boat to sail to the East will be the *U-463*. I have made recommendations to the *Führer* that a member of your party should be on that boat. That man is Goedel, but I can easily make a case for Teufel to accompany him, and for you as well. Once you are in Penang, you can get your local contacts to take you the short distance to Singapore."

Lübeck recognized that this was an order, not a request. He was not thrilled about riding a submarine to Penang, but it would give him an opportunity to learn more about Teufel.

"And if you determine that this man Teufel is a threat to the Reich, well, I will allow you to handle that matter as you see fit."

Lübeck smiled at Schellenberg.

"Yes, sir. I will get this job done."

August 2, 1942 13:31
Bay of Biscay
Imperial Japanese Navy Submarine I-30

Goedel stood on the conning tower of *I-30* next to Commander Endo Shinobu. Only a few kilometers from the submarine pens in Lorient, the end of the voyage had finally come. For Goedel, it couldn't have come soon enough.

Overhead, Junkers Ju 88 bombers patrolled the sky providing air cover for the IJN boat. On both the port and starboard sides of the submarine, German minesweepers paralleled the *I-30*'s course. Goedel thought that this was quite an escort force for one submarine.

Below, Peter Teufel was on watch as the diving officer. On Peter's breast was a shiny new IJN submarine pin. Goedel marveled at how much Two Pair had accomplished in just forty-nine days at sea. It just reaffirmed his belief that he should keep the young officer with him when he took command of his own boat.

An hour later, the *I-30* pulled into the *Keroman II* submarine bunker in Lorient. A band played as the vessel tossed lines to the handlers. Goedel could see that the brass was awaiting their arrival. *Großadmiral* Raeder was present, as was Admiral Dönitz, along with a host of other ranking submarine officers. Finally, after months of being on this mission, Goedel was finally back in Europe, where he would most certainly get his reward. From the conning tower, Goedel saluted *Großadmiral* Raeder.

For the first time in a long time, Goedel smiled.

Chapter Sixteen: Crestfallen

August 6, 1942 08:00
Near Lorient, France
Villa Kerillon

Leutnant zur See Teufel and *Oberleutnant zur See* Goedel stood at attention before Admiral Dönitz in his headquarters outside of Lorient. They had been summoned to the admiral's office by messenger and had arrived in their dress uniforms. After a weekend of ceremonial dinners in Lorient hosted by the *Kriegsmarine*, the IJN officers of the *I-30* had departed for Berlin early in the morning for an audience with the *Führer*. Goedel was glad that he was not summoned to Berlin with them. He wanted to be right where he was—in front of Dönitz. The admiral was the man who bestowed commands.

"Gentlemen, your mission to Penang has been a huge success for the Reich. I am proud to say that you have personally contributed to the German war effort. *Großadmiral* Raeder has advised me to give you the *Führer's* personal congratulations on a job well done."

Both Peter and Johann remained silently at attention. Even without looking at Goedel, Peter knew that he was beaming with pride. Peter knew the reason. This was Johann's moment in the sun.

"I must say that you two have paved the way for further cooperation with our Japanese allies in order to wage war on our enemies around the world. Your journey was a long one but well worth the time and effort. I have received word from Ambassador Ott that the two of you acquitted yourselves quite professionally during the mission."

"Thank you, Admiral. *Leutnant* Teufel and I feel that it was an honor to serve the Reich on the mission."

"The *Kriegsmarine* is going to proceed with establishing a U-boat flotilla called the *Monsun Gruppe* in Penang based on your efforts. In fact, the first U-boat will leave in a month's time and sail to Penang. Of course, it will be followed by others in short order."

Goedel was nearly bursting at the seams. He wanted to know which boat he would command, but he knew that he had to let Dönitz say his piece.

"I have also been advised by *Großadmiral* Raeder that the *Führer* himself has ordered that you two will be on that boat because of your experience in dealing with our Japanese friends."

"Which boat will I be commanding as it sails to Penang, Admiral?"

Admiral Dönitz did not respond immediately. He shuffled his feet and lit a cigarette, dropping the extinguished match into an ash tray. Goedel knew that the admiral was making him wait on purpose. He figured that this was just a way for the admiral to build up the suspense.

Dönitz inhaled and then exhaled a large puff of smoke before he continued. "You will be on the *U-463*, *Oberleutnant zur See* Goedel, but you will not be in command."

Goedel shuddered when he comprehended the words. He was being assigned to a boat but not as the commanding officer. How could this be? The last time he was in this office a boat had virtually been promised to him when he returned from Penang.

"You will be the XO of the *U-463* under *Oberleutnant zur See* Grimme."

"Grimme ... Wilhelm Grimme? He was a junior officer under me on the *U-146* on my first tour as an XO."

"I know that you will serve your captain well, Goedel. I am sure of that. *Leutnant* Teufel here will also serve the Reich as one of the ship's officers."

Goedel was shaking. His frustration was evident to all.

"Permission to speak freely, Admiral?"

"Granted, *Oberleutnant.*"

"Why? I mean, why am I not in command, sir? Before I left for Penang you said that after completing this assignment, I would be given a new boat to command. I ... I have earned it."

"You have been gone for several months, *Herr* Goedel. Things have changed. Grimme has proven his value to the *Kriegsmarine* and he is worthy of this command. Your experience with Penang and its facilities is needed to establish this *Monsun Gruppe.*"

"He has half of the time in U-boats that I do! I trained that kid and looked out for him just as his father asked me to ..."

Suddenly, it all became clear to Goedel. Wilhelm Grimme was the son of a high-ranking Nazi official. The elder Grimme was one of Joseph Goebbels' sycophants in the Ministry of Propaganda in Berlin. This was a political appointment, not a promotion based on merit.

"I am senior to Grimme, Admiral. I have been an *Oberleutnant* longer that he has been in the *Kriegsmarine.*"

"Do not disrespect me by deriding my decision, *Oberleutnant.* Your service record is excellent to date, but I will not tolerate you questioning my authority in this matter. Do you understand?"

"Yes, Admiral."

"*Kommodore* Abel and an advance contingent have been dispatched to Penang to establish our *Monsun Gruppe* support base in Penang. They will be operational by October. The *U-463* will be the first U-boat in the group. You will report to the *U-463* next Monday. Teufel, you report that day as well. You are dismissed."

August 11, 1942 19:40
Rennes, France
Rouge Canard Inn

Peter sat next to Goedel at a bar in the historic district of Rennes on the banks of the Vilaine River. It was clear to Peter that Goedel was drunk—very drunk. In Peter's heart, he sympathized for his friend. Johann had been denied his command and Peter knew that it hurt the officer in the worst way.

After leaving Dönitz's office the previous Monday, they had returned to their temporary quarters. The next day, having essentially been given the week off, they had boarded a train to Le Mans. Peter had tried to convince Goedel to go to Bordeaux, so that he could then make a break for the Spanish border, but Goedel had insisted that they stay in the north of France. Considering his friend's state of mind, Peter had decided to stick with him. He could make his run to Spain after the two of them reported aboard the *U-463*.

"We should get something to eat, Johann."

"I'm not goddamn hungry, but I could use another drink."

"No, I am pretty sure that we could use some food. I am hungry and I bet that you are, too."

"What the hell. Order us something."

Peter flagged down the waitress and ordered for the both of them. The waitress smiled at him, pleased that he ordered in her language.

"What did you get us, Two Pair, my boy?"

"Beef stew and plenty of bread to soak up the booze in your gullet."

"Good call. They make damn good bread in this country."

"We should eat and then get to bed early tonight. We have to get back to Lorient tomorrow so that we can report aboard the *U-463*."

"To hell with that! We need to make a night of it. After what has happened to me, the slap in the face, I deserve a little break. Fuck it, I might not even report to that boat."

"You are drunk, Johann. Let's eat and get back to the room. Things will look brighter tomorrow."

"No, I am serious, Two Pair. Why should I report to that boat? Why should I stay in this Navy? Obviously, I am not worthy of command in the eyes of Dönitz. I don't have the right Nazi Party connections. I should just pack up my crap and quit this chicken-shit outfit."

"You cannot just quit the *Kriegsmarine* during wartime. They shoot people for deserting, you know."

"I could just walk away. I would need a plan, but I could do it."

"Hey now, remember this: you only have a few years to go before you get a comfortable retirement once the war is finished. Now is not the time to screw that up."

"Time ... time you say? I say it is past time. They owe me now for all that I have done. They owe me a boat. Maybe I should report aboard that stinking sub and steal the son of a bitch!"

Peter spent the next twenty minutes getting Goedel to eat then helped the inebriated officer back to their hotel. After dumping Goedel on his bed, Peter watched as the drunken sailor passed quickly into a deep sleep.

Then he undressed and lay down upon his own bed. His mind was spinning with thoughts. Next week, after he reported aboard the *U-463*, he would find a way to get off of the base and make his way to Spain. He laughed to himself as he thought, *I better get off of the boat before Goedel steals it!*

August 13, 1942 07:07
Lorient, France
U-463

Oberleutnant zur See Grimme sat at the wardroom table onboard the *U-463*. At the age of twenty-three, he was younger than most U-boat commanders, but there were others who were younger. Before him stood two officers. He knew Johann Goedel. The other officer was new to Grimme, a Peter Teufel. Having finished his welcome aboard speech, he was outlining their duties aboard the boat. "Goedel, you will, of course, be my second in command. You will be responsible for navigation, damage control, and day-to-day operations of the boat."

"Yes sir, Captain."

"And you, Teufel, you will be my engineering officer. You will have responsibility for the operation and maintenance of all of the systems on this submarine. Understood?"

"Yes, sir, *Oberleutnant.*"

"Teufel, you are dismissed. *Oberleutnant* Goedel, I would like to have a word with you."

Peter left the wardroom. Grimme wanted a word alone with Goedel to establish a firm line on who was in command of this submarine.

"Sit down, Johann, please. I am aware that you are disappointed in your assignment to the *U-463* as my XO. Is that not true?"

"I am not disappointed with the *U-463*, sir, only with my position."

"I understand how you feel. You were expecting your own command and that did not work out as you had hoped."

"It certainly did not, sir."

"Let's be clear here, Johann. My career is on the rise, while yours seems to have stagnated. Your last boat did not have an enviable service record. Very few sinkings, as I recall. It nearly cost Captain Schultz his command and, of course, it reflected poorly on you."

"I know my record, sir."

"You see, I serve the *Kriegsmarine*, the Reich, the Nazi Party, and *mein Führer*. I have a duty and I will perform it to the best of my abilities. I will expect the same from every member of my crew, and even more so from you."

"Don't question my loyalties, Captain. I know where they lie."

"Onboard this boat, Johann, you have a chance at redemption. The Reich wants results and we will give them those results. If you perform well in your duties as my XO, I will have a word with my father and perhaps, just perhaps, you will get that command that you so desire."

August 20, 1942 21:41
Lorient, France
U-463

Peter sat top side of the *U-463* in the warm night air, smoking a cigarette. His new submarine was unique. The boat was built as an ocean-going submarine tanker. It was not an offensive boat. It did not have any torpedo tubes and it boasted only two 3.7cm anti-aircraft guns for protection. The boat was designed to deliver fuel oil, supplies, and spare torpedoes to operational U-boats. It was a support craft, a supply ship, not a fighting ship. Powered by two *Germaniawerft* supercharged four-stroke six-cylinder diesel engines, the *U-463* was capable of achieving nearly fifteen knots on the surface. Peter appreciated that his new boat was well designed for its mission.

In the week since reporting aboard, he had quickly settled into a routine as the engineering officer but, more importantly, he had been planning. He had mapped out a route to the Spanish border and he would cross into Spain on foot somewhere near Hendaye, France. He had decided that he would make this run to freedom on his birthday, August 22.

He would be somewhat sad to leave his friend Goedel behind. They had become quite close in the last year, but it was now a matter of self-preservation. He couldn't continue to serve on a U-boat, fighting against his own country as he masqueraded as a German officer. He needed to escape this war and to return home. He wanted to be back with his parents and, most importantly, he wanted to reconnect with Marilyn.

Peter had noticed that Goedel seemed resigned to his fate as the new XO. Over the last week, Johann had performed his duties as assigned, but gone was the vibrant, upbeat officer that he once knew. He felt bad for Goedel, but there really wasn't much that he could do for him now. Peter's mind was made up. He was leaving in two days and that was that.

August 21, 1942 13:55
Lorient, France
U-463

Peter sat in the wardroom of the *U-463*, sipping a cup of coffee. He was in a good mood. In less than twenty-four hours he would be on his way back to the United States. Committing to his plan had given him quite a bit of relief. He had wanted to get out of the European war for nearly two years. In that time, he had never been quite able to make the break, but now he was fully prepared to depart.

The chief of the boat, *Stabsoberbootsmann* Manfred Lange, poked his head into the wardroom. "The captain wants all hands topside, *Leutnant.*"

"What's going on, Chief?"

"Not sure, sir, but I wouldn't be late. The captain just returned from a meeting with Dönitz."

Five minutes later, Peter found himself in formation just outside of the U-boat bunker. He was in position in front of the engineering department, the men who worked for him. The other departments were also present. Facing Peter and the rest of the crew stood Goedel and Captain Grimme.

"All hands present and accounted for, Captain," Goedel reported.

"Very well, *Oberleutnant*. I have just received our orders for our next patrol from Admiral Dönitz and may I say that you will be pleased to learn that we have been selected for an important top-secret mission. We have been assigned to do something that no other U-boat has ever done and each of you should take pride in the fact that the *Kriegsmarine* and our *Führer* have the confidence in our ability to complete the mission. I cannot give you the complete details of our assignment today, but once we are underway in a few weeks, I will share all of the details."

Peter wondered what the mission details were. Since he was leaving tomorrow, they really were not that important to him, but he would try to learn anything that he could before he left, just to have an idea where Goedel would end up. Surely, the mission was to Penang, but was there more to it?

"I can tell you that we will have a rider with us who will have a mission of his own. We will support this man and his mission to the best of our ability. Now, due to the secrecy of our assignment, we have been ordered to take extraordinary security measures. Base security has increased. Access to and from this facility will be limited to those with official business. Additionally, from this moment on, no member of the *U-463* is allowed off of the base for any reason. Our mission is vital to the Reich and we must protect it with our lives."

Peter stood at attention, hoping that no one could see the shock and disappointment that he felt inside. Now, he had a better understanding of how Goedel felt when he didn't get his command.

Chapter Seventeen: Doubt

September 5, 1942 13:55
Lorient, France
U-463

Peter and Johann walked off of the *U-463* and climbed the stairs out of the U-boat bunker, heading for the officers' club at the end of the day. As they walked alone together in the warm fall air, Goedel broke the silence. "I have been giving it a lot of thought, Two Pair. I am done with this."

"Done with what?"

"I am done with the Navy, done with the war, done with it all."

"You want out of the Navy?"

"Yep. I want to move on with my life. There is nothing left for me here."

"What are you going to do? You can't just resign; there is a war going on."

"I know that. I would be arrested, maybe even shot. No, I have a plan."

"And … what is your plan?"

"When we get to Penang, I am going to walk off of the boat and never come back. There is virtually no one to stop me. There is no Gestapo in Penang, no SS … at least not for now. Hell, we will practically be the first Germans stationed there. I am just going to go ashore and never come back."

"Are you sure about this?"

"I have never been more sure of anything in my life."

Peter walked along in silence next to Goedel. He wondered if he should let his friend know that he, too, had a desire to escape the *Kriegsmarine*, but for very different reasons.

Goedel suddenly stopped. Peter took an extra step towards the officers' club, then turned and faced Goedel as the XO spoke. "You are the only one that I have told about this, Two Pair. I trust that you will keep my secret?"

"It is safe with me, Johann. I understand your position and would not jeopardize your right to make such a choice. Where I come from, freedom is a valued right for all men. I am curious, though, why did you tell me? You could have walked off of the boat without telling anyone."

"When I am gone, they will question you heavily because of our time together on the *U-216* and our mission to Penang. I wanted you to be prepared for that. Secondly, you have been a good friend and shipmate. Hell, you saved our lives on the *U-216*. I was convinced that if we had to stay on the surface, we would have been sunk by British air power. I owed it to you to let you get prepared."

"You owe me nothing, Johann."

Peter decided not to let Goedel know of his own desire to escape. While he was 90% certain that Goedel meant what he said, he had to be absolutely sure. He would wait and see when they got underway on the *U-463* to Penang if he still felt that way. With the base at Lorient secured, his next best opportunity to leave would also be in Penang. Perhaps then he would share his own desire to return to the United States. *Perhaps they could work together to escape?*

September 11, 1942 16:55
New York, New York
Rockefeller Center - Associated Press Headquarters

Marilyn Miller was finishing up her work at the AP. In just a few more minutes, she would be off, ready to start another weekend. This weekend, like many of her recent weekends, would be spent in the company of David Hall. They had plans to go to Peter Luger's Steakhouse this evening, a place that she had heard about but had never been. Though it was difficult to find a good steak in war time New York, David had ensured her that this was the place.

Marilyn liked David. He was tall, polite, kind, and treated her well. It was just that, well, he wasn't Peter Teufel. When she looked in David's eyes, she didn't feel the same feeling deep down in her stomach that she felt when she had made eye contact with Peter. Butterflies, she recalled; it felt like butterflies in her stomach and her heart would race whenever she looked into Peter's eyes. She believed that she was in love with him. They had written each other routinely after Danzig but the letters had stopped two years ago. Now, after the letter that she received from Anne Teufel, she understood why. Peter had joined the German Navy. She was pretty sure that she would never see Peter again.

It bothered her that his letters never mentioned a desire to join the Navy and to stay in Germany. He had always written that he wanted to return to the States as soon as he was finished touring Europe. They had planned to meet in Switzerland, but he never showed up in Basel. When he missed their rendezvous, she had not heard from him again. Was he there by choice or was he somehow trapped there?

Anne had enclosed the photograph in her letter, and it was certainly Peter in the picture. His mother intimated that Peter was now a German officer, but she had also written that, as his mother, she could not believe that he was there of his own free will. She had gone on to suggest that Peter was as much a prisoner as a sailor. *But did that make sense? How could an American become a German officer without wanting to?*

The telephone on her desk rang, jolting Marilyn out of her thoughts.

"Marilyn Miller."

"Marilyn, David here. Are you ready to go?"

"Just finishing up. Ready when you are."

"I will meet you in the lobby and we will head to dinner."

"Alright, see you in two minutes."

She placed the receiver on the cradle and put her desk in order. She picked up her purse and left her office. *Peter Teufel was a really nice guy. I once believed that he was the one for me, but it just didn't work out. Maybe it just wasn't meant to be.*

Two and a half hours later, Marilyn and David were sitting at their table at Peter Luger's Steakhouse. They had enjoyed cocktails before dinner and shared a porterhouse steak for two. It had so far been a wonderful evening.

"That was delicious, David. What a wonderful meal."

"My pleasure, dear. After all, this is a special night."

"Special?" Marilyn looked at the prices on the menu. It must be very special!

At that moment their waiter arrived with a bottle of French wine. The waiter displayed the label to David, removed the cork, and set the cork in front of him. The waiter then poured a small amount in David's glass for him to taste. David sipped the wine.

"This is good," David said to the waiter.

The waiter smiled and poured a glass for Marilyn and then filled David's glass with a standard five-ounce pour. David turned to Marilyn and lifted his glass. "To a beautiful woman."

"Why thank you, David. You make me blush."

They clinked their glasses, and each took a sip of the red wine.

"It is Chateaux Margaux, 1934. The owner told me that it was the best wine that they had. Do you like it?"

Marilyn quickly nodded. She knew that, no matter how it tasted, that manners dictated that she said she liked it. Fortunately, it was indeed pretty good.

It was not lost on Marilyn that the Chateaux Margaux was the vineyard where Peter was staying when he was in France. She again thought of Peter and how much she had loved spending time with him.

"You enjoy the wine, good. Tonight is a special night for us. At least, I wanted it to be. Have you enjoyed your evening?"

"Yes, David, it has all been very nice."

"Tonight Marilyn, I brought you here for a reason."

"To wine and dine me out of my clothes?"

She was embarrassed by her outburst. That was not like her. She had had a couple of stiff cocktails before dinner and she thought that tonight might be the night that she let David have his way with her. She hadn't been with a man since Peter and she figured it just might be the time.

"Uh, no ... I mean, well yes ... sort of. What I mean to say Marilyn is ... here."

David reached into his pocket and pulled out a small box. He slipped out of his chair and dropped to one knee next to their table. "Will you marry me?"

September 18, 1942 18:46
Lorient, France
Base Officers' Club

Wilhelm Grimme led his officer corps of the *U-463* as they marched towards the Base Officer's Club. Adorned in their dress military uniforms, an unusual occurrence for most submariners, they made quite a sight. Dinner with Admiral Dönitz was on the agenda and the new captain wanted his men to make a good impression. With the *U-463* about to depart on its secret mission, the admiral had requested that Grimme and his officers report for an official send-off dinner. It was Grimme's moment to shine.

Peter followed Goedel into the officers' club right behind Grimme. They were shown to a private party room off the main entrance. They would not be dining at the main bar in the club, where all of the other submarine officers usually hung out. This was a private gathering for the *U-463*.

Entering the private room, the men from the *U-463* were welcomed by Admiral Dönitz. The evening was a formal *Kriegsmarine* affair, but the Admiral made it clear with his greeting that Grimme's men were to have a good time, as their impending mission would be long and arduous.

Peter noticed that Admiral Dönitz was accompanied by several other officers, his chief of staff among them. All of the men present had cocktails in hand. As he scanned the room, Peter noticed two people who shocked him by their presence, *Vizeadmiral* Wilhelm Canaris and *SS Hauptsturmführer* Klaus Lübeck.

Peter quickly elbowed Goedel and whispered, "What the hell are they doing here?"

"Who?"

"Fucking Lübeck and Admiral Canaris."

"I have no idea."

The officers of the *U-463* were handed drinks as they entered the private room. Grimme immediately strolled up to Dönitz to shake his hand. The rest of the officers milled about, exchanging pleasantries. Peter avoided Lübeck and Canaris by approaching the chief of staff as quickly as he could.

Dönitz motioned for all present to take their seats. "Officers of the *U-463*, you are about to embark on a mission that has been months in planning, a mission that our *Führer* has decreed vital to the defeat of the enemy. As you are about to set out to sea, I have taken it upon myself, as your leader, to provide you with this send-off. You are my guests at this dinner, in honor of the task that you are about to undertake in the name of the *Kriegsmarine*, the Reich, and the *Führer* himself."

All glasses were raised in celebration.

"I know that *Oberleutnant* Grimme has briefed you on your mission, at least as much as I allowed him to. Tonight, I will provide you with a little more information. But, first, I would like to introduce a few guests."

Dönitz introduced his chief of staff and two other ranking officers from his command. He then continued on to introduce the other two guests.

"And I would be remiss if I did not introduce Admiral Canaris. The admiral was instrumental in the planning and execution of your mission. The support of his command, the *Abwehr*, was vital to the establishment of the groundwork needed for your endeavor. I have asked him here tonight to show our gratitude to the work that he has done in support of our U-boats.

"The last man that I want to introduce to you is *SS Hauptsturmführer* Klaus Lübeck. He will join you as you set out on your mission. He has experience in the location where you are going and will be a vital asset to your mission's success."

Peter had known that the *U-463* was going to carry a rider on this patrol, as did the other officers, but why Lübeck? He had hoped to never see that cold-blooded killer again, and now he was going to sea with him. *Could this get any worse?*

"Your mission, gentlemen, is top-secret. By now you have probably gathered that you are heading east to Penang, Malaysia. Both *Hauptsturmführer* Lübeck and *Leutnants* Goedel and Teufel have experience there. You will leave Lorient in a few days and proceed to Penang. You will be the first of many U-boats who will comprise the *Monsun Gruppe* Flotilla, our fighting force in the Far East against the British and the Americans."

The five officers of the *U-463* cheered at the admiral's words, but only three of them were very enthusiastic about it. Goedel and Peter lifted their glasses with the others, just not as high.

"You will sail south around the Cape of Good Hope and venture into the Indian Ocean. Along the way, you will supply fuel oil to our submarines operating near the Cape as you proceed to Penang. There you will operate from the port of Penang, conducting patrols supporting our attacks against enemy shipping. You will soon be joined by other U-boats, but you, men, will be the first! The honor and praise of the Reich goes with you!"

Again, there were cheers from those assembled. Then Admiral Dönitz announced that dinner was served and sat down at his table with Canaris, Lübeck, and his chief of staff.

Peter ate quietly, engaging only in small talk when requested to do so. He was worried that Canaris might recognize him and he was also concerned about Lübeck. He didn't like that man and now he was going to go to sea with that bastard. He decided to finish his meal and make an exit as soon as possible. Maybe Canaris wouldn't recognize him. He hadn't the last time they met.

When Peter finished his filet and *haricot verts,* he wiped his lips with his napkin and placed the cloth on the table as he stood to leave. "I must ensure that our diesels are at the ready, captain. Number one has been idling roughly as of late. I need to get back to the boat, sir."

"Sit down, Teufel," Grimme said easily. "You can check it in the morning. I want to know what you know about Penang. I have never been there."

Peter sat down as ordered and started to relay some of his recollections of Penang. He was interrupted by a tap on his shoulder. Peter turned to see Admiral Canaris standing behind him. Peter's heart skipped a beat as the admiral spoke.

"Forgive me, Captain Grimme, I was wondering if I could speak to *Leutnant* Teufel. I believe that I know his father. Would you grant me a moment with this young man?"

Grimme snapped to attention, almost knocking his chair over as he stood up for the senior officer. "Of course, Admiral. *Heil* Hitler!"

The other officers at the table muttered "Heil Hitler," per decorum, although Goedel did so with a less-than-respectful smile on his face. Goedel's feigned adulation for the *Führer* went unnoticed by most except Peter.

"Thank you, Captain. *Leutnant* Teufel, will you follow me? I have news of your father."

Peter followed Canaris as he made his way to the side exit of the officer's club. As they approached the door, Peter turned to see if they were being watched. He saw that Grimme was heading for admiral Dönitz's table and that Goedel was watching Peter leave with Canaris. Goedel had an odd look on his face, one of wonder. Lübeck was also watching him.

As they stepped out into the night, Peter's heart was racing. Here was the one man in the *Wehrmacht* that knew who Peter truly was, and now he was at the admiral's mercy. Should he run? Where would he go? There was no way out of the Lorient submarine base.

"Want a smoke, Peter?" Canaris offered as he lit a cigarette for himself.

Numbly, Peter accepted one from Canaris. The admiral lit it for him and continued. "I didn't recognize you last January. You had bandages on your face from wounds received while saving the *U-216* from certain destruction and you have filled out since I first met you in 1938. I took a note of the name Teufel, though. I knew that I had heard that name before."

Peter recalled their previous meeting here in Lorient with Dönitz and Schellenberg. He had been nervous then, but not as nervous as he was now. Not sure how to respond to the head of the *Abwehr*, Peter blurted, "They have good food on U-boats, Sir."

Canaris laughed. "I remember, Peter, from my days aboard a submarine in the last war. But I must ask you: What the hell is the son of an American diplomat doing on one of our U-boats?"

Peter paused. There was no point in lying. "When my parents left Berlin, I stayed to finish college, sir. I wound up in France during the occupation. I was conscripted into a labor camp building U-boats and then, well, conscripted into the *Kriegsmarine*."

"Apparently, you have done well for yourself. Most conscripts in the *Wehrmacht* do not rise to the officer ranks. When

I saw your name on the list of the *U-463*, I pulled your service record Peter. What you say is true."

"It is, sir."

"You put me in a difficult situation, young Teufel. I have knowledge of a young American, serving in the *Kriegsmarine*, whom some would consider a spy ..."

"I am not a spy, sir. I am just a man who made some youthful mistakes and who got caught up in an unusual situation."

"Unusual indeed, Peter. I don't think that you are a spy, although the knowledge that you have gained since you assisted my daughter Eva is of value to Germany's enemies."

Peter's heart raced and his mind whirled. Here he was, totally exposed, talking to the head of military intelligence for the German armed forces.

"Admiral Canaris, I have made many mistakes in my life, ones that I regret, but I believe that I have acted honorably in every instance. I am not a spy. I am not a saboteur. When asked to build boats for the Reich, I did. When asked to man a submarine against the Brits, I did. When your daughter was in peril and needed an honorable man to save her, I did. I have served your country to the best of my ability, in spite of my American heritage. I have no regrets about that. My only desire is to return to my country and live an honorable life. I just want to go home."

Peter exhaled loudly as if he were about to collapse. He had opened up his heart and soul to a man who could instantly, knowingly, have him eliminated that night. How would this play out for him—torture, firing squad?

Canaris silently lit another cigarette and walked a couple of meters away from Peter. With his back to Peter he took a long drag from his smoke and let it out. Peter stood motionless, watching the *Abwehr* chief, knowing that his life was in Canaris' hands. The admiral took one more long pull on the smoke, crushed the butt under his foot and turned back to Peter.

"I am indebted to you, *Herr* Teufel. You saved my daughter Eva when men of lesser character would not have done so. I, too, consider myself to be an honorable man. If you wish to return to your country, I will not hinder you in any way. May I ask, how do you plan to return to the United States?"

Peter was relieved. The one man who could have him arrested immediately had honored the debt of his daughter. "I do not know, sir. I had planned to try to get out of France through Spain but that has since been denied me."

"You must think hard on how you want to do this, young man. This will not be as easy as a travel pass from me and a dual citizenship passport."

"I would not be so naïve as to ask for your assistance again, sir."

"That is not what I meant Peter. I do not intend to aid you this time in that way. Deserting the *Kriegsmarine* is no easy task. You must know that if you are caught, you will be shot. If they determine that you are an American, deserting the *Kriegsmarine*, you will be shot twice."

"Once is enough, Admiral." Peter smiled weakly. He also knew that Canaris was telling the truth. He would be shot if he were caught.

"Peter, I want you to know that I appreciate what you have done for me and my family. As for our meeting tonight, we will leave it at that. You go on about your way. I will not hinder you. You have picked a good time to leave the military of Germany. Frankly, I wish that I could go with you."

"What do you mean, sir?"

"My country started this war, but I am afraid that we cannot win it. The writing is on the wall. Let's just say that Germany would be better off seeking peace with the British, and you Americans, rather than following our *Führer's* plans. Unfortunately, I am inexorably entangled in a web of Nazi intrigue demanding loyalty to the *Führer*. I am lost young Teufel, but you ... you have a chance. Honorable men deserve a chance."

"I will do my best, sir."

"We better return to the others before they get suspicious eh, Two Pair? I read in your folder that they call you that. Why?"

"It's a long story, sir, one that I will share with you some-time."

"Don't be surprised if I call your bluff sooner rather than later, Peter. I may need your services in the future. You never know," Canaris said with a smile. "Oh, and one more thing Peter, as long as we are being honest with each other. Beware of that SD officer, Lübeck. When I was looking at your records, I learned that he, too, had been looking into your background and your father's background. My friends tell me that he does not trust you and those sources are very reliable."

Chapter Eighteen: U-463

September 21, 1942 21:17
Lorient, France
U-463

The guard at the Lorient submarine base waved the German military truck through the gate to the entrance of the U-boat bunker that housed the *U-463*. Klaus Lübeck exited the truck and stationed the armed sentry at the back gate of the truck. After issuing brief orders to the sentry, he removed a duffle bag from the back of the vehicle and made his way onto the boat.

Grimme sat at the desk in his stateroom. He knew that the SD officer was reporting that night. Lübeck was one of Schellenberg's most trusted men and that would worry some, but not Grimme. The captain was connected in the Nazi Party, perhaps even better than Lübeck. He would do his best to support the SD officer. It wouldn't hurt to have a friend in Schellenberg's outfit.

Someone knocked on the bulkhead next to the captain's curtain.

"*Hauptsturmführer* Lübeck reporting aboard, Captain."

"Call me Wilhelm, if you please, Klaus."

Grimme stood to shake the SD agent's hand and motioned for him to take a seat on the captain's bunk. "I understand that you have some cargo that must be loaded. I have a work crew standing by to assist you."

"Thank you, Captain. I will need only a small space in which to store my cargo. However, it will need to be guarded at all times."

"It will be guarded until we get underway, of course."

"No, Captain, it will be guarded by an armed sentry, one of your men, for the duration of the voyage to Penang."

"*Hauptsturmführer,* I have a limited number of men on this boat and they all have functions to perform. I cannot have those resources assigned in that manner. My men are trustworthy members of the *Kriegsmarine.*"

"I am sure that you believe that, Captain. However, I have my orders. My cargo will be guarded by a sentry. No one is to approach the cargo. If the cargo is disturbed in any way, the offender will be shot, along with the sentry."

"See here now, Klaus ..."

Lübeck cut off Grimme before he could finish the sentence. "Oberleutnant, I outrank you. I do not command this submarine, but my mission takes precedence over yours. My job is to deliver this cargo and your job is to deliver me. Here are my mission orders signed by Standartenführer Schellenberg, *Reichsführer* Himmler, and the Führer. Are we clear, Oberleutnant?"

"Yes, *Hauptsturmführer.*"

"I will be occupying the XO's living quarters on this journey. He must make other arrangements. Now, where is this work party?"

September 22, 1942 02:45
Lorient, France
U-463

The *U-463* sailed out of Lorient in the early morning darkness. Her secret mission required the cover of night for the boat to slip away unseen. Her two supercharged *Germaniawerft* diesel engines hammered away as the sub proceeded out into the Bay of Biscay.

The *U-463*—a Type XIV submarine—was a refueling submersible. Her primary purpose was to resupply other submarines with needed war material. The boat was 67 meters long, with a wide beam of 9.35 meters. The boat had a machine shop in the aft end and refrigeration units for storing food. She also had huge fuel storage tanks for carrying an additional 613 tons of diesel fuel. The boat could also store thirteen tons of lubricating oil. She was crewed by six officers and fifty-four enlisted men. And for this mission, she carried one rider.

After an hour at sea, Captain Grimme secured the maneuvering watch and stationed the normal underway watch. *Leutnant zur See* Horst Richter had the officer of the deck with *Leutnant zur See* Teufel under instruction. Grimme dropped down from the conning tower into the control room and summoned his XO to the captain's stateroom.

"Have you established the guard for our passenger's cargo, *Herr* Goedel?"

"Yes, sir, I made adjustments to the watch bill. A few watch stations will be port and starboard until some of the new enlisted men get qualified. I have Chief Lange ensuring that the qualifications are completed as soon as possible."

"Very well. Oh, and until we reach Penang, you will be giving up your bunk to *Hauptsturmführer* Lübeck. You will hot rack with one of the other officers. Perhaps Teufel should share his bunk with you. He shouldn't be spending much time in his rack, as he needs to get qualified."

"Yes, sir," Goedel said, trying to hide his anger. That no good son-of-a-bitch SD man, a rider, a non-qualified hotel-load, no less, was taking his rack for the next fifty days. *This puts the icing on the cake.* "Anything else, sir?"

"No Johann, you are dismissed."

September 22, 1942 17:30
San Sebastian, Spain
Hotel Maria Cristina

Vizeadmiral Wilhelm Canaris sat in his suite in the posh Hotel Maria Cristina in the Old Town section of San Sebastian, Spain. He was not dressed in his military uniform. He had donned simple civilian clothes just before he crossed into Spain. He was on a covert mission in part for the *Abwehr* and in part for himself.

As Canaris waited for his contact to arrive, he reflected on his life. Here he sat as the head of military intelligence for a country engaged in a war that it clearly could not win. The failure to bomb Britain into submission, the senseless opening of the Eastern front, and the American entry into the war were all signs that Germany could not be victorious. Oh, the Fatherland could hold out for a while, but the end was inevitable.

Canaris also questioned his loyalty to the Nazi Party. He was an honorable man and a respected naval officer. In the beginning, he had been taken in by the professed goals of the party, but he now realized that he had been fooled. What started as a movement to improve Germany's place in the modern world had now become one man's maniacal personal quest to debase everyone else.

Canaris knew that he had been wrong, but he could save Germany from further anguish, if he could convince the British that he, and several influential Germans, were like-minded when it came to the war. The war must end, and the sooner the better for Germany.

The thought of saving Germany from further destruction was what brought Canaris to Spain on this early autumn night. He was to meet with a representative of the British Secret Intelligence Service, the MI-6. Stewart Menzies was the head of MI-6 and Canaris had conveyed messages to him previously. Now, he had arranged to meet one of Menzies's men, Sir Clive Dannenbrooke, to discuss a graceful end to the war. Additionally, Canaris was intent on establishing an exit strategy for himself.

Canaris figured that he had value to the West, given his position in German intelligence. That should be worth some sort of arrangement for himself, if the British insisted on prosecuting this war until their requested "unconditional surrender" could be achieved. He didn't want to be in Germany if that was the outcome. No. He would offer his experience, knowledge, and connections ... and perhaps something more personal, to show his honorable intentions.

Dannenbrooke arrived at the scheduled time. They spent three hours discussing Germany's future. Canaris clearly laid out the possibility of removing Hitler from office and the prospect of the new German leadership entering into negotiations to bring an end to the war. If the effort failed, the British would incur many more casualties during a prolonged war. Both men were clear that such a plan had risks, more for Canaris personally than for Dannenbrooke.

"Clive, you must recognize the position that this puts me in. Failure of such a takeover would surely result in my death. I did not rise to my position without the ability to plan for contingencies. I am hoping that I can count on your government to ensure my safety and the safety of my family if things were to go badly?"

"Wilhelm, let me be honest with you. While your family is a consideration, it is you that we see as an asset in such a situation. I cannot guarantee their safety, but I can guarantee that we would do the best that we can for your family."

Canaris sipped his cognac and took a drag on his cigarette. He had received a blunt, but honest answer from his British contact. He could live with that. Honesty was a rare trait in wartime. Perhaps he could sweeten the pot in order to improve the chances of the British securing the safety of his wife and two girls.

"My family is important to me Clive, as I am sure that yours is to you. I have some information that is of some value to you, but maybe of more value to the Americans. I offer this information to you in hopes that you will recognize that this is a personal war for me, one in which a man's family matters."

Canaris could see that Sir Clive Dannenbrooke was waiting for him to continue.

"You see, I have information that the son of an American diplomat has been caught up in the war here in Europe and he is trying to return to the United States."

"Go on, Wilhelm. I am listening."

"This is not an ordinary young man. He is educated, multilingual, and has constructed and served on U-boats. It seems he was conscripted by the *Wehrmacht* and now he is trying to make his way back home. Such a man, with his knowledge of U-boat operations and their construction, would be of some value to your country and to the Americans as well. I know him personally."

Canaris relayed the events of Christmas 1938 to Dannenbrooke. He followed that information with his meetings with Peter Teufel in Lorient. Canaris explained that young Teufel, to whom he owed a debt of honor, was a good young man who had been swept up by events. He explained that while he could not overtly help the young man to return to the United States, perhaps sharing this information with MI-6 would help him in a roundabout way.

"Where is this Teufel now?"

"He is on a U-boat headed for Penang, Malaysia. We are establishing a U-boat presence in that region. This is, of course, a secret operation."

"How do I know that what you are telling me is the truth, Admiral? I do not wish to insult you, but in our business, we hear a lot of things, some true, some not."

"I am not offended. The boat left Lorient under the cover of darkness today. In two weeks' time another U-boat will radio in its position in the North Atlantic. I know that you have broken our naval code and are monitoring our U-boat transmissions. This communiqué will be a cover to make you believe that our boat is in the Atlantic. By that time, our boat will be rounding the Cape of Good Hope."

MI6 was unaware of this information. Clive took note of the establishment of German submarine operations in the Pacific region. Almost as an afterthought, he annotated the information on Peter Teufel. "Tell me Wilhelm, what is the nature of this Pacific presence?"

"I have said much with very few words. What I have told you should suffice. It may be more than I should have told you, but, recognize that I have shared important information and, if the need should arise, I would expect that your country would remember that I did, for the needs of my family."

Dannenbrooke recognized that Canaris would not directly elaborate on this Penang submarine issue, so he tried a different tactic. "So, this young American wishes to return to the United States. Do you know how he will accomplish this task? I ask only in order to possibly assist this man to whom you are indebted."

"Honestly, I don't know. He may flee from Penang. He might jump ship in any port that they call upon. He did not share his plan, only his desire to return home."

"Do you think that he would steal the submarine?"

Canaris laughed aloud. It took a few moments before he could gain his composure.

"One man cannot steal a submarine, Clive! Heavens no! But ..."

"But what?"

"Several men, dozens actually, could steal one ... But that is very unlikely, Clive. The captain of the *U-463*, *Oberleutnant* Grimme, is an ardent Nazi. No, I think that the odds are remote. Not impossible, but very remote."

Dannenbrooke now had the number of the submarine and he noted this, too, as Canaris continued.

"I have said enough Clive. It is time for this meeting to end. I have given you information on those of us in Germany who wish to bring this war to an end. I know that you must return to England to discuss this with Menzies. You can reach me through our established channels if you wish to further this discussion. Thank you for taking the time to speak with me."

The two men shook hands. Dannenbrooke exited the room. He had gained some valuable intelligence on the desire within the *Wehrmacht* to overthrow Hitler and to end this war. The additional information about the German submarine operations in the Pacific was a bonus. Last on his debrief list for Menzies was this man Teufel.

September 30, 1942 22:21
71 Kilometers West of Freetown, Sierra Leone
U-463

The U-463 cruised on the surface of the Atlantic Ocean off the coast of Sierra Leone, rolling gently in the water as it cut through the one-meter swells. Following seas made their progress down the coast of Africa easier. They were making good time.

Aft of the conning tower out on the deck stood Johann Goedel and Peter Teufel. Goedel had come up topside for a breath of fresh air. Peter had been standing an under-instruction watch, but Richter had let him drop down on deck for a smoke with the XO.

Peter lit his cigarette. "How is it going, XO?"

"Shit, Two Pair! How do you think it is going? I have been booted from my bed by a rider, Lübeck no less, and now I am hot racking with you. Couldn't be better."

"It is the shits that Lübeck commandeered your bunk. Doesn't seem fair."

"*Ack*, fuck it. It won't matter after we pull into Penang. I will be off of this boat."

Peter looked around to see if they could be heard talking on the deck. Three or so meters above them, on the periscope sheers, stood the lookouts. They were talking with each other and Peter could not hear them. He figured that he and Goedel could not be heard either. He turned back to Goedel.

"Johann, are you seriously still considering what we talked about in Lorient? Are you going to walk away from this war?"

Goedel looked directly into Peter's eyes: "You're goddamn right I'm serious. I've had it, Two Pair. I am done with this war and this politically corrupt Navy."

"Do you really have a plan for walking away in Penang?"

"Yes and no. I will go on liberty and never come back. I plan to make my way to Argentina or Bolivia, by hopping on a steamer. It doesn't really matter. There is nothing left in Germany for me."

Peter took a drag on his cigarette. He inhaled deeply, then he exhaled the smoke from his lungs. He had wondered over the last few weeks if he should tell Goedel of his own plans to return home, to escape this war. He had thought long and hard about if he should tell Johann who he really was. Now that his plan to escape through Spain had been squashed, he needed a new plan. *Perhaps two heads would be better than one.* He decided to roll the dice with Goedel. "I'm going with you, Johann."

"What?"

"I want out of this war, too."

"What the hell are you talking about, Two Pair? You have no reason to leave the *Kriegsmarine*. You have a bright career in front of you. Jesus, I shared with you my plans because you are my friend, but I never thought that you would get the crazy idea in your head that you would follow me!"

"You don't understand, Johann."

"No, I don't! What the hell are you thinking? You are a young man, new to the service. I am an old sailor who is going nowhere. You have risen quickly, and with your education and abilities, you have a career in the *Kriegsmarine*. You are exactly what they are looking for."

"But I am a …"

Goedel, cut him off. He couldn't tolerate the thought of ruining this young German officer's career because Johann

Goedel had given into the crushing defeats of the last year or so. No, Johann Goedel would not allow it.

"Fuck that, Two Pair! What I do is my business and I have my reasons. But you, you must do the right thing. What makes you think that you should leave a very promising career in U-boats? You are talented, you are smart, you are knowledgeable, you are destined for success in this service. What makes you think that you are better off leaving the Navy?"

Peter paused for a moment. He took another drag of his smoke and flipped the butt over the side of the boat. He turned to Goedel and in perfect, flawless English said, "I am an American."

Goedel looked at Peter for a long time. Goedel didn't speak a lot of English, a smattering at best, but he understood exactly what Peter had said. "What?"

"I am an American. *Ich bin ein Amerikaner.*"

September 30, 1942 23:53
86 Kilometers Southwest of Freetown, Sierra Leone
U-463

Klaus Lübeck sat in the wardroom. He was happy that the boat was on the surface. He didn't like it when they were submerged. It was one of the few things that he had ever experienced that scared him. It was the noise that bothered him, the creaking sounds that he heard as the boat descended into the depths that unnerved the SD man. He could almost feel the pressure increasing on the hull as the boat made its daily dawn dive. He didn't like that experience at all.

Now, operating on the surface at night, it was a little easier for Lübeck. He knew that he had another month to go before he could get off of this stinking tube. It couldn't come soon enough.

He got up from the table and headed aft. It was time to check on Schellenberg's cargo and to ensure that the sentry was doing his job. He had told Schellenberg that he would get the gold to Singapore and he would. He was a man who got things done.

Lübeck stepped through the watertight hatch between the engine room and the machine shop, where the cargo was stowed. As he entered, he could see the sentry. The *Matrose* was sitting on a work bench, looking away from the hatch and more importantly, away from the gold. This lack of attention on the part of the sentry angered Lübeck.

Silently, Lübeck approached the sentry. Once he was behind the young sailor, he removed the luger from the man's holster, disarming him. In the same moment, Lübeck slipped his left arm around the throat of the sailor and raised the luger to his head with his right hand.

"Do you not understand your orders, you idiot?"

The sailor tried to get out of the hold but recognized in a second that he was outmanned and caught unaware. After Lübeck released his hold, the man protested, "I was watching the cargo, sir."

"Sure, you were. That is why you are disarmed and an instant from being dead."

"We are at sea, *Hauptsturmführer*. No one will touch this cargo."

Lübeck whispered into the young sailor's ear with a menacing tone: "I am going to inspect the cargo. If anything, fucking anything, is amiss, I will shoot you with your own weapon."

The SD man released his hold on the sailor. He looked over to the ten canvas bags that lay on the deck. The sailor stood at attention, nervously awaiting Lübeck's assessment.

Klaus took his time. He wanted to make his point. Finally, after a very long two minutes, he gave his findings to the sailor. "You live tonight, *Matrose*. But believe me, if I catch you inattentive again on this watch, even if the cargo is undisturbed, I will end your life. Slowly."

With that, Lübeck handed the pistol back to the sailor and made his way forward.

By breakfast the next day, the entire boat, including Grimme, knew of the incident. News got around quickly on U-boats, especially bad news.

October 1, 1942 18:08
321 Kilometers off of the
Coast of Freetown, Sierra Leone
U-463

Peter made his way to the officer's mess. He had been relieved on time and now he could grab a quick bite before the boat surfaced for its evening battery charge. He might even be able to get a few hours of sleep as well.

He pulled back the curtain and saw the captain, Goedel, and Lübeck already consuming their dinners. For most of the patrol, he had avoided Lübeck to the best of his ability and the SD man had made that task relatively easy.

Peter had noted that Lübeck spent most of his time in his bed reading and, when he was not there, he was in the machine shop keeping an eye on his cargo as he did calisthenics to stay in shape. In the evenings, he sometimes took a walk on deck to get some fresh air.

Their passenger for this patrol was a true "rider." He never helped out and he never missed a meal. Most riders qualify a watch station to support the mission of the ship, even officers, but the SD man had stated that his mission took priority. This lack of support for the boat was known by the entire crew. Peter had even overheard the nickname that the enlisted men had given Lübeck: *Herr Fauler Arsch*—Mr. Lazy Ass. None of the crew would say it to the SD man's face, but the moniker was routinely uttered in hushed tones.

As Peter took his seat at the table, he greeted his fellow officers. "Good evening gentlemen, and you, too, *Hauptsturmführer.*"

Peter noticed that Goedel smiled. He had caught the dig at Lübeck. No one else had.

"Ah, *Leutnant*, are the diesels ready for tonight's surface run and battery charge?"

"Yes, Captain. I checked them myself."

"Very well. Time for me to make my tour of the boat."

With that, Grimme stood up and made his way aft, leaving the three officers alone. They ate in silence, a dinner of fresh-baked bread and liver dumpling soup.

"Liver dumplings?" Peter quipped. "I was hoping for jellyfish."

Lübeck looked up from his dinner but their eyes did not meet. Peter wondered if he had pushed Lübeck too far.

Goedel changed the subject. "I heard about the incident with your sentry last night, *Hauptsturmführer*. You were pretty hard on the young sailor, don't you think?"

"He was derelict in his duties. I corrected that. He was lucky that I did not make a bigger example out of him."

"You mean by actually shooting him?"

"I have my orders and my mission. I don't need to explain myself to you, *Oberleutnant,* nor will I."

"No disrespect intended, *Hauptsturmführer*. I only suggest that the crew, who are vital in completing your mission, should be handled appropriately. If the crewman was indeed derelict, this should have been brought before the captain. We have laws at sea, you understand."

"I answer to no one, *Herr* Goedel, not even the captain. Trust me. If the event occurs again, I will handle it swiftly and directly. I have killed greater men for lesser offenses."

"Believe what he says, XO," Peter said without looking up from his soup.

"No one cares what you think, *Leutnant.* Keep your mouth shut." Lübeck snarled.

Peter could not hold his tongue. Anger rose inside of him that had been festering since Harbin. "It is quite clear to me that you don't care. You don't care about any man. You haven't lifted a finger to help on this boat at all."

"I am not going to be questioned about my conduct on-board this sewer pipe, especially by you, *Herr* Teufel! The son of a German diplomat, eh? Tell me why it is that when I searched our Federal Foreign Office records in Berlin, I could not find any reference to your father?"

Peter didn't answer the question. He just stared at Lübeck, barely masking his hate.

"Where were you born?"

"Berlin."

"But your accent does not indicate that."

"We traveled a lot when I was young."

"Bullshit! There is something odd about you and I will find out what it is. You speak German, but you lack a German accent. Perhaps you are not what you say you are."

"I am an officer in the *Kriegsmarine* and a human being, something that you are not! You are a thug and a bootlick."

Lübeck reacted so swiftly that he only appeared as a blur. He leaped from his seat and seized Peter by the neck as he slammed him into the bulkhead.

"I will fucking kill you for that, you little shit!"

Peters eyes bulged as he gasped for air. He struggled against the bigger man but he could not free himself. With one last desperate attempt to secure his release, Peter swiftly lifted a knee.

Lübeck felt the searing pain in his groin. He released his grip and staggered back, clutching himself. Hate boiled inside of him along with the pain.

"I am going to kill you, Teufel."

"ENOUGH!" Goedel shouted. "You attacked a fellow officer, *Hauptsturmführer*, without provocation. I witnessed it and I will swear by it."

Just then, Chief Lange entered the dining area with three men behind him. "Is there a problem Mr. Goedel?" the chief asked.

Goedel looked at Peter, then turned his gaze to Lübeck. "Your move, *Hauptsturmführer,* do you have a problem or would you like to complete your mission?"

The SD man thought for a moment. *This was not the time or the place.* He would see the mission through and then he would deal with the insolent Teufel.

"No problem, *Herr* Goedel. No problem at all."

"Chief, I think that our guest here could use some fresh air. Make sure that *Hauptsturmführer* Lübeck gets some fresh air up on deck."

"Yes, sir."

Five minutes later, Peter sat with Goedel alone.

"Jesus, Two Pair! What the hell is the matter with you?"

"He is an animal and a prick. He should be arrested! Why didn't you have the chief arrest him?"

"I couldn't."

"Why not? He attacked me!"

"Think about it, Two Pair. If I had him arrested and charged, he would level charges against you."

"For what, telling the truth?"

"It wouldn't matter. What matters is if any charges were brought, the both of you would be confined in Penang. Where would that leave us?"

"I suppose that you are right."

"You have to avoid him for the rest of the patrol. Do you understand me?"

"I understand."

Chapter Nineteen: Covet

October 12, 1942 08:53
24 Kilometers off of Cape Town, South Africa
U-463

Peter wiped sweat from his brow. The *U-463* had just spent nine hours refueling two U-boats near the British-controlled port of Cape Town, South Africa. Many hours of surface operations had made everyone a bit jumpy, as everyone knew that the *U-463* was the most vulnerable on the surface. The refueling had taken longer than expected and Captain Grimme was not happy. The captain had chewed ass up and down the boat. As the newly qualified officer of the deck, Peter had taken the brunt of Grimme's wrath.

Now the boat was pulling out to deeper water to continue its journey to Penang. Submerged, running on its two *Siemens-Schuckert* 2 GU 345/38-8 double-acting electric motors, the submarine glided silently beneath the waves at three knots.

Captain Grimme walked into the machine shop room in the aft end of the boat. There stood the armed sentry who was guarding Lübeck's cargo. Stacked neatly on the deck, tucked away on the port side of the compartment, were ten canvas bags. *What could be so important that an armed guard was required at sea on a submarine?* Lübeck had not shared the nature of the cargo with the captain.

"Good morning, Captain."

"Good morning. I see that you are guarding our precious cargo."

"Yes, sir."

"Good."

Grimme strolled closer to the canvas bags. He didn't see any markings on the bags. He could not tell what was in them. He had heard from the working party that the bags, though small, were very heavy. Could it be uranium, silver, or gold? He wanted to know what he was carrying to Penang for the SD officer. Should he just open a bag and look? He knew that Lübeck had given orders that no one was to disturb the cargo. *But I am the captain, I should know what is on my boat.*

Grimme reached down and grabbed the top of one of the canvas bags.

"Uh, captain? *Hauptsturmführer* Lübeck's orders were clear, sir. No one was to disturb the cargo, sir."

Grimme stared coldly at the sentry. "I am the captain of this boat, *Matrose* Braun. Now stand back."

Grimme unzipped the bag and looked inside as the sentry stood watching the entrance to the machine shop. The young guard was torn between following Lübeck's instructions and following the captain's order. The sentry prayed that Lübeck would not make an appearance.

As the opening of the canvas bag parted, Grimme could see that the bag contained ten smaller sacks. He opened one of the smaller sacks and peered into it. The sack contained gold coins from all over Europe: Swiss francs, Dutch guilders, Belgian francs, and other gold coins. He closed the sack and zipped up the canvas bag before he checked a second canvas bag. It, too, contained ten smaller sacks. Grimme zipped up the canvas bag and turned to the sentry.

"I now have a better understanding of our mission. You will not say a word to *Hauptsturmführer* Lübeck of my investigation here today. Do I make myself clear?"

"Yes, sir."

The sentry was scared. The SD man had made it very clear that no one was to mess with the cargo. He had gone on to say that the penalty was death and Braun had believed him. But this was his captain. Braun decided very quickly that he would say nothing about what had happened.

Grimme nodded at the sentry and headed back to his stateroom. He made some calculations in his head. Ten canvas bags, each containing ten sacks of gold coins. Each canvas bag weighed approximately ten kilograms, maybe a bit more. *That's at least one hundred kilograms of gold … a lot of gold.* He wondered why Lübeck was taking gold to Penang. He must be carrying out a task for one of the Nazi elites. *Why else would an SD man like that, an enforcer, be transporting gold?*

October 21, 1942 23:50
51 Kilometers North East of
Port Saint Louis, Madagascar
U-463

Peter stood on the deck of the *U-463* as the submarine cut its way across the surface of the Indian Ocean. He was having a smoke before he took the mid-watch as the officer of the deck. He had been doing a lot of thinking in the last few days, since the day that he had told Goedel that he was an American. They had not talked much in the interim. Peter needed to gauge Goedel's feelings on the subject and he was going to get his chance as Goedel stepped down onto the deck.

"Good evening, XO."

"Hey, Two Pair. What's new? Chief Lange is telling that joke again, the one about the stuttering, one-legged, syphilitic midget hooker with Tourette's named Fu-Fu-Fu … Fucking Lucky."

"It is a damn funny joke."

"Yeah, it is. Listen, Two Pair. I have been thinking a lot about our situation."

"I was hoping that you were thinking that we should work together to do so?"

"Yes, I am. Let's face it. We both need to get away ... for different reasons, but it only makes sense that we work together to make it happen. Are you in with me?"

"No, I figured that you would join with me ..."

Goedel, was taken aback at first but then he realized that Peter was kidding with him and agreeing with him at the same time.

"You ass, Two Pair! Always joking. Listen, I think that we need to make our move soon. From Penang, we need to get away quickly. There is not a large Nazi presence in our new port, but that will soon change. We need to act sooner rather than later."

"I agree. Do you have a plan?"

"I have ... *we* have several options. The best one: We walk away one night. Try to catch a coastal steamer to Singapore and, from there, make our way to Argentina."

"Argentina? The Nazis have a lot of connections in Argentina. You wouldn't be safe there, would you? Deserting from the *Kriegsmarine*, you would be on the run."

Goedel hadn't thought of that. He knew that Argentina was friendly to Germans, but what Two Pair said was true; he would be on the run.

"Well, I cannot go to America. They frown on Germans there. Maybe Bolivia or Uruguay?"

"How about Mexico? From what I have heard, that country is split politically. Some support the Germans and the other half supports the American side. If I can get to Mexico, I am pretty sure that I can make it back to America. You could vanish into Mexico and live a new life."

"Jesus, I don't know. Any place in the Americas has danger for me. Besides, no matter where we want to go, the real problem is: How do we get there?"

October 26, 1942 10:00
Washington, DC
Office of Strategic Services

Erik Teufel found himself once again with Bill Donovan, head of the newly formed Office of Strategic Services, the OSS. He had been summoned to Donovan's office by a personal visit from Byron Schoenfeld.

"We have received information from MI6 about your son. He is on a U-boat headed for Penang, Malaysia," said Donovan.

"Malaysia!"

"Although he has been serving the *Kriegsmarine* as a U-boat officer, we have information that he may be trying to desert and return to the United States."

"Jesus, Bill … that is not an easy task is it? I mean, he will be in danger and the odds of being successful, I would imagine, are pretty slim."

"To be quite honest with you, we give him about a 10% chance of making this work, maybe less."

Erik knew that the odds of Peter being able to escape the German Navy and returning safely were not good, but hearing his chances out loud shook him. His only son was in a bad spot and Erik felt guilty, unable to help him. Erik regretted letting Peter stay in Germany to finish college now more than ever.

"That is why we need your help, Erik. We want to assist him, if it is at all possible. He would have information that would benefit our war effort. Returning your son to the States would be an intelligence coup, not to mention returning him to his family."

"What can I do to help?"

"I want you to sit down with one of my men and tell him everything you know about your son. How he thinks, what he values, anything that you can think of that might help us determine how he plans to get back here. No detail is too small. As his father, you know him better than anyone."

"Tell me Bill, how did you get this information?"

"I would rather not reveal the source of the information. It would not be standard procedure for …"

"Goddamn it Bill, this is my son that we are talking about. I held a top-secret clearance when I retired. I deserve to know all that you know about my son."

Donovan thought about it. Erik Teufel was a well-known commodity. He could be trusted and his request was understandable given the circumstances.

"One of MI6's operatives met with a high-ranking German intelligence officer. He gave us the information about Peter. He apparently had spoken to Peter, shortly before the U-boat departed for Penang."

"The officer wouldn't happen to be Wilhelm Canaris, would it?"

"How did you know that, Erik?"

"I knew many in the German intelligence service during my time in Berlin. Peter knows Canaris. Peter did him a favor four years ago, right before we left Germany."

"It seems that Canaris still feels indebted to your son. This is the kind of information that helps us, Erik."

November 7, 1942 03:23
1870 Kilometers West of Penang, Malaysia
U-463

An air of relief permeated the *U-463*. Now that they were operating in Japanese-controlled waters, the crew of the boat began to relax a bit. They were on their war footing, but it was clear to all crew members that they were safer now. Captain Grimme had even run a few training drills for qualification. Drills during wartime were rare.

Klaus Lübeck was anxious to get into port and get off of this submarine. He had been at sea for forty-seven days, which was forty-seven days too long. He had enjoyed none of this trip. When the boat was on the surface, it rocked incessantly, but it was even worse when the boat was submerged. During underwater operations he could almost feel the pressure of the water above him crushing down upon his chest. He would be happy when they pulled into Penang in a couple of days.

When he reached port, Lübeck was going to meet up with his *Kenpeitai* contact and arrange for the transfer of Schellenberg's gold to Singapore. Then he would return to Germany and get back to work. Before he did, he might spend a night or two with a Chinese comfort woman. He deserved the distraction.

The boat cruised along on the surface of the Indian Ocean, heading east. On the bridge, Peter Teufel was on watch as the officer of the deck when Johann Goedel came up to shoot the stars. As the XO, Goedel served as the navigator. He would plot the course of the *U-463* using the position of the stars. When he finished taking his readings and noting the time, Goedel turned and looked at Peter.

He marveled at the young man and his ability to survive as an American in Germany for the last three years of the war. Somehow, this foreigner had fooled everyone he met into thinking that he was German. He had been conscripted into the *Kriegsmarine* and found a way to become an officer. *He is a resourceful young man.*

"It's a beautiful night, eh, Two Pair?"

"That it is, Johann."

"Are you still interested in making our journey?"

"Yes, I am. I have to."

"I think that I have a plan that will work. We need to leave Penang and make our way to Singapore. From there we can hop a ship and make our way to Central or South America, Argentina, Chile or Mexico. All of those countries have sympathies for the German cause but are not controlled by Germany. We would be welcomed there, and you could make your way home."

"We can get some information in Penang. I can speak with the Japanese there and determine which course to take."

"Perfect. We cannot wait too long. We need to move quickly."

"Right."

Chapter Twenty: Treachery

November 11, 1942 07:55
Penang, Malaysia
U-463

The *U-463* was tied up to Pier 22 in Penang. The fifty-one-day patrol had come to a successful end. On board the boat, the crew was buzzing with the word that they would receive liberty in this exotic port. They were proud to be the first to crew a German submarine to Penang during the war and they were anxious to get ashore.

Lübeck entered Grimme's state room unannounced, to the consternation of the captain. Grimme didn't like the SD man and he would be glad to see him leave.

"I am going ashore to arrange for the transfer of my cargo. I must remind you, captain, that the armed guard must be maintained until my return. Understood?"

"Understood, *Hauptsturmführer*. Your cargo will be guarded unless we are forced to abandon ship, and that is not likely, tied up to the pier as we are."

Lübeck did not appreciate Grimme's little joke. He looked perturbed.

"Under no circumstances will the security be relaxed. Got it?"

"Yes, sir."

With that Lübeck departed the ship in search of his local contacts. Grimme cursed the SD officer under his breath. He was tired of Schellenberg's man and he wished that he never came back.

November 11, 1942 12:00
Penang, Malaysia
U-463

Peter Teufel sat in the wardroom eating his lunch when he heard the alarm: "Abandon ship! Abandon ship! This is a drill. I repeat: this is a drill."

Peter looked up at Richter and Goedel, who also were seated around the table. "Is he serious? An abandon ship drill now?"

"This is the best time to run one. It is more difficult at sea. Let's go. Everyone topside," Goedel said. "We have to man the life rafts. Turn to, *Leutnants*. I will ensure that the life rafts are delivered from the engine room to topside. Let's go. Get to your stations."

Throughout the boat, men were running for the hatches and spilling out onto the deck of the submarine. Back in the machine shop, *Matrose* Braun was again standing his watch as the sentry for Lübeck's cargo. He heard the abandon ship drill announcement, but he hesitated. Should he stay with the cargo or should he muster topside? He followed his training and left the cargo unattended.

Topside of the *U-463*, sailors scurried about. Each man had an assignment to perform for the abandon ship drill. Life rafts were broken out and inflated. Emergency rations and water were loaded into the rafts and all personnel were accounted for. The captain stood on the conning tower, taking it all in. He gave an order to hurry up and to double check the emergency equipment. He then personally made a tour of the below decks to ensure that no man was left behind.

Standing at the end of the pier was a *Kenpeitai* operative. Paid by Lübeck, the operative's job was to watch the newly arrived submarine. He had spent several hours standing in the sun, watching the U-boat with nothing happening. Now, he saw that men were pouring out of the submarine. He watched as the Germans milled around on deck, inflating life rafts and dispersing emergency equipment. He noticed that the captain of the ship was pointing and directing the activities. The operative also noted that the captain headed down into the submarine. He was gone for seven minutes.

The operative took note of all that he had seen. Lübeck would be interested in this information. He was sure of that. He watched as the abandon ship drill was terminated at 12:21 in the afternoon and the sailors re-stowed the life rafts and emergency gear. Once the gear was stowed, the men entered the submarine and went about their daily business.

Grimme met with his officers in the wardroom twenty minutes after the drill. He was pleased with the crew's response to the simulated emergency.

"Well done, gentlemen. We were able to execute an evacuation in less than twelve minutes."

The officers nodded in agreement.

"XO, please arrange for liberty for the crew. Sections A and B will have liberty. Section C will have the duty. I have to go meet with *Kommodore* Abel. I will return this evening."

"Yes, sir," Goedel replied. "Richter, you have the duty tonight. I will relieve you in the morning."

With that, the U-boat men watched as the captain headed ashore. Peter noticed that Grimme carried a bulging satchel as he left the boat. The inconspicuous *Kenpeitai* operative standing on the pier noticed this as well.

November 11, 1942 19:05
Penang, Malaysia
Pier 22

A Japanese Type 94 six-wheeled truck came to a stop at the head of Pier 22. Lübeck exited the passenger side of the cab and walked over to a nondescript Asian man sitting on a crate nearby. It was the *Kenpeitai* operative Lübeck had paid to keep an eye on the submarine. The man relayed all that he had seen that day, including the abandon ship drill and the captain's subsequent departure.

After hearing the operative's report, Lübeck bolted down the pier to the submarine, straight for the machine shop in the aft of the boat. There he found the sentry in his place, alert and vigilant.

"Has anyone touched the cargo?"

"No, sir."

"How long have you been on watch?"

"An hour, sir. I relieved Braun who had the noon-to-six watch."

Lübeck bent over the canvas bags that held the cargo. He opened each of the ten bags and counted the number of smaller sacks within. When he was done with his count, he zipped up the final bag, stood up slowly, and turned to the sentry. With a lightning-fast move, he lunged at the sentry and grabbed the man by the throat, pinning the man back against a tool locker.

"Each bag is missing one item. Can you explain that?"

The sentry's eyes filled with fear. He couldn't talk with Lübeck's right hand squeezing his throat. He tried to respond, but all that came out of his mouth was a rasp and a bit of spittle. Lübeck relaxed the grip a bit.

"No one has touched this since I have been here, sir."

The SD man released his grip on the sentry. He was positive, based on what the *Kenpeitai* told him, that Grimme was the man who stole a portion of the cargo. The captain would have been the one to schedule the drill and he was seen going below decks after everyone was accounted for on deck. He would still question *Matrose* Braun later, but for now, he had to find Grimme and the satchel that he was carrying when he left the boat.

"You remain here on duty until I return."

"Yes, sir."

November 11, 1942 19:55
Penang, Malaysia
Malay Wok Restaurant

Peter Teufel and Johann Goedel sat alone, talking quietly, at the Malay Wok Restaurant in George Town. They had eaten dinner and now were enjoying a beer as they planned their departure from the *U-463*.

"So, Two Pair, tomorrow I think that you should try to get train schedules and ship schedules to Singapore. With your knowledge of Japanese, it will be easy for you. The Japanese run everything here."

"I am sure that I can do that. I will let them know that we will be in port for a few weeks and want to travel."

"Good. I will go to *Kommodore* Abel's office and see if I can get us any charts of the Pacific. They may be useful on our journey to the Americas."

"It would be a hell of a lot easier if Grimme would take the *U-463* to Chile or Mexico and drop us off."

"Not very likely to happen, Two Pair, but it is a nice idea. Let's stick with a plan where we depend on ourselves and not that Nazi Grimme."

Peter nodded. Of course, they couldn't count on Grimme to give them a ride. Then another thought crossed Peter's mind: "Johann, what if we took the *U-463*?"

"What!? We can't steal the boat."

"That's funny. You said a few weeks ago in Rennes that you were going to steal it yourself. Now I am offering to help."

"I was drunk. It would be impossible to steal the boat. Grimme would never allow it and we couldn't sail it alone. How would you convince nearly sixty other guys to steal a U-boat?"

"Yes, you were drunk, but more importantly, you were right. Look, it changes the problem dramatically. The problem is no longer how do we get from Penang to Bolivia, or wherever. The problem becomes how do we get the boat away from Penang and away from Grimme. Then we sail where we decide to go."

Goedel was lost in thought. He had never actually considered using a U-boat to make his break from the *Kriegsmarine*. He wouldn't do such a thing, *would* he? It did make sense. He wouldn't be in a foreign land trying to find safe passage to another foreign land. But how would they accomplish such a feat?

November 11, 1942 20:32
Penang, Malaysia
Monsun Gruppe Headquarters

Wilhelm Grimme left *Kommodore* Abel's office and walked out into the street. They had spent the last four hours discussing the *U-463*'s last patrol in a debrief over dinner. The *Kommodore* had been very complimentary of the performance of Grimme's boat. The refueling operations off of the South African port had been executed without incident and the boat had made its way safely to Penang. Reports from Dönitz indicated that those refueled submarines had sunk several enemy ships.

Several other U-boats were preparing to make the same voyage from Europe to Penang to complete the *Monsun Gruppe*. The plan was to have six German submarines operational in Penang by early 1943. Supplies, too, were being routed around the Cape of Good Hope to support *Kriegsmarine* submarine operations in the theatre. Within a few months, U-boats would be routinely raiding the Indian Ocean. The *U-463* would have a key role in supporting those raids.

The *Kommodore* had given Grimme orders to make any necessary repairs and to take on a full load of fuel. The second U-boat would be rounding the Cape of Good Hope soon and the *U-463* would put to sea in a few weeks to refuel this new boat. For now, the *U-463* would remain in port until it received further orders.

Grimme exited the headquarters with his satchel in hand. Inside the leather case, he carried the patrol log and a copy of his new orders. He strolled confidently along the street as he made his way back towards the boat, knowing that tomorrow he would begin to prepare his ship for the upcoming patrol. His mind was filled with all of the work that had to be done to get the ship ready for sea, taking on fuel, storing food. It was a lot to do, but he would enjoy the rewards of captaining a well-prepared ship.

As he passed a narrow, dark alley in George Town, Grimme did not see the shadowy figure waiting for him. In an instant, someone grabbed the captain by the arm and swung him into the alley with great force. His attacker slung him around and slammed his face into the wall of the building. Grimme dropped to the ground. He felt his head spinning as he was rolled over onto his back. He looked up through watery eyes to see Lübeck kneeling on his chest.

"Where the fuck is my cargo, Wilhelm?"

Grimme was still stunned by the speed and ferocity of the attack. He blinked twice without answering the SD man.

"It better be in this satchel."

Lübeck grabbed the leather case and lifted it. He knew immediately that the gold was not in the satchel. The missing gold weighed over ten kilograms. The satchel weighed less than a kilogram. Without opening it, he dropped it next to Grimme.

"Where is it, you thieving bastard?"

"Where is what?"

"The gold that you stole from me."

"I don't know what you are talking ..."

The force of Lübeck's punch broke Grimme's nose. Blood began to stream down the captain's face.

"I am only going to ask one more time *Oberleutnant* and I want you to answer me very carefully. Ten sacks of gold coins are missing. You went below decks today during the drill while everyone else was topside. Only you had the opportunity to steal it. So, I say again ... where the hell is the gold?"

"I swear to you, *Hauptsturmführer*, I do not know what you are talking about!"

Lübeck stood over Grimme. He looked down at the naval officer in disgust. *No one gets the better of Klaus Lübeck.*

It was time for more drastic action.

"You have hidden the gold somewhere. It is not on you. You must have given it to someone or stashed it somewhere and I want to know where you put it."

With that, Lübeck swiftly raised his boot and stomped on Grimme's elbow. The joint shattered. The captain screamed in agony. Lübeck quickly pulled a handkerchief from his pocket and kneeling down again, stuffed it into Grimme's mouth to muffle the scream.

"Last chance, Wilhelm. Tell me where the gold is!"

The SD man grabbed Grimme's wrist and moved the arm back and forth. He could feel the broken bones grinding against each other. Grimme's eyes widened in pain as he tried to scream, but the sound was stifled by the cloth in his mouth.

Lübeck let go of the arm and waited for the captain to calm down. Once the pain had appeared to subside, he removed the handkerchief.

"Well, where is it?"

Grimme gasped. He had never felt pain like this in his life. His eyes were watering, his nose was broken, and his left elbow was clearly shattered. He could only beg for his life now.

"Please Klaus, please. It hurts."

Lübeck knew that this was it. He had inflicted sufficient pain. Either Grimme was going to tell him where he had put the gold or the captain was never going to tell him. He did not have the time to continue torturing this man in the street. He would ask just one more time.

"Where is the gold?"

"As God is my witness, I have no idea where your shit is!"

"Then say hello to God for me."

Lübeck slammed the heel of his right hand directly into Grimme's broken nose, shoving the cartilage up into the prone man's brain. The captain died in an instant.

The SD man wasted no time. He dragged the body deeper into the alley, next to some trash cans. He removed Grimme's wallet and turned his pockets inside out to make it look like a robbery. He quickly rummaged through the satchel, looking for a key or a safe deposit box slip. Finding none, he dropped the satchel next to the body. He lifted one of the cans and covered the dead man with garbage. When he was done, he walked out of the alley towards the docks, resigned to never find the ten sacks of gold coins.

By the time that the local police found the body in the alley, the sun was already up in the east. They quickly recognized that it was a German officer. Everyone in Penang knew that the German U-boat had arrived yesterday and now one of theirs was dead.

As Grimme's body was being discovered, Lübeck was eating breakfast on an intercoastal steamer, headed for Singapore. His *Kenpeitai* contacts had arranged for his passage. He sat in his cabin, munching on eggs, rice, and potatoes with the canvas bags of Schellenberg's gold around his feet.

Chapter Twenty-One: Opportunity

November 12, 1942 13:31
Penang, Malaysia
Pier 22

Johann Goedel stood on the conning tower of the *U-463*. The warm sun beat down upon him and the work party of sailors onloaded diesel fuel into the submarine. A Japanese fuel oil barge was tied up outboard of the submarine and fuel transfer was in progress.

Goedel had relieved Richter that morning and learned that the captain had not returned from liberty. The XO figured that he spent the night in town, but it did seem a little odd. Grimme had said that he would return last night.

A man dressed in a *Kriegsmarine* uniform of a *Bootsmannsmaat* requested to board. He was granted permission by the topside watch and directed to the conning tower. The sailor approached Goedel and saluted. The XO returned the salute.

"*Oberleutnant* Goedel, sir. *Kommodore* Abel requests that you report to his headquarters at 15:00."

"What is this about?"

"I do not know, sir. I was sent with this message and told to give it to you, sir."

With that the messenger saluted and left the boat. Goedel called down into the control room and asked that Chief Lange report to him.

"What can I do for you, *Herr* Goedel?"

"I need you to take over the fuel load, Chief. I have been summoned to the *Kommodore's* headquarters. When the captain returns, let him know where I am."

"Yes, sir."

With that, Goedel headed down into the boat to shower, shave, and don his dress uniform.

An hour and twenty minutes later, Goedel was escorted into *Kommodore* Abel's office in the warehouse district of George Town.

"*Oberleutnant* Goedel, reporting as ordered, sir."

The *Kommodore* motioned for Goedel to sit. "I have some very bad news, *Herr* Goedel. *Oberleutnant* Grimme was found dead this morning in an alley not far from here."

"Dead? What happened, sir?"

"He appears to have been robbed and beaten to death. The local police are investigating. Sometime after he left this office last night he was accosted."

"Who would do such a thing, *Kommodore*?"

"I have no idea, but we are letting the local police handle this. Fortunately, we recovered his satchel which contained the *U-463*'s sealed orders. You will prepare the boat for its next mission as the temporary captain."

"Temporary captain?"

"Yes, I have already communicated with Berlin and received confirmation that a new captain is being flown here to assume command of the *U-463*, but that may take three weeks. You will ensure that the boat is ready to go to sea to support submarine operations when the new captain arrives. In the meantime, you will be temporarily in command."

Goedel was once again crushed. The death of Grimme was a shock to him, but being placed in temporary command until another officer could replace him was too much. He had always wanted his own ship, but not like this. *Fucked over again.*

Suddenly, Goedel realized that this was it. Not only had he been dealt the final insult. He'd also been offered the ultimate opportunity. Just as Two Pair had said, it would be easier to get to the Americas using their own submarine and now the *Kriegsmarine* had given him one! *Temporary* was enough, and his time in command would be more temporary than the *Kommodore* presumed.

When the briefing was finished, Abel asked if Goedel had any questions.

"Just one, sir. Our charts of the region onboard the *U-463* are very dated. The new captain will want the best charts available. I'll need to get those."

"I understand. Until our base here is fully operational, we are dependent on our Japanese friends. Try the IJN headquarters."

"Yes, sir."

November 13, 1942 16:22
Singapore
United Overseas Bank, Bonham Building

Klaus Lübeck exited the three-story Bonham Building in the heart of Singapore's Financial District. He had deposited Schellenberg's cargo in the United Overseas Bank just as he had been instructed. His mission was complete. In his pocket he kept the safe deposit box key and a deposit slip for the gold coins, ten percent less than he had when he departed Lorient.

He was still angry that ten of the sacks of gold coins had been stolen. He was sure that Grimme was the offender and it was unfortunate that he had been unable to convince the thief to talk. There was not much that he could do about it now. The bigger question was: What would he tell Schellenberg?

Several ideas ran through the SD man's head. He could tell Schellenberg that he'd had to pay the Japanese for safe passage from Penang to Singapore. That would be reasonable. Or, he could tell him the truth: that some of the gold coins had been stolen and the perpetrator had paid for his theft with his life.

Lübeck had to decide what to tell his boss soon. Following his orders, he was to contact Schellenberg from Singapore to report on his mission and to receive his next assignment. He was only a short walk away from the *Kenpeitai* headquarters in Singapore, where he was heading to make his report to Berlin. He decided that the truth was the best option. He would accept the consequences of failing to fully complete his mission for the first time in his career.

As he walked along, Lübeck chided himself for his failure. He wondered if he was losing his touch. He had always prided himself on being a man who got things done, but, this time, he had come up just a little short.

He finally reached the *Kenpeitai* headquarters and reported to the communications section. There he sent his coded message to Schellenberg with all of the details of the mission, including the missing gold. When the message was sent, he left instructions that he be contacted by the *Kenpeitai* at his hotel room when Berlin responded.

The next day a message was delivered to Lübeck at his hotel. The message was terse: *Remain in Singapore until further notice.*

November 13, 1942 18:37
Penang, Malaysia
Pier 22

It had been a hectic day for Captain Goedel. After the 07:00 morning muster, during which he had notified the crew of Captain Grimme's death and informed them of the upcoming mission, he had spent the day making preparations to ready the boat for sea as soon as possible. The crew did not know the nature of the next mission, as protocol dictated that the captain would inform them once they were underway. They only knew that Goedel wanted them to be ready to sail in a week, if necessary.

Goedel was in a hurry. He didn't want to risk having the replacement captain show up before they could get underway.

He needed to take the boat to sea as captain in order to make a break to Mexico. *Kommodore* Abel had said it would be three weeks before the replacement would arrive, but Goedel knew that it could be sooner. Dönitz would have to select a new captain. That officer would have to settle his affairs before embarking on the journey to Penang. The travel would take a couple of days at least. A week or a few days more would be the soonest his replacement could arrive.

Rather than maps of the Indian Ocean, Goedel had obtained several maps and charts of the Pacific Ocean from the IJN in order to plot his course. For the time being, he kept these charts to himself. Handing them to the quartermaster would reveal his plans to the entire crew. He just needed to figure out a way to get the boat to sea without raising Abel's suspicions.

The *U-463* was already loaded with diesel fuel, enough to travel the 17,600 kilometers to Ensenada, Mexico. But even with the excess fuel storage, he wasn't sure if the boat could make the return trip back to a friendly port. He was not going to leave the crew stranded in Mexico if he could help it.

Now they needed to obtain food. So far, the crew was having difficulty locating the needed supplies. Penang was not yet fully organized. The next couple of days would be focused on getting the needed stores loaded.

Captain Goedel sat with *Leutnant zur See* Teufel at the IJN Penang Officer's Club. They sat alone at a table in the back of the room, away from the few Japanese officers present. Goedel hadn't had a chance to talk to Peter alone about his plan to sail the *U-463* to Mexico.

"Do you think any of these officers speak German, Two Pair?"

"I don't think so. I can find out though."

"How?"

"Give me a minute."

Peter stood up and headed to the bathroom. He returned thirty seconds later, yelling: *"Feuer, Feuer, Feuer!"*

Goedel was startled but held his ground. Several Japanese officers turned and looked at Peter, but none of them looked alarmed. Peter waved to the Japanese and smiled. A couple bowed back. The rest returned to their drinks.

Peter sat back down at the table. "Nope, I am pretty sure that they don't speak German."

"Jesus, Two Pair! Yelling *fire* in a bar! Really?"

"It worked, didn't it?"

"Well, I will keep my voice down, just in case. We have our opportunity. We can take the *U-463* and make our way to Mexico, if we can just figure out a way to get the boat out of port. *Kommodore* Abel has ordered us to sit tight at the pier until the new captain can travel from Germany."

"New captain? Aren't you the captain?"

"Only temporarily. Abel made it clear that I am not highly thought of by the powers that be. That only reaffirms my decision to leave the service. We just need to find a way to get out of port. If we take the boat to sea, the harbor master will notify all commands, including Abel, of the ship's movement. They would be after us before we could submerge the boat."

"So, we need a diversion that includes a reason to take the boat to sea."

"Exactly. But I am not sure what that reason would be."

"Hell, that's easy Johann! We need a typhoon."

"How the hell are we going to get a typhoon? It's not typhoon season."

"Good point." Peter considered the problem. "If Penang were attacked by the British or the Americans, that would give you reason to take the *U-463* to sea."

"There is not a viable enemy fighting force within two thousand kilometers of here. How are we going to arrange for an attack on Penang?"

"Leave it to me. I have an idea."

"Ok, Two Pair, assuming that we do get to sea, we have several other problems to solve."

"Such as?"

"I can dream up a mission that takes the boat to Mexico, but I am not leaving the crew there. It would not be fair to them. Do they have enough fuel for the boat to make the round trip?"

"Have you plotted a course? What is the distance?"

"Yes, the course that I have plotted is about 19,500 kilometers. We have plenty of fuel to make that distance. Coming back is the hard part."

"No problem. Off hand, I would say that the boat should make it there and back. We have over six hundred tons of fuel. I will run the math on that, but it should be no issue. What else?"

"If we take off, it won't take *Kommodore* Abel very long to figure out that we are on the run. He will send the *Kriegsmarine* and maybe our Japanese friends after us. We have no real defense other that the anti-aircraft guns. The *U-463* has no torpedo tubes, which leaves us nearly defenseless. If we were found, we could not put up much of a fight."

Peter considered this problem a solvable issue. In the shipyard in Keil, he had seen several Type VII U-boats, which had an aft torpedo tube on the outside of the pressure hull. Such a weapons system could only be reloaded in port, but it was better than no torpedoes at all.

"I can build you a torpedo tube Johann, maybe two."

"What are you talking about?"

"You know, just like the Type VII boats. I can build an external torpedo tube. It shouldn't be that difficult."

"You are serious, aren't you? You really think you can?"

"It's been done before. Let me get to work on that. I think that I can have it done in a few days. How long do we have before the new captain gets here?"

"I figure it will take at least a week from today."

"Then we need to get to work. Let's pick a target date."

"To be safe, lets shoot for the eighteenth."

"Ok, Johann. By the way, what are you going to tell the crew when we get to sea?"

"Once the boat is at sea, I will inform the crew that our mission is to sail to Ensenada, Mexico, where the two of us will go ashore to make contact with Mexican operatives sympathetic to the Nazi cause. That would leave the acting XO, *Leutnant* Richter, in command with orders to pick us up in three days. Of course, when we fail to return, Richter would have orders to carry out the rest of the mission."

"Seems plausible. So, tell me, what the hell happened to Grimme?"

Johann looked down for a second. Grimme's death was weighing on him. Goedel was upset that Grimme had been given command over him, but he never wished for anything bad to happen to the man. Now, he was dead.

"I think it was that bastard Lübeck. Who else could it be, Two Pair?"

"Local thugs, or maybe the *Kenpeitai?*"

"I doubt it. We had only been in port for a few hours. Not enough time for Grimme to make enemies here. Remember, the rumor that the crew told us that some of Lübeck's cargo went missing. He must have blamed Grimme and evened the score."

"That makes the most sense." Peter lifted his glass in a toast. "To Grimme. And may that son-of-a-bitch Lübeck get what he deserves."

November 16, 1942 11:15
Penang, Malaysia
U-463

Peter tightened the last fitting on the pipe. It was snug. He stood up and wiped the sweat from his brow. His work was done.

He had spent three days constructing two torpedo tubes near the bow of the boat. With the help of Chief Lange and a few of the men, he had welded two sets of ten steel drums together into two long air-launched torpedo tubes and routed a 25mm pipe from a salvage valve in the bow compartment to the back of the tubes. With the opening of one valve, the torpedoes would fire simultaneously.

Peter did not hear Goedel as he approached.

"Well, Two Pair, how is it going with the tubes?"

"Just finished, Captain. It should work in a pinch."

Peter explained how the steel drums were welded together and contained internal bracing. The bracing would protect the tubes from deformation when the boat submerged. Each tube contained one Type G7a torpedo. Behind the torpedo was a wooden wad, stuffed with wax-coated jute fabric to protect the propeller during launch. Air was connected from the ship's bow compartment salvage valve, which penetrates the hull, to the torpedo tubes. When the valve was opened high pressure air would enter the back of the tube and force the wad forward, driving the torpedoes out of the tube. He had rigged each torpedo to arm once it left the tube. It was crude but functional.

"Jesus, Two Pair, in three days you built functional torpedo tubes?"

"It wasn't difficult. It's been done before."

"Did you tell the men that these tubes are extra torpedo storage, as we discussed?"

"Yes, sir. I explained that we needed the ability to jettison them in an emergency."

"That explains the air piping, eh?"

"I think that they believed me, although Chief Lange looked skeptical."

"Not much we can do about that. So, how do I aim them?"

"Each torpedo tube is canted two and a half degrees from centerline of the boat. The torpedoes have a zero-gyro angle, so you will have to lead the target. I suggest that you fire them with one aimed at the point of impact and the other leading. It will give you about a one-hundred-meter spread at one kilometer."

"I can do that, if needed. They are just a little protection for us. *Kommodore* Abel better believe our story on this. He has asked me to report to him this afternoon."

"Just like we discussed, it is a modification approved by the *Kriegsmarine* for all Type XIV U-boats. It increases our ability to rearm our fleet at sea. We didn't have time to install it in France before we sailed, so we did it here."

"He'd better buy it."

"By the time that he knows any different, we will be long gone, Johann. While you are with *Kommodore* Abel, I am going to make my way to the IJN communications center."

"What for?"

"I have been working on that idea to have the Americans attack Penang. I will let you know how it goes later."

"Carry on, Two Pair. Carry on."

November 16, 1942 13:00
Penang, Malaysia
Monsun Gruppe Headquarters

"*Oberleutnant zur See* Goedel reporting as ordered, *Kommodore*."

"Take a seat, Mr. Goedel. How are the preparations going to ready the *U-463* for the new captain?"

Goedel took a seat before the *Kommodore*'s desk. With no small effort, he forced a smile. "Preparations are proceeding as you commanded, sir. We are in fact a bit ahead of schedule. The boat will be ready for the captain upon his arrival."

"Excellent. I am told by Admiral Dönitz that your captain will be here by the twenty-second. Now, what is the contraption that you are installing on the deck of the *U-463*?"

"It is extra torpedo storage, sir. As you know, the boat only has four torpedoes for resupplying other U-boats. This modification increases that number by 50%. The modification was prescribed by the *Marineamt* just before we left France."

"I did not see any memo on this."

"We were not assigned to the *Monsun Gruppe* at the time. No reason for you to be sent such a modification notification, sir."

"As you know, *Kommodore*, we have plenty of fuel and supplies on our boat, but only four reload torpedoes. Think of the destruction that our fleet can do to the enemy with extra weapons."

"Very well, but I will follow up with command. I should be familiar with this modification."

"Yes, sir. Of course."

"You are dismissed, *Oberleutnant*."

Goedel stood up and saluted Abel. He turned and headed out of the *Kommodore's* office. His mind was whirling. The new captain would be in Penang in less than a week. That made getting the *U-463* underway on the eighteenth a priority. *What was Two Pair's plan for this attack? Could he make this work?*

November 16, 1942 13:20
Penang, Malaysia
Imperial Japanese Naval Communications Center

Peter walked into the IJN naval communications center and reported to the officer in charge. Speaking only in German, Peter recognized immediately that the officer did not speak that language. It took the Japanese officer several minutes to find someone to translate for Peter.

Peter explained that he was the communications officer from the *U-463* and requested that he be given the proper radio frequencies to facilitate operations from the port of Penang. He did not want to let on that he spoke Japanese. He figured it would give him more time to search for the information that he really needed.

It became apparent to Peter that the Japanese had been given orders to cater to their German friends. He was given tea and a tour of the facility. There were dozens of radios, each manned continuously. There were also several phones similarly staffed. Maps and charts were neatly pinned to the walls. One of them showed the location of all of the regional spotters the Japanese had stationed around the area to watch for ship and aircraft movements. Peter made a mental note of station number twenty-one at Kota Baharu on the east coast of Malaysia on the South China Sea. The distance was roughly two hundred kilometers from Penang.

After an hour and a half of being escorted around the facility, Peter left with the information that he needed—radio frequencies, emergency telephone numbers, including the Base Admiral's direct line, and locations of Japanese outposts. As he headed back to the *U-463*, he was convinced that he could provoke an American attack on Penang.

November 16, 1942 19:11
Penang, Malaysia
U-463

Peter walked to the end of Pier 22 with his captain. Alone just after sunset, the two men could talk in private. He explained his plan to Johann on how he was going to facilitate an American attack on Penang. Both men knew the standing order in the *Kriegsmarine* that when in port and under attack the boat must get underway and submerge.

"What are the chances that this plan of yours will work, Two Pair?"

"Pretty good. I'd say 70% in our favor. The Japanese follow protocol and orders. Hierarchy and cultural norms are a big deal with them."

"So, we are set for the eighteenth then?

"I am ready if you are, Johann."

"There is no turning back when we do this. You understand that, right?"

"Johann, I have been looking for this opportunity for years. I am all in."

"Then it is set. I will meet with *Kommodore* Able at 11:00. You launch your attack at exactly 11:35. I will just be getting back to the ship when you do. Got it?"

"11:35, got it."

November 18, 1942 11:32
Penang, Malaysia
U-463

Peter left the engine room and headed forward. He had just directed the starting of both diesel engines for their weekly run in port. They were to be operated for two hours to make them ready when they were needed. Now he had to put the plan in motion.

He sat down in the radio operator's cubicle and flipped on the master power switch. He grabbed the headphones off of the desk and placed them over his ears. As the unit warmed up, he set the main dial to the IJN air defense frequency. He looked at his watch. It was 11:35.

Peter keyed the microphone and, in perfect Japanese, called up the communications headquarters in Penang.

"Air defense control center, this is station number twenty-one. Come in. Over."

"Station twenty-one, air defense. Go ahead."

"Inbound enemy carrier aircraft headed your way!"

"Uh, station number twenty-one, can you repeat that? Can you give me a report on the numbers?"

"Air Defense, station number twenty-one, yes. I see 20 Grumman F4F Wildcats fighters, 30 Grumman TBF Avenger torpedo planes and 35 Douglas SBD Dauntless bombers. Heading 260 degrees, speed three hundred kilometers per hour."

"American planes, heading our way?"

"Yes, looks like a carrier strike-force is attacking Penang!"

Peter didn't wait for an answer. He shut the power off on the radio and headed toward the conning tower hatch. He climbed the ladder and headed down from the conning tower onto the pier. At the head of the pier he walked into the *Monsun Gruppe* supply warehouse. There he approached the sailor manning the desk.

"*Matrosenhauptgefreiter* Lepke is it? I need to use your phone."

The sailor looked disinterested and slid the phone across the desk to Peter. "Help yourself, *Leutnant*."

"*Danke.*"

Peter picked up the handset and dialed the base admiral's direct line to the Air Defense Control Center. After two rings, the officer of the day answered.

"Lieutenant Yamuri, sir. Can I help you, sir?"

"Lieutenant, this is Admiral Skikoku. I have reports of an inbound air attack on our base. What is the status?"

"I just received that report moments ago, sir."

"And you haven't sounded the air raid alarm yet! What is your name again, Lieutenant?"

Two seconds later, Peter could hear the sirens begin to wail all over the island of Penang. He placed the handset back in the cradle and headed back to the *U-463*. As he stepped out into the sunshine, he looked towards his boat. Johann was crossing the bow. *Right on time.*

Peter made his way quickly down the pier and onto the *U-463*. He climbed up to the conning tower and slipped down the hatch into the control room. The space was abuzz with activity. In the center of the room stood Goedel.

"Ah, *Leutnant* Teufel, glad you could join us. Chief Lange, now that Mr. Teufel has arrived, all personnel are accounted for, correct?"

"Aye, aye, sir."

"Good. Now release all lines. Ahead one third on the starboard engine. Take us to sea, Mr. Richter."

With the order, the *U-463* was the first ship to leave Penang.

November 18, 1942 15:17
Penang, Malaysia
U-463

The four *Kriegsmarine* officers and the chief of the boat of the *U-463* sat around the wardroom table. Captain Goedel had called the men together to discuss their mission. Only Goedel and Peter knew the true mission of the boat.

Goedel spoke to the assembled men. "Gentlemen, the air raid on Penang sent us to sea one day early. I met with *Kommordore* Abel shortly before the attack. He informed me that we are to head east on a mission vital to the Reich."

There were smiles all around the table, none brighter than Peter Teufel's.

"Since there are no U-boats to tend to yet in Penang, we are being sent on a secret mission that will help the Reich to defeat our enemies. We are heading for Mexico. Our mission is to meet up with Mexican operatives to establish an intelligence network in the Americas. I will divulge more about our assignment as we head east. For now, radio silence and avoid detection are my standing orders."

The assembled men looked pleased. Such a journey would make them famous in the submarine community.

"I also have some good news for you, *Leutnant* Richter, or should I say, *Oberleutnant* Richter. Your promotion came through channels today."

Hands were shaken and congratulations were given. At the next opportunity, Richter would have to buy a round of drinks for the wardroom officers.

"As you know, gentlemen, we are going to sea short one officer. That means that *Leutnants* Teufel and Spannagel will have to carry more duties and responsibilities. With Richter acting as XO, you will have to be the supply officer in addition to your other duties, Spannagel. Got it?

"Yes, sir."

"And you, Teufel, you will pick up weapons along with your engineering duties. Understood?"

"Yes, Captain."

"Good. Chief, I will need you to fill in as officer of the deck from time to time. Your experience is needed."

"No problem, sir. We have enough qualified watch standers after the last patrol. I will make the watch bill adjustments tonight."

"I will inform you and the crew of our exact mission soon. Now gentlemen, get some sleep. I want a status report from each of you at 06:00. Got it?"

The order was acknowledged in unison by all.

Chapter Twenty-Two: Discovered

November 20, 1942 07:06
Malacca Strait, 17 Kilometers South of Singapore
U-463

Peter stood in the engine room of the *U-463* as the boat cruised on the surface. He was monitoring both diesel engines every fifteen minutes, recording engine RPM, fuel consumption, oil temperatures, and various other parameters. He needed the data to dial in both engines to their most efficient speed. Every hour he requested that the officer of the deck increase speed slightly. Peter figured that in a couple of days he could calculate the optimal surface speed for fuel conservation. That information would be useful to Johann and, ultimately, the entire crew of the submarine.

In the conning tower, Johann Goedel glassed around the boat. To his port side, he could see Malaysia and, to the starboard side, Sumatra. The Straits of Malacca narrowed with each passing kilometer and would do so until they entered the Singapore Strait, rounded the Malay Peninsula, and entered the South China Sea. From there, Goedel planned to sail north of Borneo and skirt south of the Philippines before heading across the Philippine Sea and the Pacific. He was pleased with the progress his ship had made during the night. He would soon dive the boat for its daily trim dive.

Akio Tenaka was manning his post on the island of Pulau Senang, located in the center of the western entrance to the

Singapore Strait. The island contained an Imperial Japanese Navy observation post and the duty of the sailors manning the post was to report on all shipping transiting the strait.

Akio was good at his job. He knew almost every class of Japanese, British, Dutch, and American warship by sight. He rarely had to refer to his ship identification manuals in order to identify a ship. So, he was surprised to see a surface submarine in the strait that he did not recognize immediately.

Using his *Nippon Kogaku* naval binoculars, Akio observed the details of the submarine. It certainly was not a Japanese boat; however, it wasn't like any enemy submarine that he could remember, either. He made careful note of the hull shape, length, conning tower design, and the gun arrangement. He also noted the two strange cylinders towards the bow.

He began to search his ship identification manuals. After twenty minutes of searching through the manuals, he concluded that what he saw was a Type XIV German U-boat.

Akio looked out at the strait again. Far to the east, he could just barely see the submarine. Even with viewing through the binoculars, he could just make out the form of the vessel. Yes, he was positive; it was a Type XIV German U-boat.

Dutifully, in accordance with his training, Akio picked up his radio and reported the passage of the U-boat to the command duty officer in Singapore.

November 19, 1942 14:37
Pearl Harbor, Hawaii
United States Naval Communication Center (HYPO)

First Class Petty Officer Robert "Ping" Pinger sat at his desk, decoding messages in the basement of the Old Administration Building in Pearl Harbor. He had been assigned to this duty station shortly after the Japanese had bombed the harbor in late 1941. He was good at his job, quick with numbers and codes. Most considered him the resident expert on the IJN-25

Japanese Naval Code and everyone at Pearl Harbor knew that he was an expert poker player.

Ping's shift was ending in a couple of hours. During the day he had seen the usual radio traffic pass over his desk: fuel needs in Rabaul, ground force assignments to Mindanao, and the like. All of the message traffic was important but none of it was exciting—until he decoded the message intercepted from Singapore.

"Confirmed. German U-boat transiting the Singapore Strait into the South China Sea."

That was a new one for Ping. In the year that he had been decrypting messages in the Pacific, he had never read, or even heard of, German warship movements in this region. This was something different and important.

Ping took the message and placed it in the daily transfer file to Washington as a *Priority One*. He then called the duty officer, Lieutenant Gerold, and reported the German U-boat sighting. Finally, with Gerold's approval, he made a note on the status board for all of the other decoders to read. It informed them to monitor all traffic for German movements in the Pacific.

November 20, 1942 12:31
Penang, Malaysia
Monsun Gruppe Headquarters

Kommodore Abel received Commander Nori Kamakatsu in his office. He had not been expecting any visitors, but when his counterpart from the IJN came calling, he took the time to meet with him.

"Good afternoon, Commander."

"Good afternoon, *Kommodore* Able. Thank you for taking the time to see me on such short notice."

"I always have time for the IJN. How can I help you, Commander? Have you come to explain the air raid that didn't happen?"

Not wanting to lose face with the Germans, Kamakatsu tried to downplay the event two days before. "That is a very strange thing, a miscommunication of some sort. We received multiple reports of an imminent air attack, but no planes were ever sighted over Penang. Our air defense response was, of course, ready to repel the enemy."

"It was quite a disruption. Following standard protocol, our only unit, the *U-463*, put to sea in order to protect herself. She is a valuable asset."

"Our apologies, sir, but better safe than sorry."

"Well, she will report back today, of that I am sure. No harm done, Commander."

"Sir, let me first say that the IJN is very pleased with our German allies increasing their presence in this theatre. We believe that we have provided the needed support to get your *U-463* refitted in support of our combined war effort."

"The German high command appreciates your effort. As I said, the *U-463* should be returning to port after the air raid alarm shortly." The boat had been out since the "raid" two days earlier.

"That is why I am here, sir. We were under the impression that your U-boat would eventually be operating in the Indian Ocean to supply U-boats as they attack enemy shipping."

"That is correct. In due time."

"Do you have any other U-boats operating in this area?"

"No, the next boat isn't due to arrive for another month. Why?"

"Today, one of our spotters observed a Type XIV German U-boat transiting the Singapore Strait."

"Commander, that is impossible. Our only boat in the area is heading west."

"*Kommodore*, are you sure? The report said that the boat we saw had cylinders mounted on it, consistent with the Type XIV. We only ask that our German friends communicate openly about the locations of your military assets. We want to avoid any friendly fire incidents. Surely, you can understand that?"

"Commander, I can assure you. No U-boat passed by Singapore today. I will radio the *U-463* and verify its location. I will then let you know exactly where the boat is located."

When Kamakatsu left Abel's office, the *Kommodore* called Chief Hoffman and ordered him to go to the IJN headquarters to see which charts Goedel had acquired. He later learned from Hoffman that Goedel had only taken charts of the Pacific.

Eleven hours later, *Kommodore* Abel stood in the *Kriegsmarine* communications center in Penang. Over a dozen messages had been sent to the *U-463*. None of them were returned. His next call was to Dönitz. It was a very unpleasant call.

November 21, 1942 06:30
Near Lorient, France
Villa Kerillon

Admiral Dönitz sat alone in his office, chain-smoking cigarettes. He had spent the night fretting over the information that *Kommodore* Able had sent him. Dönitz knew that this was not a mistake. It was an act of desertion by a *Kriegsmarine* officer. *Oberleutnant zur See* Goedel had stolen the *U-463*.

Dönitz now realized just how much Goedel had been upset by not receiving a command. Succumbing to Party pressure, he had been goaded into promoting Grimme to captain the boat. Sending Goedel to Penang with Grimme had only made sense based on Goedel's experience. Dönitz was now forced to admit he had underestimated Goedel's response to being slighted.

Dönitz could not wait any longer. He knew that he needed to inform *Großadmiral* Raeder. He picked up the secure line to Berlin. When the man in charge of the German Navy answered, Dönitz explained the situation. He informed Raeder that the *U-463* had been stolen by Goedel.

"Karl, you are sure about this? This man Goedel, he has stolen our submarine?"

"I am convinced of it, sir. He has the motive and our information from the East is not suspect."

"Where do you think this man is going?"

"I'm not sure. He could be heading for Pearl Harbor. That would be a nice intelligence coup for the Americans. The possibilities are almost endless."

"I will have to notify the *Führer*. I will recommend to him that we make every effort to stop the *U-463*."

"But we have no assets in the Pacific, Admiral."

"We do not, but our Japanese friends do. I will discuss this with the high command. I will let you know what we will do to remedy this situation."

"Yes, sir."

The two men each hung up the phone. In a dark basement in Berlin, another man, who was listening to the conversation, took off his headphones. The secure line from Dönitz's headquarters was being tapped by the *Abwehr*. Within twenty minutes, Wilhelm Canaris had been informed of the situation in the east.

Canaris was in his office in Berlin when he received the news from his *Abwehr* agent that the *U-463* had apparently been stolen from the *Kriegsmarine*. He sat back in his chair and, for the first time in a long time, laughed out loud.

"Well, I will be damned! Teufel is making a run for it!"

He wanted to help young Teufel and he knew what he could do. He got out from behind his desk, grabbed his coat, and set out to contact his MI6 counterpart. He would share this information with the British and, through them, the Americans. The *U-463* was attempting to bring home an American.

November 21, 1942 19:46
Prinz-Albrecht-Strasse, Berlin
SS Main Security Office

Standartenführer Walter Schellenberg was in a foul mood. This had been a bad week for the SD man. After learning that some of his gold had been stolen on the way to Singapore, he now learned that the first submarine sent to Penang had been stolen, too. The same submarine that had carried his personal wealth to Singapore. And his man, Lübeck, had been along for the ride. The normally reliable Lübeck had somehow been duped on both accounts.

Yet, in spite of Schellenberg's desire to deal harshly with Lübeck, he now needed him more than ever. The only true asset that Germany had in the Far East was awaiting orders in a hotel in Singapore.

Earlier that evening, in a meeting with Himmler, Schellenberg had been ordered to use all available means to stop the *U-463*. Sink or capture the boat, but under no circumstances was the submarine to fall into enemy hands.

Schellenberg got to work crafting a message to Lübeck. In short, he ordered the SD operative to use his connections in the area to find and sink the *U-463*. With Berlin's support, he was to demand any necessary assistance from the Japanese to complete his mission. When the mission was complete, he could return to Germany and all would be forgiven.

November 23, 1942 07:05
Washington, DC
Office of Strategic Services

Bill Donovan sat in a well-appointed conference room receiving his Monday-morning briefing. All of his section heads reported on their developments from over the weekend. He listened to the reports from Europe, South

America, Africa, Asia, and other parts of the world. One item in particular piqued his interest.

"And finally, sir, our dispatch from Pearl Harbor contained a decoded message from the IJN indicating that a German U-boat was sighted heading into the South China Sea."

"Do we have confirmation of that, Mr. Johnson?"

"No, sir. None of our personnel have sighted that submarine. However, that transmission was followed by several more messages to all IJN fleet units to keep an eye out for a German submarine in the Pacific. From what we can gather, the message was requested to be sent out by the *Kriegsmarine*."

"Baily, does your European intelligence have any related material?"

"Not directly, Bill. There was an increase in radio traffic between Berlin and Tokyo, but we do not know the contents of those messages yet."

"Well, circle back around with your sources and see if you can get any information related to this U-boat."

"Yes, sir."

Donovan made his way down the hall to his office. His secretary had a message when he arrived. "Mr. Crouch is waiting for you, sir. He says that it is urgent."

"Thank you, Doris."

Donovan entered his office and closed the door. The man waiting for him, Reginald Crouch, was the head of the MI6 Washington office.

"Reggie, what can I do for you?"

"It seems, old chap, that we have a unique opportunity in the Pacific. One of Jerry's submarines appears to be going rogue."

"This wouldn't happen to be about the German U-boat heading into the South China Sea, would it?"

Crouch looked a bit stunned. He knew that the Americans were fairly new to this intelligence game, yet they appeared to be making progress. "As a matter of fact, old boy, it is. Would you care to swap information?"

"Absolutely, Reggie. You first."

Crouch relayed the information about the *U-463* that Canaris had passed on to his contact in MI6. The German admiral had verified that an American, Peter Teufel, was onboard and trying to return to the United States. Donovan listened until Crouch was finished.

"Tell me, Reggie, can we trust this Canaris?"

"I believe that we can. He is not a Nazi and he is from the old school. A rare German who is honorable."

"Any chance that this is all a ruse to make an attack on our ships in the Pacific?"

"Possible, yes. But not very probable. This type of submarine has no offensive capabilities, no torpedo tubes. It is a supply boat. No, Bill, I think that this submarine is trying to make its way into your backyard. That would be a huge intelligence coup if you could get your hands on that boat."

Donovan pushed the button on his intercom. "Doris?"

"Yes, Mr. Donovan."

"I need to see the President as soon as possible, and I need Admiral King there when I do."

He pulled a notebook out and jotted down a few key points that he wanted to share with Roosevelt and Admiral King. Then he made a note to contact Erik Teufel.

November 23, 1942 11:05
1600 Pennsylvania Avenue, Washington, DC
President Roosevelt's Private Quarters

Bill Donovan sat in the President's private quarters along with Admiral Ernest King, Commander in Chief, United States Fleet and the Chief of Naval Operations. He had spent the last thirty-five minutes explaining the situation with the German submarine in the Pacific. When he finished briefing the president, Donovan put his notebook in his briefcase and waited.

The president put a cigarette into his holder and lit up. He took a deep puff and exhaled. Setting the cigarette down in the ashtray, he turned to Admiral King. "Well now, Ernest, what do you think of this development?"

"To be honest Mr. President, I do not like it one bit. This whole thing smells of suicide attack, if you ask me. I think that we should sortie our available surface forces and sink this boat."

"And you, Bill? What do you think?"

"Well, sir, the admiral has a point. The low-risk option here is to destroy the sub. I, on the other hand, would support a different strategy."

"Go on, Bill."

"You see Mr. President, what the admiral here may not be considering is the intelligence boon that is in the offing here. If we were to get our hands on that U-boat, we would have access to all kinds of German secrets and technology—code books, communications gear, diesel engine technology, and even torpedoes. Our Navy has been unable to solve our poor torpedo performance for some time now. Perhaps a peek at a German warhead would help us resolve that problem."

Admiral King shuddered. He was well aware that Americans in the Pacific were struggling to get good results from their torpedoes, but he did not appreciate this OSS man poking him on it in front of the president.

"Besides, Mr. President," Donovan continued. "There is an American on board. If we could get him home, he alone would be a wealth of intelligence for us."

Admiral King responded quickly. "An American who has been in Germany for what, nine years? He joined the German Navy, for God's sake!"

The president took another drag on his smoke. "Bill, what exactly do you propose that we do in this situation?"

"Sir, I think that we make every effort to capture this boat. I think that we need to let all of our Pacific forces know that they should not fire on this U-boat, and, if the opportunity presents itself, they should provide any assistance that they can."

Franklin Delano Roosevelt leaned back in his chair, smoking. He stared up at the ceiling, deep in thought. After a minute of silence, he leaned forward and looked at Admiral King. "Ernest, in this case the rewards outweigh the risks. We are going to do exactly what Bill says. I want you to issue the orders to the fleet today. Copy me on the communiqué. We are going to do our best to get this boy home."

Chapter Twenty-Three: Foxhunt

November 22, 1942 05:22
Singapore
Hotel Xiang Xu

Klaus Lübeck awoke from his sleep, grabbed the knife under his pillow, and sprang from his bed. There was someone outside his door.

The knock on the door was polite. This took the SD man by surprise. He was expecting an intruder. He switched on the light and opened the door a crack. There he saw a familiar face, one of the *Kenpeitai* that he had met in Singapore.

"I have a delivery for you, *Herr* Lübeck," the man said in broken German.

Lübeck opened the door and grabbed the envelope.

"This came for you twenty minutes ago. It is an urgent communiqué from Berlin."

"Thank you … Satomi isn't it?"

"Yes, sir."

"Come in … I may need your assistance. Stay until I read this."

"I was told to support you any way that I can."

"Very well. Have a seat, Satomi."

Lübeck opened the envelope. He read through the message from Schellenberg. Then he read it again.

"I'll be a son-of-a-bitch! He stole the goddamn boat!"

"What, sir?"

"Uh, nothing. We need to get to your headquarters."

Lübeck dressed quickly and followed Satomi out of the room. As they walked to the *Kenpeitai* headquarters, the SD man ran the meaning of the message through his mind. *The U-463* had been stolen. Berlin believed that it was probably heading to the United States. The Reich wanted it to be stopped at all costs. Lübeck was authorized to use any means possible to prevent the boat from reaching enemy hands. He was ordered to work with the Japanese to stop that boat.

It has to be that little bastard Teufel. The man who had dared him to eat that wretched jellyfish and who spoke a strange dialect of German. He was surely involved. It dawned on Lübeck at that very moment ... *He is not German ... He is an American! That is why I couldn't nail down the man's German dialect ... It was not a true German dialect at all!*

But one man cannot steal a submarine. Clearly, *Oberleutnant* Goedel had to be involved as well. Maybe others were, too. It really didn't matter to Lübeck who was involved. He would sink the boat and dispatch that traitorous spy Teufel to the deep.

Satomi followed Lübeck into the Singapore *Kenpeitai* HQ where they proceeded directly to the station chief's office. The office was empty. They waited until the station chief arrived at six o'clock. The ten-minute wait had been agonizing for Lübeck, but the wait had given him time to rough out his plan.

The station chief did not speak German, so Satomi translated. It took a bit of time to work through the conversation but Lübeck got all of the support that he asked for. With the help of the station chief and a few phone calls, he obtained maps of the Pacific. He also acquired a contact within the IJN and obtained a seat on an air transport to Guam. Additionally, he received assurances that the IJN would support locating and sinking the *U-463*.

By three thirty that afternoon, Lübeck, accompanied by Satomi, was aboard an IJN transport flying from Singapore to Guam. He was still a man who could get things done.

November 22, 1942 19:02
Sulu Sea 53 Kilometers South of Palawan, Philippines
U-463

Johann Goedel sat in the wardroom with the officers of the *U-463*. The submarine had surfaced for the night as they were finishing dinner. Chief Lange had the watch. Goedel wanted to outline the details of their mission. He had informed the crew three days ago that they were heading to the west coast of America, the first U-boat to do so, to operate in the enemy's backyard. Now he needed to give them the rest of the cover story.

"Gentlemen, you should be honored to be on this mission. It is the first of its kind for the *Kriegsmarine*."

The officers of the *U-463* all smiled and nodded.

Richter said, "Captain, it is a very long way to Mexico." It sounded like more of a question than a statement.

"It is indeed, XO, but we have the best boat in the Reich. Are you concerned?"

"Well, sir, yes I am. Do we have the fuel to make this patrol?

"I have the same concern. Two Pair, do we have enough fuel to make it to the American coast and back?"

"I am sure that we do, sir. I have adjusted the fuel injectors on the diesels to lean out the fuel air mixture. They run a little hotter, but we use less fuel. To counteract the excess heat, I have maximized cooling water flow to the oil coolers and the jacket water cooling system. Our current fuel consumption, if we can maintain optimal operation of the diesels, will allow us to make the return voyage with plenty of fuel to spare."

"Captain, what of the American Navy?" Richter asked nervously.

"They will not be expecting us. We have the element of surprise. We will run on the surface as much as possible, but we will run submerged when it is prudent to do so. Secrecy is the key. We must remain undetected."

Goedel went on to explain the details of the mission. The *U-463* was to proceed to the coast of Mexico. It would be there that Goedel and Teufel would go ashore in a life raft to make contact with Nazi sympathizers in Mexico. Their goal would be to establish a network of spies who would relay intelligence to Germany. Such information would be valuable to the Reich. Once that was completed and the shore party had returned, the *U-463* would return to Penang.

"Remember, gentlemen, it is a great honor that awaits us. We will be the first to operate in enemy waters on their Pacific coast. Even the Japanese have not done this. And remember, *Herr* Richter, if we do not return on the third night, you are to complete the mission."

"I cannot, will not, leave you and Teufel, Captain."

"XO, your loyalty is noted. However, I order you to follow the plan. The mission is too important. If we do not return as scheduled, you will complete the orders that *Kommodore* Abel gave us. Understood?"

"Yes, sir."

"Now, we will run on the surface as much as possible, but my standing orders will be followed. If surface contacts are seen, we will dive. If airplanes are sighted, we will dive. Friend or foe, we do not want to be seen. We will maintain radio silence for the entire patrol, no matter the situation. The enemy may send fake *Kriegsmarine* radio messages ordering us to abort our mission. No messages will be sent no matter what we receive. Got it?"

Each officer nodded in agreement.

November 23, 1942 01:20
113 Miles North of New Guinea
USS Wahoo SS-238

Dudley "Mush" Morton was standing on the conning tower of the *USS Wahoo*, smoking a cigar. The Gato-class submarine of the United States Navy was prowling the surface of the Pacific Ocean for enemy ships. Next to him stood Richard "Dick" O'Kane, the officer of the deck. Mush puffed on his cigar as the *Wahoo* patrolled the waters north of New Guinea on its second war patrol.

Mush was a prospective commanding officer learning the ropes under the captain of the *Wahoo*, Commander Marvin G. "Pinky" Kennedy. Mush was in line for a command of his own boat, but he also knew that, for this patrol, he was along for the ride. Submariners had a term for such men, "riders," and Mush was well aware of the pejorative connotation of the term.

The duty radioman requested permission to come up to the conning tower. O'Kane granted permission.

"Mr. O'Kane, we have an urgent flash message from COMSUBPAC."

"Has the captain been notified, Petty Officer Rodgers?"

"First person I notified, sir."

"Very well."

O'Kane took the message from the radioman, ducked down behind the combing, and read it using his flashlight.

"What is it, Dick?" Mush asked the officer of the deck.

"You won't believe it, Mush. Apparently, we are not allowed to shoot German U-boats on this patrol."

"What?"

"It says right here that a German U-boat might transit our patrol area. We are not allowed to torpedo it. In fact, if able, we are ordered to render it any and all assistance. Can you believe that?"

"Never heard of such a thing, Dick."

"What the hell is COMSUBPAC thinking? An enemy submarine is an enemy submarine."

"If it were me, I would fire a spread if I saw the bastard. But orders are orders. In this man's Navy, we follow orders."

Both O'Kane and Morton laughed. It seemed impossible to them that a German U-boat would be prowling the Pacific. They turned their discussion to baseball.

November 24, 1942 10:35
Guam, Micronesia
Imperial Japanese Naval Headquarters

Klaus Lübeck was pleased. He had spent the last few days working with the IJN to schedule airborne and seaborne searches of the likely courses that the *U-463* would take. Using his charts, he had plotted out courses to Hawaii and to major ports in the United States. Estimating the speed of the *U-463*, he was also able to estimate where the boat would be each day, if it was indeed going to America. With the help of Satomi, he was able to establish a wide net hopefully to intercept the renegade submarine.

The Japanese had been very accommodating, more so than the SD man had expected they would be. While there was some military action in the Pacific theatre, there was apparently a relative lull in the war at sea. Both sides were licking their wounds from the recent battle for control of the Solomon Islands. From what Satomi had told him, the *Führer* had personally requested the full assistance of the IJN.

Lübeck had made the orders clear to the Japanese reconnaissance parties. Report any sighting of the U-boat first; attack second. He was sure that he was doing all that he could to find the submarine. Now all he had to do was wait.

November 24, 1942 12:00
Washington, DC
Occidental Grill

Bill Donovan walked the short distance from the White House down Pennsylvania Avenue to the Occidental Grill. He found Erik Teufel waiting at the table for him.

"Your son is an interesting young man, Erik. He has apparently commandeered a German submarine."

"He has *what*?"

"We have had another communication from your friend Canaris. He alerted MI6 that your son took a U-boat from Penang and is at this moment heading east in the Pacific towards the States. The information is substantiated by messages that we have intercepted in Europe and the Asian theatre. He is making a break for home."

"Tell it to me straight, Bill. What are his chances?"

"Well, stealing the boat was quite a feat. That might have been the hardest part. However, the Germans and the Japanese are aware of your son's plans. They are combing the Pacific, searching for the boat. I would say its fifty/fifty ... maybe a little better."

"Tell me that we, that you, are not just sitting by and waiting to see if he makes it!"

"I met with the President a few days ago. We have sent orders to our units in the Pacific to render any assistance that they can. I promise, it is the best that we can do."

Erik Teufel took a slug of the bourbon that had been placed on the table before him. He waved to the waiter for a refill. "Bill, what the hell do I tell Anne?"

"I wouldn't say a word to your wife, Erik. She doesn't have the clearance. More importantly, she would be worried more than she already is about your son. You wouldn't want to get her hopes up if, well ..."

"If he doesn't make it. Is that what you were going to say, Bill?"

"Yes. Listen, Erik. I will keep you informed of any developments that we have, but, unfortunately, this is going to be a long wait. The journey from Penang could take forty days or more and, if they are found, we may never hear anything."

Erik's second drink arrived, and none too soon.

November 27, 1942 16:56
23 Kilometers Northeast of Ulithi Atoll
U-463

Peter Teufel waited at the conning tower hatch as the *U-463* surfaced. He felt the submarine broach and settle, pushed along by the electric motors. He spun the handle on the hatch and felt the dank air rush past him as the boat's pressure equalized. He climbed up onto the conning tower and took his officer of the deck position for surface operations. Behind him, the lookouts climbed the ladder and took to their watch stations, scanning the skies and the sea for any contacts.

The sun was low in the western sky behind them, but sunset was nearly an hour away. Goedel had ordered surfacing in order to make up some distance. The *U-463* was behind his schedule.

Peter looked around the horizon, taking his time to make a 360 degree circle. The weather was sunny with scattered clouds. The wind was quartering into the boat. He saw no surface contacts. He called up to the lookouts. They, too, reported no air or sea contacts.

Peter ordered the diesels started. In minutes the *U-463* was knifing through the waves at 14.5 knots.

Peter called down to the control room, "Maintain course and speed."

The order was confirmed by the control room crew. When he heard the report, Peter relaxed a bit. Lighting a cigarette, he looked out at the vastness of the Pacific Ocean. He was happy to be on his way home. In just a few weeks, he figured, he would be back in the States. He dreamed of seeing his parents and of getting in touch with Marilyn.

"Plane off the aft port quarter, sir! It is on an attack run!"

"ALARM! Dive, Dive, Dive!" Peter shouted down to the control room.

The lookouts scrambled down from their positions and slid down the hatch as Peter secured his watch station. He

ensured that each man was below before he, too, descended
into the submerging submarine. He took one quick look up
at the plane. He could see the two bombs falling as the plane
pulled out of its dive. The red dots on the wings were clearly
visible. The bombs exploded close aboard with a thunder-
ing "WHAM!"

"Take her to 150 meters, Chief!" Peter said as he secured
the conning tower hatch.

Goedel burst into the control room as the boat was heading to the ordered depth.

"What do we have, Two Pair?"

"A plane, Captain. Japanese, a *Kawanishi* H8K seaplane I
think, sir. She came out of the clouds."

"Alright." Goedel picked up the microphone to the boat's
main communication system. "XO, damage report."

Richter replied almost immediately. "No damage, sir. We
shook a bit; the kitchen is a mess but we are fine."

"Very well."

Goedel hung up the microphone and gave his orders.

"It seems that our Japanese friends have mistaken us for
an enemy submarine. It is an unfortunate friendly fire incident.
I will report this attack upon our return to Penang. Officer of
the deck maintain your depth and heading. Call me at thirty minutes passed sunset. We will bring the boat to periscope
depth. I want to be here when we surface."

"Aye, Captain," Peter responded.

Goedel walked back to his state room. He had a lot on his
mind. Had the Japanese mistaken the *U-463* for an enemy submarine, or were they attacking the U-boat on purpose? He was
not sure, but he assumed the worst. The Reich and the Japanese
must have figured out by now that the boat was on the run.

November 24, 1942 19:21
Guam, Micronesia
Imperial Japanese Navy Officers' Club

Klaus Lübeck was sitting by himself at a table in the Officers' Club. He was drinking a beer, an Oriental beer, that was not to his taste. *Too watery.* He lifted his fork and pushed the food around on his plate. It, too, was not to his liking. He didn't think that he would ever get used to Oriental cuisine, but he had to eat something. He took a bite and forced it down.

Satomi burst into the club and rushed to Lübeck's table. "We may have sighted the boat, sir!"

"Let's go." Lübeck slammed his fork onto the table and rushed out after Satomi.

Two minutes later, Lübeck was poring over charts in the IJN headquarters. After obtaining the location of the attack from Satomi, he drew a line on the chart from Ulithi Atoll to Hawaii. He figured out about where the *U-463* should be by dawn. He drew a circle on the chart southeast of Guam.

"Satomi, I need to speak to the duty officer and then the base commander. Let's go! *Schnell.*"

Lübeck explained to the duty officer that he wanted to speak to the pilot of the patrol plane when he landed. He also wanted a list of available surface units in the area that he expected the *U-463* to transit. Satomi assured Lübeck that the duty officer understood.

Then the two men left in search of the base commander. Twenty minutes later, Lübeck stood up and shook the commander's hand. Lübeck was now in charge of the attack on the *U-463*. All available Japanese resources would be under the *Hauptsturmführer's* tactical command.

Chapter Twenty-Four: Runaway

November 25, 1942 05:43
537 Kilometers Southeast of Guam
Aichi E13A1b-S Night-Flying Float Plane

Klaus Lübeck sat in the seat behind the pilot of the *Aichi* E13A1b-S float plane that had taken off in the dark from Guam. Satomi sat in the tail gunner's seat. On the horizon, the German could see the first signs of the dawn creeping over the Pacific. The plane was flying to a rendezvous with the *Yugomo* Class Destroyer, *Takanami*. The captain of the *Takanami* had been ordered to proceed north at top speed from its location west of Truk. It was the closest ship available near the most probable track of the *U-463*.

The pilot reduced the throttles and put the nose of the aircraft down and the plane descended towards the sea. Lübeck looked around the head of the pilot but could not see a ship in front of them. He had to trust the pilot as he could not readily communicate with the man.

The pilot banked the single engine aircraft to put the nose into the wind. It was then that Lübeck could make out the shape of a destroyer. The pilot set the plane down on the water. The sponsons bounced once off of the surface and settled back down gently. The float plane slowed quickly.

The pilot maneuvered the plane to about one hundred meters from the destroyer, which already had a small motorized skiff on the water. The skiff headed to the plane and with little difficulty, Lübeck and his interpreter scrambled into the boat. They were on the deck of the destroyer four minutes later.

Lübeck was escorted to the wheelhouse of the destroyer where he was greeted by Lieutenant Commander Seishi Iwaishi, the captain of the *Takanami*. Lübeck saluted the captain and, through Satomi, paid his respects to the Japanese officer.

"Good morning, Captain. The Reich greatly appreciates your assistance in this matter."

"I am at your disposal, as is the *Takanami*. I have received my orders and we are at your service."

Lübeck pulled his marked-up chart from his pocket. He placed it on a table and explained to Iwaishi where and when he expected the *U-463* to be. As he was explaining his plan, he was interrupted by the captain.

"Two hours ago, as we were steaming to the rendezvous point, we picked up a surface contact on radar. Here—" Iwaishi pointed to the chart. "By the signal, the radar operator thought that it might be a submarine. We couldn't investigate as we were heading to pick you up."

Lübeck asked the captain to mark exactly on the chart where the contact was picked up by radar. Iwaishi made a mark on the map. The German measured the distance from where the *U-463* had been attacked last evening to where the *Takanami* had made radar contact. The track, when he extended it, was close to the Hawaiian Islands.

Then Lübeck calculated the distance between the two points on the chart. By his estimation, it was possible for the submarine to travel that far overnight. It had to be the U-boat!

Under Lübeck's direction, the captain ordered the *Takanami* to sail at top speed to the calculated location of the submarine, based on the radar contact. Once they reached that location, they were to follow the estimated track of the U-boat at slow speed, monitoring the sonar. The boat would surely dive at dawn and the destroyer would listen for the telltale sounds of a submarine. The SD officer also sent a message back to Guam to focus additional aerial searches over the projected location of the *U-463*.

November 25, 1942 06:17
Southeast of Guam
U-463

Oberleutnant zur See Johann Goedel had spent most of the night on the conning tower with the officer of the deck. The bombing the boat had received had shaken him a bit. He did not let it show, but he was on tenterhooks throughout the night. Now he stood in the control room, the boat having submerged moments ago. His plan was to spend the day submerged and hidden from prying eyes.

"Officer of the deck make your depth two hundred meters. Continue on course."

"Make depth two hundred meters, continue on course, aye, captain," Chief Lange repeated.

Goedel made a tour of the boat. He smiled as he entered each compartment, making small talk with each group of men that he passed. He assured them all that they were destined to make the Reich proud of this patrol. When his tour was complete, he entered his state room and climbed into his rack.

Sleep, though needed, would not come to Johann. His mind was alive with recent events and what they might mean for the *U-463*. The bombing most likely meant that the Japanese knew generally where his boat was. That also meant that the Germans knew of the *U-463*'s plan and had ordered the Japanese to intervene. If that was true, he needed to get the boat as far east as fast as he could. Should he have stayed on the surface? Submerged, the boat could not travel very far. Powered by the diesels, he could put a lot of distance between his boat and the attack site. So many decisions. Being a captain was more difficult than he thought.

Goedel awoke shortly after 13:00. He climbed up out of his rack and found a cup of coffee in the wardroom. As he poured his second cup, Peter entered.

"Good afternoon, Captain."

"Good day to you, Two Pair. Everything going well?"

"Yes, sir, I just got off of watch. Nothing to report. All is good."

"We need to make some distance today, Two Pair. I don't think that attack yesterday was a fluke. Call it a hunch, but I think that they were attacking us, not just a random submarine."

"Well, when we surface tonight, we can crank up the diesels to fourteen or fifteen knots or so. That would help, right?"

"I am considering it now. Five extra hours at full speed would get us that much closer to Mexico."

Peter grabbed a sandwich and a cup of coffee. He did not respond to Johann's statement. His body language showed how he felt about the idea and the captain picked up on it.

"*Ach*, Two Pair, we will stay submerged ... for now."

November 25, 1942 14:06
Southeast of Guam
IJN Destroyer Takanami

Lübeck stood on the bridge of the destroyer as it plowed through the seas at slow speed. They were searching for the U-463 with sonar sweeps. He assumed that the boat was submerged. In order to optimize the destroyer's sonar capability, Captain Iwaishi had slowed the ship. It was now a waiting game. The boat would be found with sonar or it would be found with radar when it surfaced at sunset. Patience was the order of the day.

On the horizon, the German could see that some weather was moving in. Clouds were forming in the distance and the seas were rising as the breeze picked up. He left the bridge and entered the wheelhouse.

"Captain, any reports from our aerial searches?"

Satomi relayed the message and the captain shook his head.

"He is out there, Captain. I can feel it. We will get him."

November 25, 1942 16:21
Southeast of Guam
U-463

Captain Goedel stepped into the control room. He couldn't contain himself anymore. Something was driving him to get further away. He wanted to get on the surface and run.

Goedel approached *Leutnant* Spannagel, who had the watch.

"Officer of the deck, any contacts on sonar?"

"No, sir. None have been reported all day."

"Very well. Take us to periscope depth, *Leutnant*."

"Aye, sir."

As the *U-463* leveled off at fifteen meters and slowly adjusted to periscope depth, Goedel ordered the periscope to be raised. As the scope came up, he latched onto the handles and placed his eyes against the lenses. He made a quick 360 degree scan and then he made the same observation at a much slower rate. Goedel saw nothing but open sea.

"Officer of the deck, prepare to surface."

Two minutes later, Spannagel opened the conning tower hatch. He climbed up the ladder followed by the lookouts and finally, the captain. Their initial scan of the sea showed no surface craft or airplanes. The diesels were placed online and full speed was ordered.

November 25, 1942 16:31
Southeast of Guam
IJN Destroyer Takanami

Lübeck was alerted by a message communicated to the wheelhouse. He didn't understand what was said, but by the reaction of the watch standers, it was important. He looked at Satomi, who was at his side.

"Radar contact!"

The SD man stepped forward to the window. He scanned the seas in front of the destroyer, but he did not see any submarine. He quickly turned to Satomi and asked, "What's going on?"

"We have a surface radar contact at twenty-two kilometers. The signal is weak, but they believe that it is a small vessel of some kind."

"Small, like a submarine, Satomi?"

"Yes, sir."

Just then Captain Iwaishi made his way on to the bridge. He spoke to the officer of the deck and then checked with the navigator in the wheelhouse. Then he approached Lübeck and Satomi.

"We believe that your submarine has surfaced, *Herr* Lübeck."

"Can we shoot him from here with the 127mm guns?"

"No, they are not in range. The maximum range is eighteen kilometers. I have ordered full speed. When we get to within about twelve kilometers, we will open fire."

"We should shoot when they are in range!"

"Our odds of a hit on such a target would be minimal. We will close the distance before we fire. They should not be able to see us at that distance. They will surely dive when we do open fire and we will rush in with depth charges. Trust me. I know what I am doing."

Lübeck desperately wanted to sink the *U-463* but he knew that a patient hunter was a more effective hunter. He nodded his approval. "How long until we are in range?"

"Given our speed and the targets speed, about twenty minutes."

November 25, 1942 16:47
Southeast of Guam
USS Wahoo SS-238

Dick O'Kane was standing his submerged watch on the *Wahoo*. He was on duty in the control room when his sonar operator called him.

"Con, Sonar... contact bearing 355 degrees, heading 070 degrees. Heavy screws, sir. Distance ... about 8,500 yards, sir."

"Sonar, Con, aye," O'Kane responded. He turned to the diving officer. "Bring us to periscope depth, Chief. Petty Officer Kling, get the captain."

The *Wahoo* rose to the ordered depth and, when she did, O'Kane was glued to the periscope. He searched the bearing of the contact but initially saw nothing. On his second try, he saw it. It looked like a surfaced submarine.

"Down scope, helm. Come to 040 degrees true. All ahead full."

Moments later, Captain Kennedy entered the control room followed by Mush Morton.

"What do we have, Dick?" the captain asked.

"It's a surfaced submarine, sir, heading 070 degrees at about fifteen knots Sir. She is about 8,000 yards, sir. I am closing, but we will not reach a firing solution submerged like this. Do you want me to surface and make an end around on her, Captain?"

Kennedy looked at the clock in the control room. It was still daylight. He was a cautious man.

"No, Dick. Keep closing. She may change course and we will get a shot at her then. I will get some sleep. Let me know if conditions change."

"Aye, aye, sir." But it was obvious to all in the control room that O'Kane was not happy with the order. Mush caught Dick's eye and shrugged. Both men would have given chase if they were in command.

"Con, Sonar, new contact, sir. Bearing 280 degrees, heading 070 degrees, speed about thirty knots, sir. He is on the same track as our first contact, sir."

Kennedy paused before leaving the control room. He turned to observe the new situation.

"Up scope." O'Kane rode the scope up out of the well and swung it to the new contact's bearing.

"Destroyer, making thirty knots. Japanese for sure, *Yugumo* class." O'Kane swung the scope back to the first contact. The *Wahoo* was a bit closer now.

"Contact number one is a submarine but it's not Japanese and it is not one of ours. I am not sure what the hell it is? We can't catch her, but the destroyer, we have a chance."

"Let me have a look, Dick," the captain said.

Kennedy took a look through the scope. He saw the submarine. It was unlike any that he had seen before, but it didn't matter. The sub was never going to be in range. He then turned his attention to the destroyer. He observed it for several seconds. It was Japanese alright. The *Wahoo* had a chance of getting into a firing position, but he didn't want to tangle with a destroyer. Then he ordered the periscope to be lowered.

"Dick, slow to ahead one-third. Resume our patrol. Monitor the contacts, but we will not engage."

"Aye aye, sir."

The captain left the control room, leaving O'Kane and Mush to ponder the situation. The two officers found a quiet corner of the control room to discuss what the *Wahoo* should do.

"Goddamn it, Mush, we should be closing in for an attack. What the hell is Kennedy thinking?"

"He is being cautious, Dick. A destroyer is a formidable opponent."

"Come on Mush. What would you do?"

"I think that I would do what you would do. I would press home an attack. But the thing is, we have our orders."

"When the sun sets, we will surface. We could still try an end around."

"We would never catch that destroyer at her speed, unless she slows down. But that submarine, well, we could catch her."

"That submarine was odd. It was no Japanese boat nor one of ours. I got a good look at it. It was something different. I've never seen one like it."

"Do you think it was that German boat that we were notified about?"

"It could be. I'm telling you, Mush, it was like nothing that I have ever seen."

"We were ordered to render any and all assistance to that boat. As I see the situation, that destroyer was chasing the U-boat, not escorting it. We need to get on the surface and catch up to them. Orders are orders."

"What about the captain?"

"I'll go talk to him. Maybe I can get him to at least trail these two contacts to get a better picture of the tactical situation. It's worth a shot."

Twenty minutes later, the *Wahoo* was on the surface on four engines, making 21.5 knots towards the estimated position of the contacts.

November 25, 1942 17:14
Southeast of Guam
U-463

Leutnant Spannagel heard the lookout call down to him. "Destroyer, sir!"

The officer of the deck looked directly aft of the *U-463* and on the horizon he could see a destroyer closing the distance to the U-boat at high speed.

"Ahead flank. Captain to the Conning Tower."

Seconds later, Goedel popped up through the hatch.

"What do we have, *Leutnant*?" Goedel asked as he raised a pair of binoculars to his face.

"Destroyer, sir, directly aft. She is making about twenty-eight, maybe thirty knots. Fourteen kilometers, sir."

Goedel looked at the destroyer. She was gaining on them at full speed. It was only a matter of time before she would get into gun range. He quickly scanned around the boat. The sun was starting to dip down to the horizon. In front of the *U-463* was a squall line. If they could make it into the storm, they had a chance to stay on the surface and get away.

Goedel picked up the intercom and called for *Leutnant* Teufel. In seconds, Peter stuck his head up through the hatch. "Yes, Captain?"

"Two Pair, get to the engine room and give me everything that the diesels have. Disable the overloads. I need as much speed as you can give me."

"Yes, sir."

Peter ran the diesels up to maximum RPM and disabled the overloads. He monitored all of the relevant parameters on the two machines and, once he was satisfied that the diesels could take the punishment, he increased the speed even more. When he was finished with his adjustments, the *U-463* was skimming along the surface at 16.2 knots.

November 25, 1942 17:31
Southeast of Guam
IJN Destroyer Takanami

Lübeck was trying to be patient. He wanted to sink the U-boat and he wanted to do it now. He paced in the wheelhouse as the chase unfolded before his eyes. Finally, he couldn't take it anymore.

"Captain Iwaishi, shouldn't we open fire?"

"Just a few more minutes."

"We are losing light, sir. If we are in range, we should attack."

"Ready all gun mounts. Ready all depth charges. On my command, gunners ... Fire!"

Lübeck thought to himself, *It's about goddamn time.*

On Iwaishi's orders, the forward twin 127 millimeter gun mounts opened fire. The projectiles shot from the cannons and arced out over the Pacific towards the racing submarine.

November 25, 1942 17:32
Southeast of Guam
U-463

"She is firing at us, Captain!"

Goedel had seen the flash of the guns. Moments later, two explosions occurred 150 meters aft of the *U-463*. He knew that the Japanese would correct their aim. He looked ahead of the *U-463* at the squall line. It was close, but not close enough. They were not going to make it into the relative safety of the rainstorm. He had to pull the plug.

"ALARM! Dive! Dive! Dive! Take me to periscope depth, NOW!"

The men on the conning tower scrambled down the hatch, urged on by a second salvo from the destroyer. The two rounds landed fifty meters in front of the *U-463*. Goedel was the last to leave the bridge and he pulled the hatch closed behind him.

As he climbed down into the control room, Goedel began issuing orders. "Ahead one third. Starboard 30 degrees rudder. Bring her to course 165 degrees."

The *U-463* leveled off at periscope depth. She now cruised slowly ahead on her electric motors.

"Up scope."

Goedel rode the periscope up with his eyes affixed to the viewer. In the fading light, he could see the destroyer rapidly closing on their position. He had hoped to bring his makeshift torpedo launcher into a firing position, but was there time?

"Bearing 250 degrees, range six kilometers, angle on the bow 0 degrees."

Goedel looked around the control room. He could see that the men were nervous. Adrenaline was running high in each man. He realized then that he was the captain of a U-boat under attack and he had to set the example. "Emergency deep. Take her down to two hundred meters. Helm, rudder hard to starboard. Bring her to course 210 degrees."

Goedel watched as the boat descended into the deep. In his mind he was calculating how long it would take for the destroyer to close the distance. *Could he get deep enough if they attacked?*

It would be close.

Chapter Twenty-Five: Plunge

November 25, 1942 17:35
Southeast of Guam
IJN Destroyer Takanami

"Depth charges manned and ready, Captain."

Iwaishi nodded his approval and barked his orders. "Ahead two thirds. Sonar, let me know when you acquire the submarine. We will make our first pass over their last position."

Lübeck stood silently in the back of the wheelhouse. His mind was focused on the attack. He wanted desperately to sink the *U-463*. He had traveled halfway around the world and now he was zeroing in on his quarry. This kill would set him right with Schellenberg.

"On my command, launch depth charges ... fire!"

On the stern of the *Takanami*, barrel-shaped depth charges rolled off of the racks in pairs. At each six-second interval, another pair would drop. The destroyer deployed ten depth charges in that manner.

Lübeck smiled as the first set of charges exploded.

November 25, 1942 17:36
Southeast of Guam
U-463

"Con, Sonar. They are dropping depth charges, sir!" Sonar, Con... very well," Goedel responded. This was the time that all submariners dreaded. Waiting for depth charges to explode, not knowing if one will end your life, was a dreadful experience. Goedel waited.

The thunder came moments later. "Klick…WHAM! Klick…WHAM!" The boat shook from stem to stern. The charges were close, but not that close.

"Passing 180 meters, Captain."

"Level off at two hundred meters and continue on course. Be ready to turn when I say."

"Klick…WHAM! Klick…WHAM!..Kl-WHAM, WHAM!"

These were very close and Goedel knew it. The boat shook violently and rolled to starboard about 15 degrees before righting itself. "Damage report."

Peter picked up the microphone in the engine room. "Auxiliary sea water leak and an oil leak on diesel number two, Captain. We are taking on water."

"How bad is it, Two Pair? Can the pumps keep up with it?"

"For now, I think so, Captain. Let me take a closer look and I will get back to you."

"Depth 210 meters, sir and we are still headed down. I can't control the depth."

"Ahead two-thirds. Up 10 degrees on the planes. Get me back to two hundred meters, Richter."

"Yes, sir. Trying, sir."

Peter surveilled the damage. There was a crack in the auxiliary sea water pipe and a flanged joint on the lube oil system was separated on the number two diesel. Outboard of the diesel, he could see that the pressure hull was dished in from the force of the explosion. Another foot or two and the boat would have been holed. He picked up the microphone. "Control, engine room. No status changes. We can keep up with the pumps, but it is close."

"Engine room, Control. Understood," Goedel replied.

"We leveled off at 230 meters, Captain. We are fighting depth control with the water that we are taking on aft."

Goedel acknowledged the report. He ran through the situation in his mind. They were near test depth. They needed speed to keep the boat steady. The drain pump was running constantly to pump out the engine room. All of this meant noise—noise that the destroyer would be listening for.

"Con, Sonar. She is making another run at us, sir."

"Helm, hard to port, come to 040 degrees."

"Con, Sonar. Depth charges, sir."

Goedel looked around the control room. The men were all at their duty stations. Sweat was dripping off of every man. They were in a pickle, no doubt about it. He prayed as he waited for the inevitable explosions. Maybe they wouldn't be close.

"K-WHAM! K-WHAM, K-WHAM, WHAM!!!"

Again, the *U-463* shook violently. Lightbulbs burst and dust filled the air. The destroyer had them zeroed.

In the engine room, Peter had been knocked to the floor. He raised himself up and saw that the auxiliary sea water pipe had sheared. Sea water was now gushing into the boat. He scrambled to the microphone.

"Flooding in the engine room!"

Goedel had had only seconds to make the decision. He trusted Two Pair's assessment.

"Emergency blow. Take her up, Mr. Richter, now! We will fight it out on the surface," Goedel said with more confidence than he felt. He again picked up the microphone and announced to the ship. "Ready for surface action. Gun crews, report to the control room. Engine room, ready number one diesel. Give me top speed when we surface."

The diving officer pulled down on the "chicken switches," forcing compressed air into the ballast tanks. The *U-463* began to slowly rise from the depths. Goedel, along with the crew, knew that they were committed to a surface battle where they would be outgunned. They had a chance, but it was a long shot.

November 25, 1942 17:53
Southeast of Guam
IJN Destroyer Takanami

The sun had just set over the horizon as the *Takanami* finished another depth charge run. Lübeck was practically salivating at the scene before him. Sonar had a solid contact on the U-boat and Iwaishi was pressing home the attack. It was only a matter of time. He was sure of it. He was a man who got things done.

"Captain, Sonar. The contact is surfacing. She is blowing her ballast tanks."

Lübeck smiled broadly. Now was the time. He would get his revenge on that bastard Teufel. The submarine would only surface if it were in trouble and, once she did, she would be an easy target. She would be sunk within minutes ... *or captured*?

Lübeck spoke to Iwaishi through Satomi.

"Captain, if the boat is coming to the surface, we can force it to surrender. We can capture the boat and return it to the Reich."

"If she fights, if she shoots at us, I will return fire. I will not risk my ship when the orders are to stop the U-boat at all costs."

"The *U-463* has no torpedoes, just anti-aircraft guns. She is no match for us. Stay abeam of her and rake her gunners and conning tower with machine gun fire. We can board the son-of-a-bitch!"

Iwaishi hesitated.

"Submarine on the surface to port, Captain!"

Both Iwaishi and Lübeck saw the submarine surface on the port side at about fifteen kilometers. The bow of the boat was quartering away from the destroyer.

"Let me remind you, Captain, that I am in tactical command here. Order your men to shoot them with machine guns. No cannon fire. I want that boat!"

November 25, 1942 17:56
Southeast of Guam
U-463

"All ahead flank. Hard to port. Give me one shot at that bastard. Gun crews on deck, no lookouts. Mr. Teufel, direct fire on that destroyer when ready."

Goedel's orders were executed as he headed up to the conning tower hatch. He opened the hatch and burst onto the conning tower deck, followed by the gun crews and the weapons officer, *Leutnant* Teufel. There he could see the destroyer directly on the port beam. He had to get the boat turned for one shot with the make-shift torpedo launchers. That was really his only hope. Diesel number one roared to life and the boat slowly began to turn. Goedel watched as the destroyer countered his move. The Japanese ship was cutting off his turn.

Just then, a hail of machine gun fire swept across the conning tower. Goedel ducked behind the combing and yelled down the hatch. "Hard to starboard. Bring her around, goddamn it! Gun crews, fire on the bridge of that destroyer."

He planned to reverse his course and turn inside the destroyer, hoping to get off a torpedo shot. It was there only hope.

Peter took his position near the forward 37mm gun. He directed the crew to fire on the bridge of the destroyer. Just as the *U-463* opened fire, the boat was raked with a hail of small arms projectiles. The barrage was intense. Peter watched in disbelief as one of the gun crew fell after being shot in the head. It seemed to happen in slow motion.

Something stung Peters left shoulder with enough force to spin him around. He dropped to the deck and saw that blood was dripping from his shoulder onto the deck. *I think that I have been shot.*

November 25, 1942 17:58
Southeast of Guam
IJN Destroyer Takanami

Lübeck saw what he had prayed that he would see. In the failing light of dusk on the Pacific, he could make out the submarine. It was without a doubt the *U-463*. He had found his prize.

The German watched as the destroyer laid down a hail of small arms fire onto the deck of the submarine. He watched as two of the U-boat's gun crew fell under the barrage. The others tried in vain to bring the guns to bear but they were pinned down by the intense Japanese fire.

"Captain, cease fire and stop the ship. Put me on speaker. I will order them to surrender."

Iwaishi ordered his guns to cease fire and all stop on the main engines. The destroyer immediately began to slow down.

November 25, 1942 17:59
Southeast of Guam
U-463

Goedel prayed that they could bring the torpedoes into a firing position, but, on one engine, the boat was turning slowly. He was outmatched by the maneuverable destroyer. He looked down to the deck and saw that his gun crew was in disarray. Two men were down and the others were struggling to return fire as bullets whizzed by them.

Then, just as quickly as the shooting began, it stopped. All Goedel could hear was the shouting of the gun crew on deck. Then he heard a familiar voice:

"*U-463*, this is *Hauptsturmführer* Lübeck. I order you to surrender. Raise a white flag or you will be sunk."

Lübeck? How the hell did that asshole get out here?

No matter. Goedel looked around and saw that the destroyer was slowing down. His situation appeared hopeless.

Should he fight it out? If his torpedoes missed, it would be a battle that he couldn't win. The lives of fifty sailors were in his hands. He couldn't be the cause of the deaths of these innocent men. They had one chance, but he needed more time to swing the boat around. *Should I fight or should I surrender?*

"You have one minute to comply. Surrender your ship or be fired upon."

Goedel called for a white sheet and a megaphone to be brought to the conning tower.

November 25, 1942 17:59
Southeast of Guam
USS Wahoo SS-238

Captain Kennedy looked through the periscope at the situation on the surface. He had enough light to make out a Japanese destroyer firing on a surfaced submarine. He took a long look at the sub.

"By God, it is a German U-boat."

"Captain, our orders were clear. We are to render aid to that U-boat," said O'Kane.

Kennedy swung the scope over to the destroyer.

"We will shoot a spread of three. Bearing 140 degrees, range 5,900 yards, angle on the bow port 70 degrees. Do we have a firing solution?"

"Yes, Captain, but we are still out of range."

"Engine room, control, ahead flank. We have to close the distance. We will fire at three thousand yards. Down scope."

November 25, 1942 17:59
Southeast of Guam
U-463

Goedel knew that he had to act quickly. He called down to the control room.

"Five degrees to port, ahead one third, come to heading 255 degrees. Get me pointed at that destroyer. "

The *U-463* slowed to a crawl and slowly began turning towards the destroyer. Goedel just needed a little time to turn the boat and he needed Peter to man the torpedo launching valve.

"Gun crew below decks. Two Pair, get to the launching valve. Be ready when I give the command to fire."

The gun crews scrambled for the hatch.

Peter picked himself up off of the deck. Oddly, his shoulder did not hurt. He climbed up to the conning tower. "Remember, Johann, fire one at the target and lead it with the second one. I will be on the phones at the valve."

"It better fucking work, Two Pair, or we are done."

"It will work. But we need them aimed correctly."

Peter headed down the hatch. As he entered the control room, a white sheet and a megaphone were passed up to Goedel. Peter raced forward through the boat into the bow compartment. He grabbed a headset and put it on then reached his right hand up and held onto the salvage valve. He was confident that the makeshift torpedo launcher would work. As he waited, his left shoulder began to throb with pain. He could hear Goedel over the phones.

"Be ready, Two Pair."

"Awaiting your orders, Captain."

November 25, 1942 18:00
Southeast of Guam
IJN Destroyer Takanami

Lübeck waited. There was no signal from the *U-463*. *What were they waiting for?*

"Captain, fire a warning salvo over his bow."

Seconds later, the 127mm guns roared to life. Lübeck watched as two explosions blasted plumes of water into the air two hundred meters off of the submarine's bow. Moments later, he recognized Goedel's voice echoing across the water.

"*Hauptsturmführer* Lübeck, this is *Oberleutnant zur See* Goedel. We are turning to come alongside your ship. We request no more shooting. We expect that you will board our ship. We have injured men."

Lübeck beamed with joy. He saw a white sheet hanging from the embattled conning tower. He now had that little bastard Teufel and his traitorous captain right where he wanted them. Capturing the *U-463* would make things right with Schellenberg and, more importantly, he could settle his score with Teufel.

"Satomi, tell Captain Iwaishi to prepare a boarding party. Ten men, armed. I will lead them. Let the submarine come alongside. We have captured the traitors. I want that son of a bitch, Teufel, taken alive."

Lübeck smiled as he picked up the microphone for the ship's speaker. "Captain, pull your boat alongside and prepare to be boarded."

November 25, 1942 18:00
Southeast of Guam
U-463

Goedel watched as the destroyer sat motionless in the water. He estimated that the distance was about eight hundred meters. The Japanese ship was nearly broadside to the submarine. He just needed to turn the *U-463* a few more degrees. Goedel called down to the control room. "Keep bringing her about, Mr. Richter, slowly."

The *U-463* was pointed at the destroyer. Goedel knew that he needed a couple of more degrees in order to point the starboard torpedo at the ship, with the port torpedo leading it by five degrees. The moments passed like hours. Finally, he picked up the phone.

"Fire, Two Pair. Fire! Shoot him now!"

Peter turned the handle on the ball valve ninety degrees to open it. He heard the air rushing through the pipe and up to the fabricated torpedo tubes. He prayed that it would work.

In the conning tower, Goedel watched as the lids on the front of the torpedo tubes popped off and banged onto the deck. He waited but nothing happened. Had it failed? Why is it not—

Suddenly both torpedoes shot out of the tubes. The starboard torpedo hit the water and began its run at the destroyer. The port torpedo hung up a bit as it exited the tube. It did not launch with the same force. As it dropped from the tube, its propeller banged against the hull, sending the torpedo twenty degrees off track.

Goedel looked at the errant torpedo, then switched his focus back to the weapon heading directly at the destroyer. The run time would be short, about twenty-five seconds. *Could the destroyer evade the hit by going to ahead flank?*

Goedel wasn't sure.

November 25, 1942 18:00
Southeast of Guam
USS Wahoo SS-238

Captain Kennedy did not like the idea of taking on a destroyer, yet he had his orders. He was to help the U-boat at all costs and that still did not sit well with him.

"Captain, we should surface and pull the attention away from the U-boat. Submerged like we are, we will never get into firing range."

"Mr. O'Kane, we will maintain depth course and speed."

"But, Captain?"

"Enough, mister. Your recommendation is noted. Up periscope."

Kennedy rode the scope up as it broke the surface. He was still out of range. He could see that the U-boat had a white flag hanging from the conning tower. Apparently, the fight was over.

"All stop. The boat has surrendered. Let's see what unfolds."

November 25, 1942 18:01
Southeast of Guam
IJN Destroyer Takanami

Standing next to Captain Iwaishi, Lübeck smiled as he checked his pistol. The magazine was full and a round was in the chamber. He would be prepared, but he did not plan on using his weapon. He wanted to get his bare hands on Teufel and make him pay dearly. He heard the loudspeaker crackle to life. The announcement was in Japanese, to which the sailors snapped into action.

"What is it, Satomi?"

More so than anyone, he was surprised by what Satomi said next: "Torpedo in the water!"

Just then the tell-tale trail of bubbles from a G7a steam torpedo crossed the bow of the *Takanami*. It had missed by a hundred meters.

"Where did that come from!?" Iwaishi shouted. "Ahead flank. Hard to starboard."

It was too late. The second torpedo struck amidships four seconds later with a thunderous boom. The destroyer's back broke in two. The bow of the ship pushed forward as it rolled on its side to port. The stern of the destroyer turned to starboard before it went under.

In the wheelhouse, there was panic. Lübeck found himself lying on the tilting deck. He was stunned by the explosion and his ears were ringing. *How could this have happened*? He scrambled around in the wheelhouse, slipping on blood, trying to find a way out as the ship began to sink. Water began to rush in. He had to get out.

November 25, 1942 01:17
Pearl Harbor, Hawaii
United States Naval Communication Center (HYPO)

Petty Officer Pinger liked working the night shift in Pearl Harbor. All of the boats in the Pacific were surfacing to re-charge their batteries and to send off their nightly contact reports. It made for a busy night, which made the shift seem to go by faster.

Pinger processed each report as it crossed his desk. The fourth message that he came to was one from the *Wahoo*. It gave a synopsis of the battle southeast of Guam with a destroyer and confirmed that a German U-boat had escaped. The *Wahoo* reported that the submarine returned to its easterly course.

I'll be a son of a bitch. This is it.

He immediately called the duty officer.

Chapter Twenty-Six: Border

December 18, 1942 22:18
1.5 Kilometers off of the Coast of Ensenada Mexico
U-463

More than three weeks had passed since the attack by the destroyer. The *U-463* was now surfaced off of the coast of Mexico. The sub rolled gently on the waves in the dark. Topside, Peter helped as members of the crew inflated a raft. His shoulder wound had been superficial and healed quickly.

Peter loaded two backpacks into the raft. Goedel had filled them with provisions for their journey—food, water, ammunition, and pistols. The raft was nearly ready to go. Peter looked up to the conning tower and waived at the two officers there.

Goedel stood with Richter on the conning tower. He issued his last orders to his XO as the commanding officer of the *U-463*. "Pick us up three nights from now, XO, at this exact spot."

"Yes, sir."

"Remember, if we are not back, for whatever reason, you are to return to Penang as the CO. Understood?"

"Yes, sir. If that happens, Captain, I have enough fuel to make it, but will the Japanese attack us again, sir?"

"I don't think so. Once you have cleared the area, you can break radio silence. Give *Kommodore* Able your intentions. Trust me, they will be eager to hear from us."

"Good luck, Captain. I will see you in three days."

"You can count on it, Richter."

With that, Goedel climbed down onto the deck of the submarine. He and Two Pair clambered into the bobbing raft and began to paddle. It took them a couple of hours to get to shore.

The two men hauled the raft up onto the beach along the rocky coast. They removed their gear and then deflated the raft.

Goedel said. "We shouldn't need this anymore, Two Pair." They folded the raft up and hid it amongst the rocks. "Come on, we want to get into Ensenada before sunrise."

Goedel handed him a pack. "Food and water, Two Pair. Survival supplies."

Peter lifted his pack and slung it over his shoulder. It was damn heavy. He walked along behind Johann as the German headed East.

December 19, 1942 18:30
Ensenada, Mexico
Hotel Del Rey

Johann and Peter sat in their hotel room on the outskirts of Ensenada. They had finished their dinner and had opened a bottle of celebratory tequila. It was a first for both of them. With glasses filled with the fermented agave juice, the two former *Kriegsmarine* officers toasted to their good fortune.

"We made it, Two Pair. All the way to Mexico. Who would have guessed?"

"No one would have guessed, but we did it!"

They both drank to their good luck. The tequila went down with a slow warming burn.

"Where are you going to go tomorrow, Johann?"

"I am going to make my way to Brazil. Just sounds like a nice place to live."

"I am going to make my way to Tecate and cross into the United States there. I called my parents today to let them know that I was coming. They said that they would try to meet me there. I figure that I can make it there in two days. Send me a card when you get settled. After the war, who knows … We may meet again someday."

"Maybe someday, but this is goodbye for now, isn't it, Two Pair? This has been one hell of a run! Hand me your backpack, will you? I need to show you something."

The two tipped their tequila glasses one more time and then Peter set the pack on the table in front of Johann, who dug around and pulled out a small sack with the word "ammunition" written on it.

"What are you going to do with the ammo, Johann?"

"We are going to spend it."

Johann opened the sack and dumped the contents on the table. It was not ammunition. There on the table sat a pile of gold coins.

"No wonder my pack was so heavy! You took the gold. You did it," Peter said in amazement. "You made me haul Lübeck's gold."

"It's not Lübeck's. It's ours. I call it severance pay."

"How did you get it?"

"During the abandon ship drill, I went to the engine room to break out the rafts. I saw the sentry going forward to get topside. As the rafts were being taken topside, I slipped into the machine shop and liberated it."

"You have some balls Johann, some balls."

Goedel laughed. He felt bad that Grimme had been killed, but that truly was all Lübeck's doing. *There was no way to predict that. What is done is done.*

"Here, Two Pair, half of it is in your backpack. It is yours."

"I cannot take it, Johann. I can't."

"Why not?"

"I will be home in a few days. I have family there and my family has money. You are starting over. You keep it. Consider it my gift to you for helping me get home."

"Are you sure?"

"I am sure, my friend. Keep it. You will need it."

"Fuck, now I have to carry it all!"

The two men laughed and poured more tequila. They toasted to their friendship.

December 20, 1942 14:00
New York, New York
Rockefeller Center Associated Press Headquarters

Harvey Benkleman looked out the window of his seventh-floor office. A light snow drifted down onto the city below. His years in the newspaper business had given him a myriad of contacts. One of them was a high-ranking Navy official in the War Department. He had learned from his source that an American who had escaped from the Japanese was being repatriated to the United States. It was a feel-good, human interest story and he had to send someone to cover it.

"You sent for me, Mr. Benkleman?"

Harvey turned to see Marilyn Miller standing in his doorway.

"Come in, Marilyn. I have a job for you."

This was her chance to be a photographer and a reporter. He told her that he had secured a flight to San Diego through one of his connections. He had to call in all of his IOUs to make it happen.

"When do I leave, sir?"

"This afternoon. You will return by train."

"But I won't get back til after Christmas. I am supposed to meet my fiancé David's parents at Christmas."

"Do you want to be a goddamn journalist or not, Miller?"

Marilyn thought for just a second and then nodded *yes*.

December 21, 1942 12:07
Pacific Ocean
Southwest of Guam

The sun beat down unmercifully on the ocean. Unrelenting and unbearable for the two men who had survived the sinking of the *Takanami*. In a raft, adrift for the twenty-seventh day, Klaus Lübeck and a Japanese sailor whose name he couldn't pronounce floated along. They had seen no planes or ships. Nothing but the endless sea and the punishing sun.

Klaus pondered his situation. They had no food left. It had been gone for over a week. Their water was running low. If their luck didn't change, and soon, they would die out here.

The German was tired and sunburned. His lips were cracked and his skin was a peeling mess. He wasn't sure how much longer he could take this torture. Hunger pangs made his entire body ache. Starvation was consuming him slowly.

Lübeck looked at his companion. He could kill the man and eat. He could do that. He was a man who got things done. He decided he would wait one more day before he would resort to cannibalism, but just one.

The sailor noticed Lübeck staring at him. Something in his eyes worried the sailor. He looked away to avoid the German's gaze. Looking out to sea, he saw something … a column of smoke on the horizon. He shielded his eyes from the sun with his hands and stared at the smoke. It was a ship!

Lübeck watched his companion as the Japanese man began waving his arms frantically. The German turned to look in the direction that the man was waving. Klaus began to wave as well.

December 22, 1942 08:05
Tecate Mexico
United States Border Crossing

A green 1931 Ford pickup rumbled up the dirt road towards the border. A plume of dust partially shrouded the truck as it came to a stop. In the back, a dust-covered man with a beard stood up and hopped off of the tailgate. The man said something to the driver and walked towards the border crossing.

Erik Teufel stood on the US side of the border. He and Anne had been waiting there for two hours. With them stood two of Donovan's men, along with a reporter from the Associated Press, who had arrived less than ten minutes ago. He looked on as the reporter readied her camera and took readings with her light meter. The elder Teufel watched several people make the crossing, but none of them were Peter.

Peter swatted the dust from his clothes as he approached the crossing. He looked up and saw his mother. She looked worried. His father was next to her. When he saw Marilyn Miller, he broke into a run.

Halted by the border guard, Peter tried to explain who he was. One of Donovan's men whistled at the guard. He let Peter pass.

Anne Teufel looked at the man running towards them. It took her a minute to recognize her own son. She began to cry.

"Marilyn!" Peter yelled.

Marilyn Miller was taking a picture as she heard her name called. She lowered her camera to get a better look. She couldn't believe what she was seeing: Peter!

Peter was intercepted by his mother before he could get to Marilyn.

Anne hugged her son as tightly as she could and cried tears of joy.

Peter felt the hand of his father on his shoulder.

"Welcome home, son."

"I am sorry, dad … I am so sorry. I was wrong."

"You are home now, son. That is all that matters."

His mother finally released her grip on him and he hugged his father.

"There are some men here, Peter, from the Office of Strategic Services. They are going to want to talk to you."

"Just a minute, ok? There is someone that I have to say hello to."

Peter stepped away from his parents and went to Marilyn. He hugged her with all of his might. A hug that he had saved for two years, just for her.

"Peter …." She blinked back tears.

"I am so sorry, Marilyn. I can explain everything."

He leaned over and kissed her on the lips and she held the kiss for a moment, but then backed away.

"There is something that I need to tell you, Peter. I'm engaged."

Peter took a step back and looked down at her left hand. There he saw the ring. He had struggled to get back to her for two years and now, she was marrying someone else. His heart sank lower than he could ever remember.

"I'm sorry, Peter … I didn't know what happened to you."

"But all of this time, I have thought of no one but you. I only wanted to be with you."

"Peter, I never heard from you. I thought that something happened."

"The war happened. I couldn't find a way out."

Peter stopped talking. He looked into Marilyn's eyes. He could see the hurt, the pain and realized that she was right. He had been out of touch for two years. *Of course, she moved on, she had to.*

His heart was broken. What should have been a joyous reunion with the woman he loved had turned into a crushing blow. He held in tears that desperately wanted to flow and decided to do his best to put her mind at ease.

Peter gave her a tender hug and lied to her and to himself. "It's ok. I understand. Good to see you, Marilyn. I am happy for you."

He turned back to his parents, stifled a tear, and nodded towards the OSS men. "Are these the guys who want to talk to me?"

Had Peter looked back, he would have seen Marilyn crying. He never looked back.

CPSIA information can be obtained
at www.ICGtesting.com
Printed in the USA
LVHW032335060222
710417LV00015B/110